Praise for Elmore Leonard

'**Like no one else in the business**, Elmore Leonard tells his readers a story'   Ian Rankin

'He has invented a style of storytelling all his own, **burning with energy and imagination**. His dialogue is unmatched by any other writer'   *The Times*

'There's **no cooler, slicker thriller writer** than Elmore Leonard'   Geoffrey Wansell, *Daily Mail*

'The master of American crime writing'   *Guardian*

'**The crime laureate**'   *Independent*

'He can get to the heart of his characters so fast and straighter than almost any writer you could think of'   *Scotsman*

'The great American writer' Stephen King

'How does Leonard do it? He just keeps on getting **better and better**'   *Evening Standard*

'There is **no greater writer of crime fiction** than Elmore Leonard, and no one who has more resplendent energy'
Philip Hensher

'One of the true icons of crime literature'   Patricia Cornwell

'A crime writer whose work made it abundantly clear that a mystery novel or a western could have literary merit. **He was flat out one of the best writers of dialogue that has ever lived**'   Mark Billingham

'The world's greatest living crime writer'   *Daily Mirror*

Elmore Leonard was born in New Orleans in 1925. He wrote forty-five books during his phenomenal career, including the bestsellers *Mr Paradise*, *Tishomingo Blues*, *Be Cool* and *The Hot Kid*. Many have been made into successful movies, including *Get Shorty* with John Travolta, *Out of Sight* with George Clooney and *Rum Punch*, which became Tarantino's *Jackie Brown*. In 2017, *Get Shorty* was made into a TV series starring Chris O'Dowd and Ray Romano. Leonard is the recipient of the Cartier Diamond Dagger Award and the PEN USA Lifetime Achievement Award. He died in 2013 in Detroit.

Get Shorty

ELMORE LEONARD

WEIDENFELD & NICOLSON

First published in 1990 by Delacorte Press
First published in Great Britain in 1990 by Viking
This paperback edition published in 2017
by Weidenfeld & Nicolson
an imprint of the Orion Publishing Group Ltd
Carmelite House, 50 Victoria Embankment
London EC4Y 0DZ

An Hachette UK Company

1 3 5 7 9 10 8 6 4 2

A CIP catalogue record for this book
is available from the British Library.

ISBN (Mass Market Paperback) 978 1 4746 0539 7

Typeset at The Spartan Press Ltd,
Lymington, Hants

Printed in Great Britain by Clays Ltd, St Ives plc

www.orionbooks.co.uk

For Walter Mirisch,
one of the good guys

When Chili first came to Miami Beach twelve years ago they were having one of their off-and-on cold winters: thirty-four degrees the day he met Tommy Carlo for lunch at Vesuvio's on South Collins and had his leather jacket ripped off. One his wife had given him for Christmas a year ago, before they moved down here.

Chili and Tommy were both from Bay Ridge, Brooklyn, old buddies now in business together. Tommy Carlo was connected to a Brooklyn crew through his uncle, a guy named Momo, Tommy keeping his books and picking up betting slips till Momo sent him to Miami, with a hundred thousand to put on the street as loan money. Chili was connected through some people on his mother's side, the Manzara brothers. He worked usually for Manzara Moving & Storage in Bensonhurst, finding high-volume customers for items such as cigarettes, TVs, VCRs, stepladders, dresses, frozen orange juice . . . But he could never be a made guy himself because of tainted blood, some Sunset Park Puerto Rican on his father's side, even though he was raised Italian. Chili didn't care to be made anyway, get into all that bullshit having to do with respect. It was bad enough having to treat these guys like they were your heroes, smile when they made some stupid remark they thought was funny. Though it was pretty nice, go in a restaurant on 86th or Cropsey Avenue, the way they knew his name, still a young guy then, and would bust their ass to wait on him. His wife Debbie ate it up, until they were married a few years and she got pregnant. Then it was a different story. Debbie said with a child coming into their lives he had to get a regular job, quit associating with 'those people', and bitched at him till he said okay, all *right*, Jesus, and lined up the deal with Tommy Carlo in Miami. He told Debbie he'd be selling restaurant supplies to the big hotels like the Fontainebleau and she believed him – till they were down here less than a year and he had his jacket ripped off.

This time at Vesuvio's, they finished eating, Tommy said he'd see him at the barbershop – where they had a phone in back – turned up the collar of his Palm Beach sport coat for whatever good it would do him and took off. Chili went in the checkroom to get his jacket and all that was in there were a couple of raincoats and a leather flight jacket must've been from World War Two. When Chili got the manager, an older Italian guy in a black suit, the manager looked around the practically empty checkroom and asked Chili, 'You don't find it? Is not one of these?'

Chili said, 'You see a black leather jacket, fingertip length, has lapels like a suitcoat? You don't, you owe me three seventy-nine.' The manager told him to look at the sign there on the wall. WE CANNOT BE RESPONSIBLE FOR LOST ARTICLES. Chili said to him, 'I bet you can if you try. I didn't come down to sunny Florida to freeze my ass. You follow me? You get the coat back or you give me the three seventy-nine my wife paid for it at Alexander's.'

So then the manager got a waiter over and they talked to each other in Italian for a while, the waiter nervous or he was anxious to get back to folding napkins. Chili caught some of what they were saying and a name that came up a few times, Ray Barboni. He knew the name, a guy they called Bones he'd seen hanging out at the Cardozo Hotel on the

2

beach. Ray Bones worked for a guy named Jimmy Capotorto who'd recently taken over a local operation from a deceased guy named Ed Grossi – but that was another story. The manager said to the waiter, 'Explain to him Mr Barboni borrow the coat.'

The waiter, trying to act like an innocent bystander, said, 'Somebody take his coat, you know, leave this old one. So Mr Barboni put on this other coat that fit him pretty good. He say he gonna borrow it.'

Chili said, 'Wait a minute,' and had the waiter, who didn't seem to think it was unusual for some asshole to take a jacket that didn't belong to him, explain it again.

'He didn't take it,' the waiter said, 'he borrow it. See, we get his coat for him and he return the one he borrow. Or I think maybe if it's your coat,' the waiter said, 'he give it to you. He was wearing it, you know, to go home. He wasn't gonna keep it.'

'My car keys are in the pocket,' Chili said.

They both looked at him now, the manager and the waiter, like they didn't understand English.

'What I'm saying,' Chili said, 'how'm I suppose to go get my coat if I don't have the keys to my car?'

The manager said they'd call him a taxi.

'Lemme get it straight,' Chili said. 'You aren't responsible for any lost articles like an expensive coat of mine, but you're gonna find Ray Bones' coat or get him a new one. Is that what you're telling me?'

Basically, he saw they weren't telling him shit, other than Ray Bones was a good customer who came in two three times a week and worked for Jimmy Cap. They didn't know where he lived and his phone number wasn't in the book. So Chili called Tommy Carlo at the barbershop, told him the situation, asked him a few times if he believed it and if he'd come by, pick him up.

'I want to get my coat. Also pull this guy's head out of his ass and nail him one.'

Tommy said, 'Tomorrow, I see on the TV weather, it's gonna be nice and warm. You won't need the coat.'

Chili said, 'Debbie gave me it for Christmas, for Christ sake. I go home, she's gonna want to know where it's at.'

'So tell her you lost it.'

'She's still in bed since the miscarriage. You can't talk to her. I mean in a way that makes any fuckin sense if you have to explain something.'

Tommy said, 'Hey, Chil? Then don't fuckin tell her.'

Chili said, 'The guy takes my coat, I can't ask for it back?'

Tommy Carlo picked him up at the restaurant and they stopped by Chili's apartment on Meridian where they were living at the time so he could run in and get something. He tried to be quiet about it, grab a pair of gloves out of the front closet and leave, but Debbie heard him.

She said from the bedroom, 'Ernie, is that you?' She never called him Chili. She called him honey in her invalid voice if she wanted something. 'Honey? Would you get my pills for me from the sink in the kitchen and a glass of water, please, while you're up?' Pause. 'Or, no – honey? Gimme a glass of milk instead and some of those cookies, the ones you got at Winn-Dixie, you know the chocolate chip ones?' Dragging it out in this tired voice she used since the miscarriage, three months ago. Taking forever now to ask him what time it was, the alarm clock sitting on the bed table a foot away if she turned her head. They had known each other since high school, when he'd played basketball and she was a baton twirler with a nice ass. Chili told her it was three-thirty and he was running late for an appointment; bye. He heard her say, 'Honey? Would you . . .' but he was out of there.

In the car driving the few blocks over to the Victor Hotel on Ocean Drive, Tommy Carlo said, 'Get your coat, but don't piss the guy off, okay? It could get complicated and we'd have to call Momo to straighten it out. Okay? Then Momo gets pissed for wasting his time and we don't need it. Right?'

Chili was thinking that if he was always bringing Debbie her pills, how did they get back to the kitchen after? But he heard Tommy and said to him, 'Don't worry about it. I won't say any more than I have to, if that.'

He put on his black leather gloves going up the stairs to the third floor, knocked on the door three times, waited, pulling the right-hand glove on tight, and when Ray Bones opened the door Chili nailed him. One punch, not seeing any need to throw the left. He got his coat from a chair in the sitting room, looked at Ray Bones bent over holding his nose and mouth, blood all over his hands, his shirt, and walked out. Didn't say one word to him.

Ernesto Palmer got the name Chili originally because he was hot-tempered as a kid growing up. The name given to him by his dad, who worked on the docks for the Bull Line when he wasn't drinking. Now he was Chili, Tommy Carlo said, because he had chilled down and didn't need the hot temper. All he had to do was turn his eyes dead when he looked at a slow pay, not say more than three words, and the guy would sell his wife's car to make the payment. Chili said the secret was in how you prepped the loan customer.

'A guy comes to see you, it doesn't matter how much he wants or why he needs it, you say to him up front before you give him a dime, "You sure you want to take this money? You're not gonna put up your house or sign any papers. What you're gonna give me is your word you'll pay it back so much a week at interest." You tell him, "If you don't think you can pay at least the vig every week when it's due, please don't take the fuckin money, it wouldn't be worth it to you." If the guy hesitates at all, "Well, I'm pretty sure I can—" says

5

anything like that, I tell him, "No, I'm advising you now, don't take the fuckin money." The guy will beg for it, take an oath on his kids he'll pay you on time. You know he's desperate or he wouldn't be borrowing shylock money in the first place. So you tell him, "Okay, but you miss even one payment you're gonna be sorry you ever came here." You never tell the guy what could happen to him. Let him use his imagination, he'll think of something worse. In other words, don't talk when you don't have to. What's the point?'

It was the same thing getting his coat back. What was there to say?

So now it was up to Ray Bones. If getting his nose busted and his teeth pushed in pissed him off he'd have to do something about it. Some things you couldn't prevent. Tommy Carlo told him to get lost for a while, go fishing in the Keys. But how was he going to do that with Debbie an invalid, afraid to take a leak she might see blood?

He imagined different ways Ray Bones might try for him. Eating at Vesuvio's, look up, there's Bones pointing a gun. Or coming out of the barbershop on Arthur Godfrey Road where they had their office in back. Or, no – sitting on one of the chairs while he's shooting the shit with Fred and Ed, which he did sometimes when there weren't customers in the place. That would appeal to Ray Bones, with his limited mentality: the barbershop was here and it was the way guys had gotten hit before, like Albert Anastasia, that Ray Bones would know about. Chili said shit, went over to S.W. Eighth Street and bought a snub-nosed .38 off a Cuban. 'The famous Smit and Wayson model *treintaseis*.'

It happened when Chili was in the backroom office making entries in the collection book. Through the wall-board he heard Fred say, 'Paris? Yeah, I been there plenty of times. It's right offa Seventy-nine.' Ed saying, 'Hell it is, it's on Sixty-eight. It's only seventeen miles from Lexington.' Fred saying,

'What're you talking about, Paris, Kentucky, or Paris, Tennessee?' Then a silence, no answer to the question.

Chili looked up from the collection book, listened a moment to nothing, opened the desk drawer and got out the .38. He aimed it at the open doorway. Now he saw Ray Bones appear in the back hall, Bones in the doorway to the office, his face showing surprise to see a gun aimed at him. He began firing the big Colt auto in his hand maybe before he was ready, the gun making an awful racket, when Chili pulled the trigger and shot him in the head. The .38 slug creased Ray Bones, as it turned out, from hairline to crown, put a groove in his scalp they closed up at Mt. Sinai with more than thirty stitches – Chili hearing about it later. He pried two slugs out of the wall and found another one in the file cabinet he showed Tommy Carlo.

Tommy called Momo and Momo got in touch with Jimmy Cap, taking the situation to the table, so to speak, discuss whether Ray Bones had been shown disrespect by an associate from another crew, or was it his own fault he got shot. Otherwise it could get out of hand if they let it go, didn't make a judgment. The two bosses decided this coat thing and what came out of it was bullshit, forget it. Jimmy Cap would tell Ray Bones he was lucky he wasn't dead, the guy's wife had given him the coat for Christmas for Christ sake. That was the end of the incident, twelve years ago, except for one unexpected event that came out of it right away, and something else that would happen now, in the present.

The unexpected event was Debbie walking out on Chili, going home to Bay Ridge to live with her mother over a clothing store.

It happened because during the discussion period Momo called Chili to get his side – as a favor to Tommy Carlo, otherwise he would never have spoken to him directly – and

7

Debbie listened in on the extension. All Momo told Chili was to cut out the schoolyard bullshit, grow up. But that was enough for Debbie to know Chili was still connected. She went so far as to get out of bed to keep after him, wanting to know what he was doing with Momo and 'those people,' becoming screechy about it until finally he told her, so he was working for Momo for Christ sake, so what? Thinking it would shut her up and he'd get the silent treatment for about a month, which he could use. But instead of that she became hysterical, telling him. 'That's why I had the miscarriage, I knew it. I *knew* you were back in that life and the baby knew it from me *and didn't want to be born*!'

What? Because its dad was operating a quick-loan business? Helping out poor schmucks that couldn't get it from a bank? How did you talk to a woman who believed an unborn kid would know something like that? He tried. He told her she ought to see a doctor, get her fuckin brain looked at. Debbie's last words to him, she said, 'You think you're so smart, let's see you get a divorce, big shot.' In other words she would pass up alimony and live with her mother over a clothing store to prevent his ever remarrying. Debbie, too dumb to realize the world had changed with rock and roll and the pill, believed it would keep him from ever getting laid again.

Chili, from then until now, went with a succession of women, some on a serious basis, some not. There was one named Rose, a bartender, who lived with him a few years. One named Vera, a go-go dancer he fell in love with, but he couldn't stand other guys watching her and they broke up. He took out women who were waitresses, beauticians, sales clerks at Dadeland Mall, would take them to dinner and a movie, sometimes to bed. There was a singer named Nicole he liked a lot, but her whole life seemed to be rock and roll and he never knew what she was talking about. Chili liked

8

women and was comfortable with them without putting on any kind of act. He was who he was and they seemed to go for him. What some of the women didn't go for was seeing so many movies, practically every time they went out. They would get the feeling he liked movies more than he did them.

The other thing that came out of the coat incident, now twelve years later, happened right after they got word about Momo, shot dead as he left a restaurant on West 56th in Manhattan, and Tommy Carlo went to attend the funeral. The day after that Chili had a couple of visitors come in the shop looking for him, a big colored guy he had never seen before and Ray Bones.

'They cut straight hair in this place,' Bones asked Chili, 'or just fags?'

Times changed. Fred and Ed were gone and a couple of guys named Peter and Tim were doing hair of either sex in an art deco backstage-looking setup, light bulbs around rose-colored mirrors. They were okay. They had Chili combing his hair straight back, no part, like Michael Douglas in *Wall Street*.

Chili had changed too in the past dozen years, tired of showing respect to people he thought were assholes. Momo had been okay, but guys in his crew would come down to Miami on vacation and act like hard-ons, expecting him and Tommy to show them around, get them broads. Chili would tell the hard-ons, 'Hey, I'm not your pimp,' and they'd give Tommy a bad time because he was Momo's nephew and had to go along. The result of this situation, Chili was phasing himself out of the shylock business, only handling a few regular customers now who didn't give them any trouble. He was also doing midnight car repossessions for small loan companies and some collection work for local merchants and a couple of Las Vegas casinos, making courtesy calls. He had chilled down a few more degrees too.

Still, he couldn't help saying to Ray Bones, 'The way you're losing your hair, Bones, you oughta let these guys style what you have left, see if they can cover up that scar. Or they can fit you with a rug, either way.'

Fuck him. Chili knew what was coming.

There weren't any customers in the shop. Ray Bones told Peter and Tim to go get a coffee. They left making faces and the big colored guy backed Chili into a barber chair, telling him, 'This man is the man. You understand what I'm saying? He's Mr Bones, you speak to him from now on.'

Chili watched Mr Bones go into the back hall toward the office and said to the colored guy, 'You can do better'n him.'

'Not these days,' the colored guy said. 'Not less you can talk Spanish.'

Bones came out with the collection book open, looking at all the names of who owed, the amounts and due dates in a green spiral notebook. He said to Chili, 'How you work it, you handle the spies and Tommy the white people?'

Chili told himself it was time to keep his mouth shut.

The colored guy said, 'The man's talking to you.'

'He's outta business but don't know it,' Bones said, looking up from the book. 'There's nothing around here for you no more.'

'I can see that,' Chili said. He watched Bones put his nose in the book again.

'How much you got working?'

'About three and a half.'

'Shit, ten grand a week. What'd Momo let you have?'

'Twenty percent.'

'And you fucked him outta what, another twenty?'

Chili didn't answer. Bones turned a page, read down the entries and stopped.

10

'You got a miss. Guy's six weeks over.'

'He died,' Chili said.

'How you know he died, he tell you?'

Ray Bones checked the colored guy to get some appreciation, but the guy was busy looking at hair rinses and shit on the counter. Chili didn't give him anything either. He was thinking he could kick Mr Bones in the nuts if he came any closer, then get up and nail him. If the big colored guy would leave.

'He got killed,' Chili said, 'in that TransAm jet went down in the Everglades.'

'Who told you?'

Chili got out of the chair, went in the back office and returned with a stack of *Miami Herald*s. He dropped them on the floor in front of Bones and got back in the chair.

'Help yourself. You find him on the list of victims, Leo Devoe. He's Paris Cleaners on Federal Highway about 124th Street.'

Bones nudged the stack of newspapers with a toe of his cream-colored perforated shoes that matched his slacks and sport shirt. The front page on top said 'TransAm Crash Kills 117.' Chili watched Bones toe his way through editions with headlines that said 'Winds Probed in Crash' . . . 'Windshear Warning Was Issued' . . . 'Nightmare Descends Soon After Farewells' . . . getting down to a page of small photographs, head shots, and a line that read, 'Special Report: The Tragic Toll.'

'His wife told me he was on the flight,' Chili said. 'I kept checking till I saw, yeah, he was.'

'His picture in here?'

'Near the bottom. You have to turn the paper over.'

Bones still wasn't going to bend down, strain himself. He looked up from the newspapers. 'Maybe he took out flight insurance. Check with the wife.'

11

'It's your book now,' Chili said. 'You want to check it out, go ahead.'

The colored guy came over from the counter to stand next to the chair.

Ray Bones said, 'Six weeks' juice is twenty-seven hunnerd on top of the fifteen you gave him. Get it from the guy's wife or out of your pocket, I don't give a fuck. You don't hand me a book with a miss in it.'

'Payback time,' Chili said. 'You know that coat? I gave it to the Salvation Army two years ago.'

'What coat?' Bones said.

He knew.

The colored guy stood close, staring into Chili's face, while Bones worked on the Michael Douglas hairdo, shearing off a handful at a time with a pair of scissors, telling Chili it was to remind him when he looked in the mirror he owed fifteen plus whatever the juice, right? The juice would keep running till he paid. Chili sat still, hearing the scissors snip-snipping away, knowing it had nothing to do with money. He was being paid back again, this time for reminding Ray Bones he had a scar that showed white where he was getting bald. It was all kid stuff with these guys, the way they acted tough. Like Momo had said, schoolyard bullshit. These guys never grew up. Still, if they were holding a pair of scissors in your face when they told you something, you agreed to it. At least for the time being.

Chili was still in the chair when the new-wave barbers came back and began to comment, telling him they could perm what was left or give him a moderate spike, shave the sides, laser stripes were popular. Chili told them to cut the shit and even it off. While they worked on him he sat there wondering if it was possible Leo Devoe had taken out flight insurance or if the wife had thought about suing the airline. It was something he could mention to her.

But what happened when he dropped by their house in North Miami – the idea, see what he could find out about any insurance – the wife. Fay, stopped him cold. She said, 'I wish he really was dead, the son of a bitch.'

She didn't say it right away, not till they were out on the patio with vodka and tonics, in the dark.

Chili knew Fay from having stopped by to pick up the weekly four-fifty and they'd sit here waiting for Leo to get home after a day at Gulfstream. Fay was a quiet type, from a small town upstate, Mt. Dora, not bad-looking but worn thin in her sundress from working at the cleaner's in that heat while Leo was out betting horses. They'd sit here trying to make conversation with nothing in common but Leo, Chili, every once in a while, catching her gaze during a silence, seeing her eyes and feeling it was there if he wanted it. Though he couldn't imagine Fay getting excited, changing her expression much. What did a shy woman stuck with a loser think about? Leo would appear, strut out on the patio and count the four-fifty off a roll, nothing to it. Or he'd come shaking his head, beat, saying he'd have it tomorrow for sure. Chili never threatened him, not in front of the woman and embarrass her. Not till he left and Leo would know enough to walk him out to his car parked by the streetlight. He'd say, 'Leo, look at me,' and tell him where to be the next day with the four-fifty. Leo was never to blame: it was the horses selling out or it was Fay always on his back, distracting him when he was trying to pick winners. And Chili would have to say it again, 'Leo, look at me.'

He owed for two weeks the night he didn't come home. Fay said she couldn't think where Leo could be. The third week she told him Leo was dead and a couple weeks after that his picture was in the paper.

This visit sitting on the patio, knowing Leo was not going

to appear, strutting or otherwise, the silences became longer. Chili asked what she planned to do now. Fay said she didn't know; she hated the drycleaner business, being inside. Chili said it must be awful hot. She said you couldn't believe how hot it was. He got around to asking about life insurance. Fay said she didn't know of any. Chili said, well . . . But didn't move. Fay didn't either. It was dark, hard to see her face, neither one of them making a sound. This was when she said, out of nowhere, 'You know what I been thinking?'

Chili said, 'Tell me.'

'I wish he really was dead, the son of a bitch.'

Chili kept still. Don't talk when you don't have to.

'He's called me up twice since going out to Las Vegas and since then I haven't heard a goddamn word from him. I know he's there, it's all he ever talked about, going to Las Vegas. But I'm the one stuck my neck out, I'm the one they gave the money to, not him. I'm talking about the airline company, the three hundred thousand dollars they gave me for losing my husband.' Fay paused to shake her head.

Chili waited.

She said to him on that dark patio, 'I trust you. I think you're a decent type of man, even if you are a crook. You find Leo and get me my three hundred thousand dollars back if he ain't spent it, I'll give you half. If he's hit big we split that, or whatever he has left. How's that sound as a deal?'

Chili said, 'That's what you been thinking, huh? Tell me why the airline thinks Leo got killed if he wasn't on the flight.'

'His suitcase was,' Fay said, and told Chili everything that happened.

It was a good story.

14

2

Harry Zimm believed if he kept his eyes closed and quit listening that sound coming from somewhere in the house would stop and pretty soon they'd go back to sleep.

But Karen wouldn't leave it alone. He heard her say, 'Harry?' a couple of times, maybe not sure if she was hearing something or not. Then, '*Harry*—' still a whisper but putting more into it. This time when he didn't answer she gave him a poke in the back, hard. 'Harry, God damn it, somebody's downstairs.'

They hadn't slept in the same bed on a regular basis in over ten years, not since they had lived together, and Karen still knew when he was faking. The only other time, in this same bed, was right after she and Michael were divorced and Michael, a star by then, gave Karen the house. There was no way to hide from her. So he rolled over and there she was in her Lakers T-shirt, sitting up on her side of the king-size bed, a soft white shape in the dark, a little porcelain doll.

'What's wrong?'

'Be quiet and listen.'

A tough little porcelain doll under that loose T-shirt.

'I don't hear anything.' It was true, he didn't at the moment.

'I thought at first it might be Miguel,' Karen said. 'My houseman. But he's visiting his mom in Chula Vista.'

'You have a houseman?'

'Miguel does everything, cleans the house, takes care of the outside . . . *There*,' Karen said. 'If you can't hear that, Harry, you're deaf.'

He wanted to ask her how old Miguel was and what he looked like. Miguel . . . and thought of Michael, her former, now a superstar. Michael had lived here and slept in this bed. He wondered if Miguel ever got in it with her. Karen was closing in on forty but still a knockout. She kept in shape, had given up dope for health food, switched from regular cigarettes to low-tar menthols.

'Harry, don't go to sleep on me.'

He said, 'Have I ever done that?' Was quiet for a moment and said, 'You have any idea what that is?'

'Those are *voices*, Harry. People talking.'

'Really?'

'On television. Somebody came in and turned the TV on.'

'You sure?'

'Listen, will you?'

Harry raised his head from the pillow, going along, hearing a faint monotone sound that gradually became voices. She was right, two people talking. He cocked his head in the bedroom silence and after a moment said, 'You know who the one guy sounds like? Shecky Greene.'

Karen turned her head, a slow move, to give him a look over the shoulder. 'You're still smashed, aren't you?' Judging him, but the tone not unsympathetic, a little sad.

'I'm fine.'

Maybe half in the bag but still alert, with a nice glow. The headache would come later if he didn't take something. He must have put away half the fifth of Scotch earlier, down in the study where the TV was on, while he told Karen about his situation, his thirty years in the picture business on the brink. He was about to become either a major player or

16

might never be heard from again. And she sat there listening to him like a fucking Teamsters business agent, no reaction, no sympathy. He thought of something else and said:

'Maybe, you know how you go downstairs in the morning sometimes you see pictures cockeyed on the wall? You're thinking, This is some hangover, wow. Then you see on the news there was an earthquake during the night over near Pasadena someplace. Not a big one, like a four-point-two. You know? Maybe it's something like that, an atmospheric disturbance turned on the TV.'

Karen was listening, but not to him, staring at the bedroom doorway, pitch-dark out there, her nice slim back arched.

'Or maybe it's only the wind,' Harry said.

That got her looking at him again because she knew the line, intimately. From *Grotesque, Part Two*, one of his highest-grossing pictures. The maniac's up on the roof ripping out shingles with his bare hands; inside the house the male lead with all the curly hair stares grimly at the ceiling as Karen, playing the girl, says to him, 'Maybe it's only the wind.' She hated the line, refused to say it until he convinced her it was okay, it worked.

'I love your attitude,' Karen said. 'What do you care if somebody broke in, it's not your house.'

'If you think somebody broke in, why don't you call the police?'

'Because I don't intentionally allow myself to look stupid,' Karen said, 'if I can help it. Not anymore.'

The way she kept staring at him, over the shoulder, was a nice angle. The dark hair against pale skin. The lighting wasn't bad either, Karen backlit with the windows behind her. It took at least ten years off her age, the tough little broad a sweet young thing again in her white T-shirt. She

17

was telling him now, in a thoughtful tone, 'When I came upstairs, you stayed to finish your drink.'

'I didn't turn the TV on.'

'You said you wanted to watch a few minutes of Carson.'

She was right. 'But I turned it off.'

'Harry, you can't be sure what you did.'

'I'm positive.'

Yeah, because he had turned it off the moment he thought about getting in bed with Karen instead of sleeping in the guest room: the idea, start talking again, work on her sympathy . . .

'I used the remote control thing and laid it on the floor,' Harry said. 'You know what could've happened? The dog came in and stepped on it, turned the TV back on.'

'I don't have a dog.'

'You don't? What happened to Muff?'

'Harry, are you going down, or you want me to?'

He wanted her to but had to be nice, obliging, to have any hope of using her.

Getting out of bed his boxer shorts hiked up on him and he had to work them down, get the elastic band under his belly. Karen thought he was fat.

In the study, earlier, he had told her about the story he'd optioned that could change his life, an original screenplay: no fiends or monsters, this one straight-up high-concept drama. He told her he was taking it to a major studio and Karen said, 'Oh?' He told her – making it sound like an afterthought – yeah, and guess who read the script and flipped over it? Michael. No kidding, loves it. Her ex, and she didn't say a goddamn word, not even 'Oh?' or make a sound. She stared at him, smoking her cigarette. He told her he did have a few problems. One, getting past Michael's agent, the prick, who refused to let Michael take a meeting with him. And, there was some sticky business to clean up

18

that involved money, naturally, not to mention getting out from under his investors, a couple of undesirables who'd been financing him. Which he did mention, in detail. This was his career on the launch pad, about to either fly or go down in flames; and Karen sat there letting the ice melt in her drink, blowing menthol smoke at him. Didn't comment outside of that one 'Oh?' or ask one question, not even about Michael, till he was through and she said, 'Harry, if you don't lose thirty pounds you're going to die.' Thanks a lot. He told her he was glad he stopped by, find out all he had to do to save his ass was join Vic Tanny.

'Harry? What're you doing?'

'I'm putting my shirt on.'

He moved to a window to be moving, doing something while he worked on the goddamn buttons.

'Is that okay? So I don't catch cold? But I'm not gonna get all dressed for some friend of yours thinks he's funny.'

'Friends don't break in, Harry, they ring the bell.'

'Yeah? What about stoned they might.'

Karen didn't comment; she was clean now, above it. Harry looked out the window at the backyard, overgrown around the edges, a tangle of plants and old trees surrounding the lawn and the pale oval shape of the swimming pool. It looked full of leaves.

'Does Miguel skim the pool? It needs it.'

'Harry—'

He said, 'I'm going,' and got as far as the door. 'If somebody broke in, how come the alarm didn't go off?'

'I don't have an alarm.'

'You have it taken out?'

'I never had one.'

That's right, it was the house in Westwood, where Karen had lived with him. She'd come in, forget to touch the numbers to turn it off . . . Marlene had the alarm system now and the house that went with it. He had married Marlene, his director of development, after Karen left to marry Michael. Then when both marriages ended at about the same time he told Karen it was a sign, they should get back together. Karen said she didn't believe in signs. Which was a lie, she read her horoscope every day. Marlene was married to a guy who at one time ran production at Paramount and was now producing TV sitcoms, one of them a family with a Chihuahua that could talk. Tiny little dog with a tiny little fake Puerto Rican accent. Why chew look hat me like dat? The dog always fucking up. He was thinking of Karen in the Westwood house instead of this one, her own place, a semi-French chateau high up in Beverly Hills, above the lights of LA. Built in the late twenties for a movie star and passed on to others.

From the doorway he said to Karen, 'Why chew make me do thees?'

'Because I'm a girl,' the pale figure on the bed answered, 'and you're bigger than I am. A lot.'

Harry moved down the curved staircase in his shirt and boxer shorts, the monotone sound of voices becoming more distinct; he could hear words now and what sounded like audience response, the volume turned up to be heard on the second floor. He believed it was the Letterman show. The tile in the foyer was cold on his bare feet. Mexican tile now and primitive art, hardwood floors except in the study, all the fat comfortable slipcovered furniture from Michael's time gone. And yet there were pictures of him in the study, among the dozens of photographs of movie people and movie posters covering the paneled walls.

He crossed to the study, the door open partway, dark inside except for the glow from the big thirty-two-inch Sony. There, David Letterman talking to someone – not Shecky, it wasn't his voice.

Harry couldn't see the desk, where he and Karen had sat with the bottle of Scotch, schmoozing, Karen telling him she was reading a script she might do. Oh, really? Want to get back into it, huh? Great. Biding his time until finally making his presentation: here is my tremendous opportunity, but here are the problems. Pause. Waiting then for her to say, Maybe I can help. No, she tells him he ought to lose weight.

Still, there was hope. Asking him to spend the night was a good sign. Looking after him, saying he was in no condition to drive. It meant she cared. Though not enough to let him sleep with her when he suggested it, as kind of a trip down memory lane. Spunky Karen said, 'If you think nostalgia's going to get you laid, forget it.' He could take the guest room or a cab. Fine, sleeping with her wasn't that important anyway; they were back on familiar ground with one another. When he did slip into her bed, later, Karen said, 'I mean it, Harry, we're not going to do anything.'

But, she didn't kick him out.

So he felt pretty good pushing open the door to the study, telling himself there was no one in here. If there was it would be one of Karen's friends, no doubt stoned, some bit-part actor thinking he was funny. Okay, he'd nod to the guy very nonchalantly, turn the TV off and walk out.

Moving into the glow from the big Sony now, most of the room dark, he saw David Letterman talking to Paul Shaffer, his music guy, the two of them acting hip. Harry felt his bare feet in the warm carpeting. Felt himself jump and said, 'Jesus Christ!' as Letterman and Paul Shaffer vanished, the screen going to black in the same moment the desk lamp came on.

A guy Harry had never seen before was sitting there, hunched over a little, his arms resting on the desk. A guy in black. Dark hair, dark eyes, that lean, hard-boned type. A guy in his forties.

He said, 'Harry Zimm, how you doing?' in a quiet tone of voice. 'I'm Chili Palmer.'

3

Harry pressed a hand against his chest. He said, 'Jesus, if I have a heart attack I hope you know what to do,' convinced the guy was a friend of Karen's, the way he was making himself at home, the guy staring at him out of those deep-set dark eyes but with hardly any expression.

He said, 'Where you been, Harry?'

Harry let his hand slide down over his belly, taking his time, wanting to show he had it together now, not the least self-conscious, standing there without his pants on.

'Have we met? I don't recall.'

'We just did. I told you, my name's Chili Palmer.'

The guy speaking with some kind of East Coast accent, New York or New Jersey.

'Tell me what you been up to.'

Harry still had a mild buzz-on that made him feel, not exactly reckless, but not shy either.

'You mean what am I doing here?'

'You want, you can start with that.'

He didn't appear upset or on the muscle. But if he had a key to get in – Harry assuming that – the guy was closer to Karen than just a friend, Karen maybe going in for rough trade now.

Harry said, 'I'm visiting, that's all. I'm up in the guest room, I hear the TV . . . You turned it on?'

The guy, Chili, kept staring, not saying anything now.

23

Typecast, he was a first or second lead bad guy, depending on the budget. Hispanic or Italian. Not a maniac bad guy, a cool bad guy with some kind of hustle going. But casual, black poplin jacket zipped up.

The answer came to Harry and he said, 'You're in pictures, right?'

The guy smiled. Not much but enough to show even white teeth, no doubt capped, and Harry was convinced of it. The guy was an actor friend of Karen's and she was in on it – the reason she was so anxious to get him down here – setting him up for this bullshit audition. The guy scares hell out of you to prove he can act and you give him a part in your next picture.

'Did you stop to think what if I had a heart attack?'

The guy didn't move, still doing the bit, no expression, very cool.

He said, 'You look okay to me, Harry. Come over here and sit down. Tell me what you been up to.'

The guy wasn't bad. Harry took one of the canvas director's chairs by the desk, the guy watching him. He knew how to stare without giving it much. The angle was nice too: the guy lean and dark, the bottle of Scotch, the ice bucket and the glasses he and Karen had left, in the foreground. Harry raised one hand and passed it over his thinning hair. He could feel it was losing its frizz, due for another permanent and touch-up, add some body and get rid of the mousy gray trying to take over. The guy had a full head of dark hair, as that type usually did, but close-cropped so you could see the shape of his head, like a skull. It was a nice effect.

He said, 'Harry, you looking at me?'

Harry brought his hand down. 'I'm looking at you.'

'I want you to keep looking right here, okay?'

'That's what I'm doing,' Harry said, going along. Why not?

The guy was from Brooklyn or the Bronx, one of those. If he was putting it on he had it down cold.

'Okay, so tell me what's up.'

He was good, but irritating.

'I don't have a script,' Harry said, 'so I don't know what you're talking about. *Okay*?'

'You don't have a script,' Chili said. 'How about, you happen to have a hunnerd and fifty big ones on you?'

Harry didn't answer.

'You're not saying nothing. You remember being in Vegas November twenty-sixth of last year, at Las Mesas?'

It was starting to sound real. 'I go to Vegas, that's where I stay, at Mesas,' Harry said. 'Always have, for years.'

'You know Dick Allen?'

'Dick Allen's a very dear friend of mine.' It still could be a script, something Karen put together. 'How far you want to go with this?'

The guy gestured, his hands limp, very natural.

'We're there, Harry. You signed markers for a hunnerd and a half, you're over sixty days past due and you haven't told anybody what the problem is.'

It wasn't a script.

Harry said, 'Jesus Christ, what're you, a collector? You come in here, walk in the house in the middle of the fucking night? I thought you were some actor, au*dition*ing, for Christ sake.'

The guy raised his eyebrows. 'Is that right?' He seemed about to smile. 'That's interesting. You thought I was acting, huh?'

'I don't believe this,' Harry said. 'You break in the house to tell me I owe on some *markers*? I know what I owe. So what? I go to Mesas I get comped, the whole shot. I got a credit line for as much as I owe – and they send you here to *collect*?' Harry felt an urge to move, do something. He pushed up out

25

of the chair to look down at the guy, get an advantage on him. 'We'll see about this,' Harry said, picked up the phone and punched the 0. 'Operator, how do I get Las Vegas Information?' He listened a moment and hung up.

Chili said, 'Lemme give you some advice, okay?'

Harry looked up, the phone in his hand again, about to punch the number.

'You don't want to act like a hard-on you're standing there in your undies. You know what I'm saying? You got enough to handle. You got the markers and you got another outstanding debt if I'm not mistaken. What you wanta do, Harry, is use your head, sit down and talk to me.'

It stopped him. 'What outstanding debt?'

'Put the phone down.'

'I want to know what you're talking about,' Harry said, getting a peeved tone now, indignant, 'outside of what I owe at Mesas, which they know I'm good for.'

'They know you're good up to your last trip. After that, as they say, nobody knows nothing.' Chili waited.

Harry hung up the phone. He felt the chair against his bare legs and sat down.

'A marker's like a check, Harry . . .'

'I know what a marker is.'

'They don't want to deposit yours and have 'em bounce, insufficient funds, or they find out the account's closed. That's embarrassing. So your customer rep, your very dear friend Dick Allen's been calling, leaving messages on your machine, but you never get back to him. So basically, you want to know why I'm here – I don't actually work for Mesas, but Dick Allen asked me as a favor would I look you up. Okay, I come to LA, try your apartment, your office, you're not anywhere around. So I contact some people I know of, get a few leads—'

'What people?'

'You have high blood pressure, Harry? You oughta lose some weight.'

'*What* people?'

'You don' know 'em, some people I was put in touch with. So I start calling around. I call here, Karen tells me she hasn't seen you. So we talk, I ask her if this's the Karen Flores used to be in the movies. Yes, it is. Well, how come I haven't seen you? . . . I remember her in *Grotesque* with the long blond hair. I start to think, this is where I'd come if I was Harry Zimm and I want to stay off the street.'

'You think I'm hiding out?'

'What're you getting excited about?'

'I don't like the insinuation, I'm hiding.'

'Well, that's up to you, what you like or what you don't. I called your former wife, the one in Westwood? She goes, "I hope you're a bill collector and you find the cheapskate." '

'You have fun talking about me? Jesus,' Harry said, 'that broad used to work for me. She's supposed to know the business, but apparently has no idea what I was going through at the time.' His gaze moved to the bottle of Scotch thinking of Marlene, who liked her booze, also thinking he wouldn't mind having one.

'You're not looking at me, Harry.'

'Why do I have to keep looking at you?'

'I want you to.'

'You gonna get rough now, threaten me? I make good by tomorrow or get my legs broken?'

'Come on, Harry – Mesas? The worst they might do is get a judgment against you, uttering a bad check. I can't imagine you want that to happen, man in your position.'

'I've won there and I've lost,' Harry said, staying with the peeved tone, 'They carry me and I always pay what I owe. But now all of a sudden they're worried I'm gonna stiff 'em?

Why? They don't give you a credit line of a hundred and a half unless they know you're good for it.'

'What's that, Harry?'

'You heard me.'

'What I heard,' Chili said, 'your credit line's an even hunnerd and they gave you the extra fifty TTO, this trip only, 'cause you had front money, that cashier's check for two hunnerd thousand, right? Four hours later, the night's still young, it's all gone, the two you rode in on and the hunnerd and a half. It can happen to anybody. But now a couple months go by, Dick Allen wonders if there's a problem here, if Harry Zimm was playing with scared money. He says you never put down more than ten on a basketball game in your life. You come in this time and drop the whole load, like you're not doing it for fun.'

'I didn't have to twist any arms. I told 'em what I wanted to put down and they okayed it.'

'Why not? It's your money.'

'They tell you what game it was and the point spread? Lakers and the Pistons, in Detroit. Which happens to be where I grew up. Now I'm out here I follow the Lakers, had seats up to last year. Not down there with Jack Nicholson, but they weren't bad seats. You don't recall the game?'

'I mighta read about it at the time. What was the spread?'

The guy showing interest. It picked Harry up.

'The sports book line had the Pistons by three and a half. The bad boys from Motown over the glamor boys from showtown.'

'You live here,' Chili said, 'but you like the Pistons. I can understand that. I don't live in New York anymore, I'm in Miami, but I still follow the Knicks, put a few bucks on 'em now and then. Even though it's been years.'

'I don't happen to bet that way,' Harry said, 'emotionally. I like the Pistons this time 'cause they're at home, twenty

28

thousand screaming fans on their ass. Also the fact they beat the Lakers four zip in the finals last year.'

He had the guy's attention; no question about it, waiting to hear about a basketball game that was played more than two months ago.

'You know how I bet it?'

'You went with the Pistons and the Lakers won.'

'I went with the Pistons,' Harry said, 'and the Pistons won.'

Right away Chili said, 'The point spread.'

Harry sat back in the director's chair. 'The Pistons by three and a half. The score was one-oh-two to ninety-nine. They won and I lost.'

Now Chili sat back. 'That was close. You almost did it.'

The guy showing sympathy. Good. Harry wanted him to get up now, shake hands and leave. But the guy was staring at him again.

'So then you go through your credit line playing black-jack,' Chili said, 'chasing what you lost, going double-up to catch up. But when you have to win, Harry, that's when you lose. Everybody knows that.'

'Whatever you say,' Harry said, tired of talking about it. He yawned. Maybe the guy would take the hint.

But Chili kept at it. He said, 'You know what I think? You went in the hole on some kind of deal, so you tried to bet your way out. See, I don't know anything about your business, Harry, but I know how a guy acts when he's facing a payment he has to make and he doesn't have it. You get desperate. I know a guy put his wife out on the street, and she wasn't bad-looking either.'

'You don't know anything about my business,' Harry said, showing some irritation, 'but you don't mind sticking your nose in it. Tell Dick Allen I'll cover the markers in the next sixty days, at the most. He doesn't like it, that's his problem.

29

First thing in the morning,' Harry said, 'I'm gonna call him, the prick. I thought he was a friend of mine.'

Harry paused, wondering whether or not he should ask the guy how he got in the house, and decided he didn't want to know. The guy says he broke a window – then what? Harry waited. He was tired, irritable, not feeling much of a glow. He said, 'We gonna sit here all night or what? You want me to call you a cab?'

The guy, Chili, shook his head. He kept staring, but with a different kind of expression now, more thoughtful, or maybe curious.

'So you make movies, huh?'

'That's what I do,' Harry said, relieved, not minding the question. 'I produce feature motion pictures, no TV. You mentioned *Grotesque*, that happened to be *Grotesque, Part Two* Karen Flores was in. She starred in all three of my *Slime Creatures* releases you might've seen.'

The guy, Chili, was nodding as he came forward to lean on the desk.

'I think I got an idea for one, a movie.'

And Harry said, 'Yeah? What's it about?'

4

At first, all Karen heard was Harry's side of whatever was going on. As soon as she came out of the bedroom she heard his voice. Harry saying. *'Jesus Christ!'* and it gave her goose bumps standing in her T-shirt and panties, one hand on the railing that curved around the open upstairs landing. Her eyes held on the foyer, directly below: dark except for a square of light on the floor, coming out of the study. A few minutes passed. Karen was about to step back into the bedroom to call the police when she heard Harry's voice again, Harry saying, *'What people?'* and then repeating it, *'What people?'* With an edge this time, Harry acting tough. A good sign. He wouldn't use that tone with a burglar. Little Harry Zimm, with his perm, his frizzed hair, loved to act tough. But then Karen began to wonder if Harry could be talking to himself. Harry into the Scotch again.

What people?

Meaning the people he wanted to get out from under, his investors, the undesirables. Harry trying to convince himself there was no problem.

What people?

As if to say, What, those guys? Seeing if he could make the mess he was in seem trivial.

It was possible. He used to talk to himself sometimes when he was loaded, or rewriting dialogue in a script, look at the line and recite it to her aloud, when they were living together. She liked the idea of Harry boozing, trying to reassure himself. She liked it a lot better than thinking someone had broken in and was still in the house. Harry talking to himself made sense.

Until his voice, raised, came out of the study again.

'*You heard me.*'

Karen listened, holding on to the railing.

That was it. *You heard me*. Then silence.

Would he say that to himself? She didn't think so. Unless he was acting out his own kind of scene, imagining what he would like to tell his money guys. *You heard me*. Harry hating to be controlled, especially by outsiders, people not in the movie business. Harry called investors a necessary evil. Talking to him earlier he had sounded okay . . .

But looked awful.

In the past ten years he'd become a fat little sixty-year-old guy with frizzy hair. The same guy she once thought was a genius because he could shoot a ninety-minute feature in ten days and be looking at a workprint two weeks later . . .

Harry doing the first of the *Slime Creatures* in Griffith Park when she read for him in bra and panties, he said to give him an idea of her figure, and she got the part. Karen asked him if he did horror or T and A and Harry explained to her the philosophy of ZigZag Productions. 'Zig for the maniac, escaped lunatic and dope-crazed biker pictures.' No vampires or werewolves; she would never get bitten or eaten. 'Zag for the ones featuring mutations fed on nuclear waste, your slime people, your seven-foot rats, your maggots the size of submarines. But there's nothing wrong with showing a little skin in either type picture.' She told him if he was talking about full frontal nudity, forget it, she didn't do porn, hard or soft. If she had to go to bed with him, okay, one time only, but it would have to be an awfully good part. Harry acted insulted. He said, 'You ought to be ashamed of yourself, I'm old enough to be your uncle. But I like your spunk and the way you talk. Where you from, somewhere in Texas?' She told him he was close, Alamogordo, where her dad was a rocket man and her mom was in real estate. Karen told him she left to study drama at New Mexico State, but since coming here had done nothing but wait on tables. Harry said, 'Let's hear you scream.' She gave him a good one and he gave her a big smile saying, 'Get ready to be a star.'

Karen was slimed to death within twenty minutes of her first appearance on the screen.

Michael, who had also read for a part and was turned down, told her she was lucky, not have to hang around the set. It was where she first met Michael, when they were casting *Slime Creatures* fifteen years ago, saw him a few other times after, but they didn't seriously get it on until Michael was a star and she was living with Harry . . . tired of it, saying mean things and arguing by that time, picking at dumb lines that had never bothered her before. Like the one Harry threw at her in bed, out of nowhere . . .

'Maybe it's only the wind.'

Knowing she'd remember it.

Instead of giving him a look, she should have said, 'What're you up to, Harry? What can I do for you?'

Make him come out and say it instead of trying to take her down memory lane. It was so obvious. Harry wanted her to use her influence with Michael to set up a meeting. But wanted it to be her idea, happy to do him this favor because she owed him, theoretically, for putting her in pictures, making her a ZigZag Productions star.

But it was weird – hearing that line again.

When she first read it she said to Harry, 'You've got to be kidding.' It was his line, he was always rewriting, sticking in additional dialogue. Harry said, 'Yeah, but it works. You hear the roof being torn off, you look up and say to the guy, "Maybe it's only the wind." You know why?'

'Because I'm stupid?'

'Because you want it to be the wind and not that fucking maniac up there. It may sound stupid, but what it does, it gives the audience a chance to release nervous laughter.'

'At my expense,' Karen said.

And Harry said, 'You going to sulk? It's entertainment, babe. It's a put-on, the whole business of making pictures. You ever catch yourself taking it seriously you're in trouble.'

Karen recited the line. It got a laugh and a picture that cost four hundred thousand to make grossed over twenty million worldwide. She told Harry it was still schlock. He said, 'Yeah, but it's my schlock. If it doesn't make me famous, at least it can make me rich.'

She might ask Harry in the morning, 'Who's taking it seriously now?' Harry dreaming of a twenty-million-plus production he'd never get off the ground. And a star he'd never sign. With or without her help.

She might ask him, 'Remember I told you last night about a picture I've been offered?' After a seven-year layoff. She had expected Harry to at least be curious, show some interest. 'You remember I wanted to talk about it and all you said was "Yeah? Great"?'

Now she was the one taking it seriously, standing on the upstairs landing in her T-shirt . . . listening, beginning to see the stairway and the foyer below as a set.

It would be lighted to get eerie shadows and she would have on a see-through nightie rather than a T-shirt. She hears a sound and calls out softly, 'Harry? Is that you?' She starts down the stairs and stops as a shadow appears in the foyer, a moving shadow coming out of the study. She calls again, 'Harry?' in a stupid, tentative voice knowing goddamn well it isn't Harry. If it's a Zig shadow, now the maniac

34

appears, looks up, sees her. A Zag shadow is followed by a gross, oversized mutation. Either one, she stands there long enough to belt out a scream that will fill movie theaters, raise millions of goose bumps and make Harry a lot of money.

Karen cleared her throat. It was something she always did before the camera rolled. Cleared her throat and took a deep breath. She had never screamed for the fun of it because it wasn't fun. After only three takes – Harry's limit – her throat would be raw.

The house was so quiet.

She was thinking, Maybe do one, hang it out there for about five beats. See what happens.

And in almost the same moment heard Harry's voice coming from the study.

'We gonna sit here all night?'

Now she heard a faint murmur of voices, Harry's and another voice, but not the words, Harry carrying on a conversation with someone who had walked in her house, or broken in. You could take that seriously. Now she heard Harry's voice again, unmistakably Harry.

'Yeah? What's it about?'

Those familiar words.

A question she heard every day when they were living together and Harry got her involved in story development because he hated to read. *What's it about?* Never mind a script synopsis, coverage to Harry meant giving him the plot in three sentences, fifty words or less.

Karen went back through the bedroom to the bathroom and turned the light on. She stared at herself in the mirror as she took a minute to run a comb through her hair.

What's it about? . . . It's what Hollywood was about. Somebody making a pitch.

5

While they were still in the other room, the study, getting ready to come out here, Harry said to him, 'You're Chili? . . . I don't think I caught your last name.'

Chili told him it was Chili Palmer and saw Harry give him that look. Oh? Like he was wondering what the name was before somebody changed it.

They were in the kitchen now. It was as big as the kitchen in the Holmhurst Hotel, Atlantic City, where he had washed dishes a couple of summers when he was a kid, back before they tore the place down to make a parking lot. The fifth of Dewar's, what was left of it, and a tray of ice were on the butcher-block table. There were all kinds of pots and pans hanging from a rack right above them. He saw Harry, who was sitting at the end of the table facing the door to the hall, look up as he was about to take a drink and stop.

Harry said, 'Karen?' sounding surprised. He took the drink then and said, 'Karen, say hello to Chili Palmer. Dick Allen sent him. You remember Dick, at Mesas? Chili, this is Karen Weir.'

'Flores,' Karen said.

'That's right,' Harry said, 'you changed it back.'

Chili had been telling his movie idea until this interruption, which he didn't mind at all, a chance to meet Karen Flores. He sat with his arms resting on the table, looking past his shoulder now at Karen in the doorway, the

36

hall behind her dark. She looked smaller in real life than in movies, about five-two and no more than ninety-nine pounds. She was still good-looking, but where was all the blond hair? And the boobs he remembered as big ones for her slim figure. He nodded, saying to her, 'Karen, it's a pleasure. How you doing?'

She didn't say anything, looking at him as if trying to figure out if she knew him. Or she was giving him a pose, standing there with her arms folded in a Los Angeles Lakers T-shirt that came down just past her crotch and was like a little minidress on her. Middle of the night, never saw him before in her life – she could be on the muscle without showing it. Her legs were nice and tan.

Harry was telling her, 'Chili's the one called you the other day. He says just from talking to you on the phone he had a feeling I'd show up here sooner or later. You imagine that?'

Harry seemed in a better mood since coming out here to get ice and they sat down with their drinks, Harry more talkative. Listening to the movie idea he kept sticking his own ideas in.

Chili straightened, touched the front of his jacket to smooth it down. He thought of getting up but now it was too late. He liked the way Karen kept looking right at him without appearing nervous or emotional, putting on any kind of act. No, this was her. Not anything like Karen the screamer facing the maniac with a butcher knife or seven-foot rats or giant ticks gorged on human blood. He liked her hair, the way it was now, thick and dark, hanging down close to one eye. He noticed how thin her neck was and took a few more pounds off, got her down to around ninety-five. He figured she was now up in her thirties, but hadn't lost any of her looks to speak of.

'He's telling me an idea for a movie,' Harry said. 'It's not bad, so far.' He motioned with his glass. 'Tell Karen, let's see what she thinks.'

'You want me to start over?'

'Yeah, start over.' Harry looked at Karen again. 'Why don't you sit down, have a drink?'

Chili watched her shake her head.

'I'm fine, Harry.'

He liked her voice, the quiet way she spoke. She was looking at him again, curious, doing a read.

'How did you get in the house?'

'The door from the patio, in back.'

'You broke in?'

'No, it was open. I mean it wasn't locked.'

'What if it was?'

That was a good question. He didn't have to answer it though, Harry saying, 'He works for Dick Allen. Got sent here to check up on me.'

Karen said, 'Oh,' and nodded. 'That makes it all right to walk in my house.'

Chili didn't say anything. He liked the way she was handling it. If she was pissed off you couldn't tell.

'He knew I was gonna turn up here,' Harry said, 'just from talking to you on the phone.'

'Why, what did I say?'

'Something about your voice. It was a feeling he had, a hunch. You want to hear his idea?'

Chili watched her. His feeling now was Karen'd say no and tell him to get the hell out of her house. But she didn't say anything. Or Harry didn't give her a chance.

'It's about a guy,' Harry said, 'who scams an airline out of three hundred grand. Go on, tell her.'

'You just did.'

'I mean the way you told it to me. Start at the beginning, we see how the story line develops.'

38

'Well, basically,' Chili said, 'this guy owes a shylock fifteen thousand, plus he's a few weeks behind on the vig, the interest you have to pay, on account of he doesn't have it. The guy runs a drycleaner's but spends everything he makes at the track.'

Chili could see Harry ready to cut in and let him.

'You understand what he means,' Harry said. 'The guy borrowed money from a loan shark. It's the kind of situation, you don't pay you get your legs broken.'

'Or the guy thinks he could get 'em broken,' Chili said. 'You have to understand the loan shark's in business the same as anybody else. He isn't in it looking for a chance to hurt people. He's in it to make money. You go to him, you understand that, you're gonna pay him every week. You don't like that idea, you don't have any business going to him.'

Karen said, 'Yeah?' Telling him to go on.

'But you don't make your payments,' Harry said, 'you can get your legs broken, or worse.'

'It can happen,' Chili said, looking at Karen, 'but it's not, you know, the usual way. Maybe once in a while you hear about it.'

'If the guy doesn't think it's gonna happen to him,' Harry said, 'you don't have a story. That's the only reason he gets on the plane, he's scared to death, he's running for his life.'

'That's right,' Chili said, 'the guy's scared. I just meant he wouldn't necessarily get his legs broken in that kind of situation, a few weeks behind. The guy doesn't know any better, so he gets on the plane.'

'This's Miami,' Harry said. 'He's going to Vegas. He's got a few bucks and he's thinking maybe it's his only chance.'

'He gets on the plane,' Chili said, watching Karen's eyes come back to him, 'ready to go, and the plane sits there at the gate, doesn't move. They announce over the PA there's some kind of mechanical problem, they'll be there maybe an hour, but keep your seats in case they get it fixed sooner. The guy's nervous, in no shape to just sit there, sweat it out. So he gets off the plane, goes in the cocktail lounge and starts throwing 'em down, one after the other. He's in there when the plane takes off . . .'

'Without him,' Harry said. 'The guy's so out of it he doesn't even know it's gone.'

'That's right,' Chili said. 'As a matter of fact, he's still in the cocktail lounge when he hears people talking about a plane crash. But the shape he's in, he doesn't find out right away it's the plane he was on. It didn't gain altitude on account of something to do with the wind and went down in the Everglades, the swamp there, and exploded. Killed everybody aboard, a hunnerd and seventeen people counting the crew. Then when the guy finds out it was his flight, he can't believe it. If he'd stayed on that plane he'd be dead. Right then he knows his luck has changed. If everybody thinks he's dead he won't have to pay back the fifteen or what he owes on the vig, four and a half a week. He'd be saving himself a pile of dough.'

Karen was about to say something, but Harry beat her.

'Not to mention saving his ass.'

She said to Chili, 'The interest is four hundred and fifty a week on fifteen thousand?'

'That's right. Three percent.'

'But a week,' Karen said. 'That's a hundred and fifty percent a year.'

'A hunnerd and fifty-six,' Chili said. 'That's not too bad. I mean some'll charge you more'n that, go as high as six for five on a short-term loan.'

He watched her shrug without unfolding her arms.

'What the guy does,' Chili said, 'is look in the *Herald* for his name on the list of victims. See, the way the plane

40

exploded and went down in the swamp, they're not only having trouble identifying bodies, they can't find 'em all. Or a lot of 'em, they find like just parts of bodies, an arm . . . Others, they're burned beyond recognition. So when the guy doesn't see his name in the paper right away, he has his wife call the airline and say her husband was on that flight. What they do, they bring her out to the airport where they're identifying bodies and going through personal effects, whatever wasn't burned up. See, the guy's bags were on the plane. Oh, the bodies they keep in refrigerated trucks right there in the hangar. They don't show the wife any bodies, they tell her to get her husband's dental chart from his dentist. She says Leo hasn't been to a dentist for as long as they're married. The guy's name is Leo, Leo Devoe.'

Karen moved to lean against the doorjamb and Chili noticed she was barefoot. He wondered if she wore anything under that T-shirt she slept in.

'So what the wife does, she identifies stuff from Leo's bags. Tells 'em what to look for and there it is, his monogrammed shirts, what kind of razor he used, things only she would know about. So Leo's identified and gets his name in the paper. A couple days go by, people from the airline come to see the wife, tell her how sorry they are and all and offer her a settlement, the amount based on what he would've earned operating the drycleaner's the rest of his life. Leo had some kind of trouble with his kidneys, so they were giving him about ten years.'

'Yeah, but wait,' Harry said. 'The best part, the guy hadn't even thought about a settlement, he's so happy to get out from under the shylock. All of a sudden he realizes he can sue the airline, go for at least a million. It's the loser's grandiose dream, see, but now he's pressing his luck . . .'

Karen said, 'How much is the wife offered? . . .'

Chili started to tell her as Harry said, 'Three hundred

41

grand, and they take it, money in the hand, babe. The guy has his wife cash the check and he takes off for Las Vegas with the dough. Gets there, he's supposed to call her, tell her when to come out . . . Wait, he does call her a couple of times.'

'Twice,' Chili said. 'Basically stringing her along.'

'After that, nothing,' Harry said. 'She never hears from him again. Meanwhile, the guy's hot. Runs the three hundred grand up to almost half a million . . .'

'He comes to LA,' Chili said, and stopped as Harry raised his hand.

'It drives the guy nuts, he's winning but can't tell anybody who he is. You show in a back story his motivation, his desire to be famous, pal around with celebrities, the head-liners doing the big rooms. Now he's got the dough to buy his way in, mix with celebs and he can't resist the tempta-tion. Even if it means he's liable to be revealed as a fraud, and very likely shot dead by the shylock, he makes up his mind to go for it. Where else but Hollywood. That wouldn't be a bad title, *Go for It*.' Harry said all this to Karen. Now he looked at Chili again. 'So, he comes to LA . . .'

'I don't know about his wanting to meet celebrities,' Chili said, 'that's something new. But, yeah, he comes to LA. Then, after that, I don't know what happens.'

He saw Karen waiting. She seemed patient, moved only that one time. He turned his head to see Harry looking at him, Harry saying after a moment, 'That's it? That's your great idea for a movie?'

'I said I had an idea, that's all.'

'That's half a movie, with holes in it.' Harry looked at Karen. 'Maybe forty minutes of screen time.'

Karen said, 'How did you know Harry was here?'

Like that, getting back to it.

'His car's in the garage,' Chili said.

'You called, that was four days ago. How did you know he'd be here this evening?'

'I've been stopping by. See if there's a gray '83 Mercedes around with ZIGZAG on the license plate.'

'So you walked in. What if all the doors were locked?'

'I would've rung the bell.'

'Hey, it's okay,' Harry said. 'The guy's a friend of Dick Allen's. He's not gonna take anything.'

'It might be okay with you,' Karen said. 'What you're doing, Harry, you're bringing your dirty laundry into my house and I don't want it.'

Chili felt she was going to keep talking but Harry moved in saying he should've rung the bell. Why didn't he? Chili said he wanted to surprise him, catch him with his pants down, so to speak. A little humor there. Nobody laughed though or even smiled. Karen asked, what if she had called the police? Chili told her Harry would've explained to them it was okay, just like he explained it to her now. She stared at him and he stared back at her until Harry told him, well, anyway, he had the beginning of an idea but it was full of holes.

'In the first place,' Harry said, 'it's not believable the wife would get a settlement that fast. From an insurance company? Without them checking her out?'

'They did,' Chili said. 'I didn't tell you all the details, how nervous she was about it and all.'

'Harry doesn't realize it's a true story,' Karen said.

They were both looking at her now.

'That Miami flight that went down in the Everglades, it was on the news every day for about a week, covering the investigation, interviews with witnesses, relatives of the victims from around here . . . Harry was busy.'

Chili caught the tone. So she knew about Harry's problems, but wasn't exactly crying over them.

Harry was squinting, as if to get his memory to work, saying, 'Yeah, on the news . . .' and then turning to Chili. 'That's where you got the idea.'

'Part of it, yeah.'

'And you made up the rest.'

'No, it's all true, Harry, everything I told you.'

This got him squinting again. Chili could see his mind working. He expected to hear from Karen, but Harry was staying with it.

'The part about the shylock?'

'Everything.'

'Wait a minute. You're not the guy, are you?'

Chili said, 'You mean Leo?' shaking his head. It was getting good.

'You wouldn't be talking to me if you were.'

'I'm not the guy, Harry.'

Again he expected Karen to jump in and say something as Harry started thinking, looking up at the pots and pans before getting an idea.

'You know the wife?'

'Yeah, I know her. Fay.'

Harry seemed to like that. It got him hunched over the table. 'You're related to her. Wait – you're her brother.'

Chili shook his head, not giving him any help.

'But you're a close friend. She asked you to help her find her husband.'

'I talked to her, that's all.'

Chili waited. Harry was still thinking of it as a movie instead of real life. You could see him going over the story in his head, trying to come up with the answer. Staring at his glass now to see if it was in there.

Harry said, 'Okay, the guy goes to Vegas . . .' Then stopped and looked at Chili. 'How's the wife know for sure that's where he went?'

'Take my word for it.'

'Okay, he's in Vegas,' Harry said, 'he can't trust any-body, . . . So he uses an assumed name. Right?'

'Larry Paris.'

'How do you know?'

'Trust me.'

'Okay, he starts gambling, gets hot right away . . . Wait a minute, you made that part up. The guy *doesn't* win. That's it – he not only doesn't win he blows the entire three hundred thou, gets into Mesas for a chunk of dough and they send you to find him.'

Now he was back to real life, putting in things he knew, but still making it sound like a movie. Chili felt like saying to him, See? Not a bad idea, huh? At least so far. But Harry was still talking.

'It's what you do, working for the casino. It's why you're here tonight.'

'You're close,' Chili said, 'but you're coming at it wrong. I'm looking for the guy, yeah, but it wasn't the casino sent me. They asked would I look *you* up, that's all.'

'Which I resent,' Harry said, 'and believe me Dick Allen's gonna hear about it.'

'Okay, but getting back,' Chili said, watching the way Harry was staring at him, still interested, 'where you think I fit in the picture?'

Karen said, 'Harry, for God's sake,' sounding bored.

They both looked over at her, Harry saying, 'What's the matter?'

'He's the shylock,' Karen said.

She was staring at him again as Harry said, 'Is that right, that's what you do for a living?'

'What I did up till recently,' Chili said, still looking at Karen. 'After I get done here I'll think about what I'm gonna do next.'

Karen straightened, where she was leaning against the doorjamb. 'With your experience,' she said to Chili, 'you could always become an agent. Right, Harry?'

'Yeah, that's what we need,' Harry said, 'more agents.'

Still looking at Chili she said, 'Well, if I don't see you again . . .' gave him kind of a shrug and walked away, left them.

'She's upset,' Harry said.

'You think so?'

She didn't seem upset to Chili; he thought she had it together, handled it just right.

'You should've rung the bell,' Harry said, hunching over the table. 'But getting back for a minute – it was the guy's wife told you where he went, huh?'

'Yeah, Fay. She felt it was her money more'n it was his,' Chili said. 'So she offers me half of whatever I bring back, if I find Leo and he has any of it left.'

'You didn't mention this before.'

'You said keep it simple.'

'But what it does,' Harry said, 'it adds a whole new dimension to the story. So you went to Las Vegas but didn't find him. The guy stayed a jump ahead of you.'

'No, I found him,' Chili said, and paused.

Harry, waiting, seemed more interested now than he did before.

'You want to hear about what happened in Vegas?'

6

The next evening after the visit with Fay he was in Las Vegas, checked into the Golden Nugget and on the phone with Benny Wade, the man in charge of collections at Mesas. Chili knew him well enough to call his house, tell him he was in town looking for a Leo Devoe and didn't have much time, a couple of days . . .

'Never heard of him.'

Chili said to Benny somebody must know of a flashy kind of guy comes to town with three hundred grand. Benny said high rollers left their money at home and played on credit; this guy sounded like a runaway, the kind dreams of making a score and then flying down to Rio by the sea-o.

'Can you check for me? I'll do you one gratis.'

'That's what I like to hear. Where are you?'

'The Nugget, downtown.'

'What's the matter with Mesas? Give you casino rate.'

'The Strip,' Chili said, 'you have to get a cab to go anywhere. Here, you walk out the door you're in Vegas.'

Right there out the window, the Pioneer, Binion's, Sassy Sally's, all the grind joints, hot slots, discount prime ribs, keno, bingo, race and sports book . . . cleaning and pressing While-U-Wait . . .

'Downtown, you get it out of your system, why you're here, in less'n twenty-four hours.'

'Not to mention it's cheaper,' Benny said. 'You could stay

in your room, watch TV, you want to save money. Or you could've stayed home.'

'I wouldn't be here,' Chili said, 'if I didn't have to find this guy. He took a walk, so the new management tells me he pays or I do.'

Benny said, 'Let me get on it. Leo Devoe?'

'Yeah, but listen, he could be using a different name,' Chili said, looking at While-U-Wait in red neon down on the street. 'You don't score with Devoe, try Paris. It's the name of his drycleaning place.'

Chili wasn't going to get dressed up but changed his mind, put on a dark suit and tie, white shirt – so he wouldn't look like a tourist – a giant neon cowgirl watching him through the window. The suit picked him up, made him feel like going out, find some broad to have dinner with him, nice bottle of wine . . . He was studying himself in the mirror, smoothing his short hair forward to lie flat, wondering why people didn't like to get dressed up anymore, when Benny Wade called back.

'You ought to put down some bets tonight, you're lucky. Did you know that?'

'I try to be.'

'There's a Larry Paris keeps changing hotels, moving up the Strip. Stayed a few nights at the Trop, left and went to the Sands, the Desert Inn, Stupak's Vegas World. Currently he's appearing right up the street from you, at the Union Plaza.'

'So is "Nudes on Ice," ' Chili said, feeling himself getting more into a Vegas mood. 'How's he doing?'

'Nobody knows. He didn't apply for a credit line anywhere he stayed.'

'Not with a phony name. It must be the guy.'

'I mentioned "Larry Paris" and the night manager at Stupak's knew right away who I meant. He said Mr Paris

48

rented a bodyguard to carry his cash. They do that, pay some local stiff ten bucks an hour, try and impress you.'

'That's Leo,' Chili said. 'He must think he died and went to heaven.'

Benny Wade said he sounded like the kind you'd find shooting craps, where you can draw a crowd. Check the dice tables at the Plaza.

It made sense, but didn't take into account this was Chili's lucky night. He went downstairs, walked across that flowery Nugget carpeting and there was Leo playing roulette, a lady's game, Leo betting numbers while his bodyguard, a guy who looked like a young dressed-up weight lifter, held his briefcase.

Chili stood away from the table, behind Leo and a little to one side. Two women in their thirties, wearing party dresses but not too attractive, were across the table from Leo, who was trying to get something going. He'd shake his head at their betting one chip at a time, saying you had to take risks if you wanted to score big. Leo was playing what they called the action numbers, 10 through 15 and 33, the numbers scattered evenly around the wheel. His chips were a shade of green to match his outfit, but there was no way to tell what the chips were worth or how much he was betting. The two women were playing with blue and pink chips. A lot of color at the table, Leo looking like the Easter bunny in a pale green sport coat with gold buttons, an open pink shirt with one of those high Hollywood collars, Leo's face hunched in there behind sunglasses, hair slicked back. Chili watched the wheel spin and stop. The house won. As the two women walked away Leo told them the dinner offer was still on. They said thanks anyway and turned to each other rolling their eyes. Leo watched them go, the poor little drycleaner trying to be a high roller. The bodyguard, a young guy with shoulders that filled his suit, was opening the briefcase now. He brought out a stack of 100s in a paper strap and handed it to Leo, the dealer waiting. Leo tore the strap, wet his thumb and counted out twenty bills he passed to the dealer, who gave Leo his stack of twenty green chips. So he was betting a hundred a spin on each of the seven action numbers, looking for a hit that would pay him 35 to 1. Chili watched. Leo hit and put three chips on each number, his idea of a system. He hit again, collecting over ten grand, tried three chips again on the seven numbers and lost. Now he went back to betting a hundred on each and was covering the numbers when Chili walked up behind him, said, 'Look at me, Leo,' and Leo spilled his chips. The dealer looked over.

Leo, getting himself ready, didn't turn right away. When he came around he was adjusting his sunglasses over a casual expression that showed just enough surprise – a guy who scams three hundred thousand ready to put on whatever kind of act was needed – though all he managed to say was 'Well, well . . .' The bodyguard, with his build and his hair shorter than Chili's, stepped in to put his hand on Leo's shoulder.

Chili said, 'What's this guy do, Leo, stop traffic you want to cross the street?'

'Well, this is a surprise,' Leo said, 'believe me. What're you doing here?'

'I'm collecting,' Chili said. 'Twenty grand even.'

Leo pushed his sunglasses up on his nose. He seemed to be squinting, puzzled. 'I owe you twenty? How you figure that?'

'Expenses,' Chili said, 'and a late charge I'm adding on.'

The young weight lifter had his eyes narrowed, giving Chili his ten-bucks-an-hour bodyguard look.

'Mr Paris, is this guy bothering you?'

Leo waved him off. 'It's okay, Jerry.' Still looking at Chili.

'I was gonna call you, it slipped my mind. Listen, when I'm through here we'll have a drink. I'll write you a check.' Turning to the table he said, 'It's good seeing you, Chil,' and began picking up his chips.

'You'll write me a check,' Chili said. 'You serious? Leo, look at me, I'm talking to you.'

'I'm busy at the moment,' Leo said, studying the table layout. 'Okay? You mind?'

He was serious.

It didn't make sense till Chili began to think about it, staring at Leo's shoulders rounded inside that sporty green jacket, his sprayed hair hanging over the Hollywood collar, and said, 'Lemme ask you something, Leo.'

'You heard Mr Paris,' the ten-dollar bodyguard said. 'He don't want to talk to you.'

'Okay, you ask him,' Chili said, watching Leo reach over the table to cover his action numbers. 'Does he think I just happened to run into him . . .' He saw Leo begin to straighten, bringing his arm in. 'Or I knew where to look?'

Leo turned from the table. The old Leo once again, Leo the loser. He took the case from the bodyguard.

'How much you want?'

'What you owe me. I'm not into extortion, Leo. I will give you one piece of advice you can take any way you want. Call Fay. And I mean tonight, soon.' He felt the bodyguard start to move in and said to him, 'Keep out of this. There's no problem.' Now the bodyguard didn't know what to do. Leo was bringing a stack of currency from the briefcase. 'We're old friends,' Chili said to the bodyguard. 'I knew him when.'

Leo handed him the currency saying, 'Fay told you, huh?'

'What'd you expect?' Chili said, looking hard at Leo, wondering what was going on in the little drycleaner's head. 'What're you doing, Leo? You nuts or something? Can you tell me?'

Leo raised his face, sunglasses shining in the light. 'What am I *do*ing? You kidding? I'm doing what I never dreamed in my whole life I'd ever have a chance to. That's what I'm doing.'

The dealer, watching them with his arms folded, said, 'We have a problem here, gentlemen? I can get the floor-man.'

Benny Wade told him on the phone to go in the door next to the cage, the cashier's window, take a left at the hard count room, go down past the coffeemaker and the Xerox machine and you're there. Benny came out from behind his computer terminal – gray-haired, easygoing, not at all what Chili thought an ex-FBI agent should look like. He didn't act like a guy who'd once been a hard-on in wing tips, either.

'So you found him.'

'I found him,' Chili said, 'then lost him again.'

'You told me on the phone you collected.'

'I did. I wanted to see him about something else. He was suppose to call his wife last night – it's a long story. I talked to her and found out he never called, so I wanted to see him again. This morning I go over the Plaza, he's gone, checked out.'

'Maybe he's back on the Strip.'

'No, he left, went to LA.'

'Let me see what we have there,' Benny said, sat down at the computer and began tapping keys. 'Yeah, one of Dick Allen's customers, guy owes us a hundred and fifty K, over sixty days. You want to talk to Dick? I mean if you're going to LA.'

'Yeah, why not.'

Benny sat there staring at him. 'You found this guy Leo and collected. But you don't seem too happy about it. What's the matter?'

'I don't know if I told you, I had my ass in a crack when I came here.'

'You mentioned it in passing.'

'It's still there,' Chili said. 'You remember your saying to me last night I was lucky, should lay down some bets?'

'Don't tell me the rest,' Benny said, 'I don't want to feel responsible.'

'I'm not blaming you, I'm the one did it.'

'Okay then, how much you lose?'

'What I collected, less some change.'

7

'You know why it doesn't work?' Harry said. 'I mean even before I find out you don't know how it ends. There's nobody to sympathize with. Who's the good guy? You don't have one.'

Chili said, 'The shylock's the good guy.' Sounding surprised.

Harry said, 'You kidding me? The shylock's the heavy in this. Leo's the victim, but we don't give a shit about him either. You don't have a good guy, you don't have a girl in it, a female lead . . . you have a first act, you're partway into the second.'

Chili said to him, 'I guess I better tell you about my coat getting ripped off and this guy named Ray Bones I shot one time and wants to pay me back.'

Harry said, 'Jesus Christ.' He said, 'Yeah, I think you better.'

They were still in the kitchen, three A.M., drinking coffee now and smoking Chili's cigarettes till he ran out and Harry found a pack of Karen's menthols.

'That's everything?' Harry said.

'Pretty much.'

'You have scenes that appear to work, but don't quite make it,' Harry said, wanting to know more about this guy without encouraging him too much. 'The one in the casino, for example, at the roulette table. You don't do enough with the bodyguard.'

'Like what?'

'The scene,' Harry said, 'that type of scene in a picture, should build a certain amount of tension. The audience is thinking, Jesus, here it comes. They know you're a tough guy, they want to see how you handle the bodyguard.'

'Yeah, well in real life,' Chili said, 'you start something in a casino, you get thrown out and told don't come back. What I didn't mention, the next day it was the bodyguard, Jerry, told me Leo got on a flight to LA. I had to find him first, check the different companies rent out bodyguards.'

'You have to threaten him?'

'You want me to say I beat him up,' Chili said, 'this guy bigger'n I am. What I did, I took him out to breakfast. I even asked him how Leo did. Jerry goes, "Oh, not too bad. I put him on that airplane with four hundred fifty-four thousand dollars, that's all." '

'Why would he tell you that?'

'The kid was dying to tell me, it made him feel important. It's like saying you know where a movie star lives, being on the in.'

Harry said, 'I know where all kinds of movie stars live. It doesn't do a thing for me.'

Chili said, 'Yeah? I wouldn't mind driving past some of their homes sometime.'

'You know who used to live right here? Cary Grant.'

'No shit. In this house?'

'Or it was Cole Porter, I forget which.'

Harry was lighting another one of Karen's menthols, tired, getting a headache now, but staying with it.

'So you have no idea where Leo is, other than he's in LA.'

'I don't even know that for sure. Fay, his wife, still hasn't heard. I called her again, she gave me a name to check, some

55

broad she knows Leo met at a drycleaners' convention. It's why I'm staying at the motel over on Ventura Boulevard. It's near Hi-Tone Cleaners, the broad's place, but she's out of town. I'm hoping she's with Leo and they'll be back sometime.'

'Say you find him, then what?'

Chili didn't answer right away and Harry waited. He saw the guy himself having far more possibilities than his idea for a movie.

'There are different ways I could go with it,' Chili said. 'Basically, you might say it's the wife's money. It was paid to *her*.'

'Basically,' Harry said, 'it's the airline's money. That doesn't bother you?'

'Bother me – I didn't cop it, they did.'

'Yeah, but you're talking about going halves with the wife.'

'No, I said that's what she offered. I never said anything else about it. There might even be a few things, Harry, I haven't told you.'

Starting to get cagey on him.

Harry had to think a moment, go at it another way. He said, 'The plot thickens, huh? You have a girl in it now, even though she doesn't do much. See, it gets better the more details you give me. So you're at the roulette table, he pays off his debt . . . You didn't discuss the wife?'

'He realized I must've talked to her. That's what brought him back to earth.'

'I mean you didn't say anything about basically it was her money.'

'It looked like management was gonna get involved, so I left. But I told him, yeah, he better call her.'

'So then you took the twenty gees in your hot little hands,' Harry said with some pleasure, 'and blew it.'

'I dropped a little over seventeen,' Chili said, 'before my brain started working again. But the thing that got me about Leo, he looks me right in the eye and goes, "When I'm through here I'll write you a check." Like he's telling me he'll do it when he has time, so get off my back. This drycleaner, been on the hook to us for years, talking to me like that. I couldn't believe it.'

Harry said, 'He must've thought you ran into him by accident.'

'Yeah, like I don't know he's suppose to be dead. But what I'm talking about, *he* knows he's six weeks behind on the vig. That has to be right in the front of his head. But what's he do, he cops an attitude on me. I couldn't believe it. He comes on to me like there was no way I could touch him.'

'It made you mad,' Harry said.

'The more I thought about it, yeah. At the time, it surprised me. I never saw him act like that before. Then after, I got pretty mad thinking about it.'

'That kind of attitude,' Harry said, 'is called delusions of grandeur, or, trying to play the power game. Having the bodyguard carry his bag was the tip-off. Out here it's very common. You see it in actors – guy making a hundred grand a picture gets lucky, his next one turns out to be a hit and his price goes up to a million. Pretty soon he's up to several million a picture plus a cut of the gross. He's the same schmuck who made it on his tight pants and capped teeth, but now all of a sudden he knows everything there is about making pictures. He rewrites the script or has it done. He tells the director how he's gonna play his part, and if he doesn't like the producer he has him barred from the set. But directors, producers, anybody can play the power game, especially agents. You keep score by getting so many points for being seen with the right people, driving a Ferrari or a Rolls, what table you get at Spago or The Ivy, what well-known actress blew you on location, how many of your phone calls to the real power players in town are returned, all that kind of bullshit.'

Harry paused. He was getting off the track, wasting time.

'But when Leo tried to play the game, you pulled it out from under him. That was pretty neat, it's a good scene.'

Harry paused again and was aware of the refrigerator humming in the silence. It was too bright in here, uncomfortable and his head ached. He didn't want to move, though. Not now.

'I like the coat story, too, you mentioned. It plays, but would work better if it wasn't a flashback. What it does, though, it shows you know how to handle yourself in that kind of situation. I imagine in your line of work there were other times . . .'

'I'm out of that now.'

'But there were times, right, you had to get tough? Say one of your customers stopped paying?'

'They always paid,' Chili said. 'Oh, I've smacked guys. Smacking was common, just an open-hand smack, I'm talking to a guy trying to get my money, he looks away and I smack him in the face. "Hey, you look at me when I'm fuckin talking to you." Like that, get their attention. See, the kind of people we were dealing with, a lot of 'em thought they were tough guys, you know, from the street, guys that were basically hustlers, thieves, or they were into drugs. We had them besides the legit people, who ordinarily didn't give us any trouble, always paid on time. I think what you're getting at, Harry, you have the same attitude as some of the legitimate people I did collection work for. Like a car dealer, or a guy runs a TV store . . . They're carrying a deadbeat, they want you to get the money and they don't care how, break his fuckin legs. That's the first thing they think of, come up with that statement. I say to 'em, "How's he gonna pay you he's in the hospital?" They don't think of that. They want a piece of the guy *and* their money.'

Harry said, 'Well, you've been in some tight spots. The business with Ray Bones – that's a good name for a character. I meant to ask you, you weren't arrested for shooting him that time?'

'Bones had the idea of doing me on his own,' Chili said. 'He told the cops it happened out on the street, an unknown assailant come up to him. He still wants to do me, it's on his mind.'

'And you still have to pay him?'

'Yeah, only we have a different arrangement now. I talked to Tommy Carlo on the phone . . . You have to know Tommy, his personality, he gets along with everybody. Jimmy Cap I mentioned, Capotorto? He always liked Tommy. But he has to go along with Ray Bones up to a point, Ray's his guy. So Jimmy Cap says split what the dead guy owes, me and Tommy, fuck the running vig, a flat eight grand each and that's it, forget it.'

'You spoke to Tommy,' Harry said, leaning over the table on his arms. 'So now he knows Leo's still alive.'

'Did I say that?'

Harry sat back again, questions popping in his mind along with the headache, but wanting to appear relaxed, the producer showing a certain amount of interest in a story.

'So you didn't happen to mention it to him,' Harry said and grinned at the deep-set eyes staring at him. 'You want Leo Devoe for yourself.'

'What I *don't* want,' Chili said, 'is Ray Bones finding out. Tommy, he'd think it's pretty funny, this drycleaner taking an airline. He'd swear he wouldn't tell a soul, but I know he would. So why put him in that position?'

'But you still have Ray Bones to think about.'

Chili moved his shoulders. The deep-set eyes didn't change.

'You gonna pay him?'

'Maybe, when I get around to it.'

'What if he comes looking for you?'

'It's possible. The guy's got a one-track mind.'

'Have you been involved in any shootings since Ray Bones?'

Chili's eyes moved and he seemed to be thinking about it or trying to remember, looking off for a moment.

'Well, there was one time, it was when me and Tommy were running a club in South Miami, a guy came in looking for another guy, not me, but I was in the way.'

'What happened?'

'Nothing. He shot the guy and left.'

Now Harry paused. Chili Palmer had been sent to him from heaven, no question about it.

'You were running a club?'

'Belonged to Momo. We had entertainment, different groups'd come in, catering mostly to the younger crowd.'

Harry had the next question ready.

'You pack a gun?'

Chili hesitated. 'Not really.'

'What does that mean?'

'Not ordinarily. Maybe a few times I have.'

'You ever been arrested?'

'I've been picked up a few times. They'd try to get me on loan-sharking or a RICO violation – you know what I mean? Being in what they call a racketeering kind of activity, but I was never convicted, I'm clean.'

'Racketeering, that covers a lot of ground, doesn't it?'

'What do you want to know?'

Harry hesitated. He wasn't sure.

'Why don't you get to the point, Harry? You want me to do something for you, right?'

8

Here was a man had made forty-nine movies and named a bunch of them earlier, when he was making coffee. Chili remembered having seen quite a few. The one about the roaches – guy turns on the kitchen light, Christ, there's a fuckin roach in there as big as he is. He had seen some of the *Grotesque* movies, about the escaped wacko who'd been in a fire and was pissed off about it. The one about the giant ticks trying to take over the earth. The one about all the people in this town getting scalped by an Indian who'd been dead over a hundred years, *Hair-raiser* . . . Forty-nine movies and he looked more like a guy drove a delivery truck or came to fix your air-conditioning when it quit, a guy with a tool kit. When he'd gone over to the range to get the coffee in his shirt and underwear showing his white legs, skinny for a fat guy, he looked like he should be in detox at a booze treatment center. Chili had seen loan customers in this shape, ones that had given up. Harry's mind seemed to be working okay, except all of a sudden he wasn't as talkative as before.

'Tell me what you're thinking, Harry.'

Maybe he didn't know how to say it without sounding like a dummy.

'Okay, you want me to help you out in some way,' Chili said. 'How do I know – outside of your asking me questions here like it's a job interview. I happened to mention – we were in the other room – I said when I came out here I talked to some people and you kept saying "What people?" having a fit. You remember that? Well, they were a couple lawyers I was put in touch with. I told you I talked to Tommy Carlo . . .'

Harry was listening but making a face, trying to understand everything at once.

'What's he got to do with it?'

'I go to your apartment, your office on Sunset, ZigZag Productions, you're not either place and nobody knows where you are. So I call Tommy, now in tight with Jimmy Cap, and ask him, see if he can get me a name out here, somebody that knows somebody in the movie business. Tommy calls back, says, "Frank DePhillips, you're all set." You ever hear of him?'

Harry shook his head.

'Don't go to sleep on me, okay?'

'I got a headache, that's all. Who's Frank DePhillips?'

'He's to some part of LA what Jimmy Cap is to South Miami. But I don't meet with him, he's on a level only talks to certain people. I meet with one of his lawyers down at the courts, criminal division. Young guy, he comes running out of a courtroom loaded down with papers and shit, looks at me, says, "What do you want?" Fuckin lawyers, they're always rushing around the last minute. I remind him Mr DePhillips set this up, also I happen to represent one of the biggest casinos in Vegas. That gets me about two minutes of his time. He says, "I'll see what I can do. Gimme a phone number." I tell him I'll call him, otherwise I'd never hear. Also I don't want him to know I'm staying at this dump on Ventura. Two days later I meet him and another lawyer in a restaurant in a hotel that's Japanese. I mean the entire hotel, not just the restaurant, a Japanese hotel right in the middle of downtown LA.'

Harry said, 'Yeah, the Otani.'

'Right by the city hall. These two lawyers eat there all the time. I watch 'em dig into the raw fish, suck up bowls of noodles . . . The noodles weren't bad. So this other lawyer gives me addresses and phone numbers, yours and anybody you ever been intimate with on a single sheet of paper. He says, "You're not the only one looking for old Harry Zimm," and mentions your investors have been trying to find you for two months. I said, "Oh, what's the problem?" Guy says, "It looks like Harry skipped with two hunnerd thousand they put in one of his movies."'

Harry was shaking his head. He looked worn out.

'That doesn't surprise me. This town loves rumors, everybody knows everything, just ask them. My investors have been trying to find me for two months? I spoke to them, it wasn't more than two weeks ago.'

Chili said, 'You mention the Piston-Lakers game?'

Harry said, 'Look, these guys came to me originally, I mean before. They already put money in two of my pictures and did okay, they're happy. Which you can't say about most film investors, the ones that want to be in show biz, get to meet movie stars and they find out, Christ, it's a high-risk business.'

Harry was easing into it, watching his step.

Chili said, 'Yeah? . . .'

'These guys already know movie stars, celebrities; they run a limo service. So they come in on another participation deal – this was back a few months ago when I was planning what would be my next picture. About a band of killer circus freaks that travel around the country leaving bodies in their wake. The characters, there's a seven-hundred-pound fat lady who wouldn't fit through that door, has a way of seducing guys, gets them in her trailer—'

Chili said, 'Harry, look at me,' and waited to see his watery eyes in the kitchen light, frizzed hair standing up.

'You're trying to tell me how you fucked up without sound-ing stupid, and that's hard to do. Let's get to where you're at, okay? You blew their two hunnerd grand on a basketball game and you haven't told 'em about it Why not?'

'Because they're not the type of guys,' Harry said, 'would take it with any degree of understanding or restraint.'

'They scare you.'

'What'd I just say?'

'I'm not sure. You want to say something to me, Harry, say it, don't beat around the bush.'

'Okay, they scare me. I keep thinking the first thing they'd do is break my legs.'

'You got that on the brain. What's the second thing?'

'Or they'd have it done – you don't know these guys. They're not exactly financial types.'

'Harry, I prob'ly know 'em better than you do. What you're telling me,' Chili said, 'they got more out on the street than limos. They're dealing, huh? Selling dope to movie stars and using you to launder their dough. Put it in a Harry Zimm production, take it out cleaned and pressed.'

Chili waited.

Harry eased back. The chair creaked and that was the only sound.

'You don't know or you don't want to or you're not saying,' Chili said. 'But from what you tell me, that's what it sounds like.'

He smiled, wanting Harry to relax.

'You have my interest aroused. I wouldn't mind knowing more about these guys, if they're real hard-ons or they're giving you a buncha shit. Or what their connections are, if they have any. But what I want to know first,' Chili said, 'is why you took their two hunnerd grand to Vegas, put yourself in that kind of a spot. I mean if you're scared of these guys to begin with . . .'

65

'I had to,' Harry said, sounding pretty definite about it. 'I've got a chance to put together a deal that'll change my life, make me an overnight success after thirty years in the business . . . But I need a half a million to get it started.'

'A movie,' Chili said, wanting to be sure.

'A blockbuster of a movie.'

'You don't want to ask your limo guys?'

'I don't want them anywhere near it,' Harry said. 'It's not their kind of deal, it's too big.' Harry was hunching over the table again. 'See, what happened . . . This's at the time I'm getting *Freaks* ready for production. I've got a script, but it needs work, get rid of some of the more expensive special effects. So I go see my writer and we discuss revisions. Murray's good, he's been with me, he wrote all my *Grotesque* pictures, some of the others. He's done I don't know how many TV scripts, hundreds. He's done sitcoms, westerns, sci-fi, did a few *Twilight Zones* . . . Only now he can't get any TV work 'cause he's around my age and the networks don't like to hire any writers over forty. Murray has kind of a drinking problem, too, that doesn't help. Likes the sauce, smokes four packs a day . . . We're talking – get back to what I want to tell you – he happens to mention a script he wrote years ago when he was starting out and never sold. I ask him what it's about. He tells me. It sounds pretty good, so I take the script home and read it.' Harry paused. 'I read it again, just to be sure. My experience, my instinct, *my gut*, tells me I have a property here, that with the right actor in the starring role, I can take to any studio in town and practically write my own deal. This one, I know, is gonna take on heat fast. The next day I call Murray, tell him I'm willing to option the script.'

'What's that mean?'

'You pay a certain amount to own the property for a year, take it off the market It's an option to buy. I paid Murray five hundred against twenty-five thousand if I exercise the option, then another twenty-five at the start of principal photography.'

'That doesn't sound like much.'

'It's an old script, been shopped around.'

'Then why do you think you can get it made?'

'Because on the other hand it's so old it's new. The kid studio execs they have now had just come into the world when Murray wrote it.'

'So you don't buy it,' Chili said, 'till you know you have a deal. Is that right?'

'Or raise the money independently,' Harry said, 'which is the way I prefer to go. You retain control. But with the actor I have in mind, I know I'm looking at a twenty-million-dollar picture, minimum, and that means going to one of the majors. Otherwise I wouldn't go in a studio to take a leak.'

'You're so sure it's a winner,' Chili said, 'what's the problem?'

'I told you, I need a half a million to get started,' Harry said. 'See, the guy I want is the kind of star not only can act, he doesn't mind looking bad on the screen. Tight pants and capped teeth won't make it in this one. If I could get Gene Hackman, say, we'd be in preproduction as I speak. But Gene's got something like five pictures lined up he's committed to, I checked.'

Chili thought of his all-time favorite. 'What about Robert De Niro?'

'Bobby De Niro is possibly the finest actor working today, right up there with Brando. But I don't quite see him for this one.'

'Tom Cruise?'

'Wonderful young actor, but that's the problem, he's too young for the part. I'll have to show you my list, the ones I've considered are at least good enough and the right age. Bill Hurt, Dreyfuss, who happens to be hot at the moment,

Pacino, Nicholson, Hoffman . . . Dustin I saw as a close second choice.'

'Yeah? Who's your first?'

'Michael Weir, superstar.'

Chili said, 'Yeah?' surprised. He said, 'Yeah, Michael Weir,' nodding then, 'he's good, all right. The thing I like about him, he can do just about anything, play a regular person, a weirdo . . . He played the mob guy in *The Cyclone* that turned snitch?'

'One of his best parts,' Harry said.

Chili was nodding again. 'They shot that in Brooklyn. Yeah, Michael Weir, I like him.'

'I'm glad to hear it,' Harry said.

'He's a different type than your usual movie star. I think he'd be good,' Chili said, even though he didn't know how to picture Michael Weir in this movie, whatever it was about. 'Have you talked to him?'

'I took a chance, sent the script to his house.' Harry sat back, brushing a hand over his frizzy hair. 'I find out he not only read it, he flipped, absolutely loves the part.'

'You found out – he didn't tell you himself?'

'Remember my saying I need half a mil? I have to deposit that amount in Michael's name, in a special escrow account before he'll take a meeting with me. This is his fucking agent. You have to put up earnest money to show you're serious, you're not gonna waste his time.'

'That's how it's done, huh? Make sure you can handle it.'

'It's how this prick does it, his agent. He says, "You know Michael's price is seven million, pay or play." That means if he signs and for any reason you don't go into production, you still have to pay him the seven mil. You make the picture, it's released, and now he gets ten percent of the gross. Not the net, like everybody else, the fucking gross. Hey, but who cares? He loves the script.'

'How'd you find out?'

'From the guy who's cutting the picture Michael just finished, the film editor. We go way back. In fact, I gave him his start on *Slime Creatures*. He calls, says Michael was in the cutting room with the director, raving about a script he had with him, *Mr Lovejoy*, how it's the best part he's read in years. The cutter, the friend of mine, doesn't know it's my property till he notices *ZigZag Productions* on the script. He calls me up: "You're gonna do one with Michael Weir? I don't believe it." I told him, "Well, you better, if you want to cut the picture." I don't know yet who I want as my director, Jewison, maybe. Lumet, Ulu Grosbard . . .'

Chili said, 'What's it called, *Mr Lovejoy*?'

'That's Murray's title. It's not bad when you know what it's about.'

Chili was thinking it sounded like a TV series, *Mr Lovejoy*, about this faggy guy raising a bunch of kids of different nationalities and a lot of that canned laughter. He wondered if they got people to come into a studio, told them to go ahead, laugh, and they recorded it, or if they told them jokes. He remembered a TV program about how movies were made that showed people kissing their hands, the sound of it being recorded to go in a love scene the hand kissers were watching on a screen. Movies were basically fake. The sounds in a fight scene weren't anything like what you heard nailing some guy in the mouth. Like the fight scenes in the *Rocky* movies, Stallone letting some giant asshole pound him, he'd be dead before the end of round one. But there were good movies too, ones that had the feeling of real life . . .

Harry was saying once he had a development deal at a studio, that would satisfy Mesas, they'd quit bothering him. Harry saying now if he could get to Michael Weir through Karen he wouldn't need to raise the half a mil . . .

Wait a minute. 'What?'

'You knew she was married to Michael at one time.'

'Karen? No . . .'

'Four years, no kids. This is the house they lived in till Michael walked out on her.'

'No, I didn't know that,' Chili said. 'So you want her to call him, set up a meeting?'

'That's all – put in a good word.'

'They get along okay?'

'They never see each other. But he'd do it, I know.'

'Then what's the problem? She won't ask him?'

'I haven't asked *her*,' Harry said. 'If I did, I'm pretty sure she'd turn me down. See, but if she thinks about it a while and it becomes her idea, then she'd do it.'

'I don't follow.'

'That's 'cause you don't know actors,' Harry said, 'the way their minds work. Karen can't just call Michael up cold and ask him. She wasn't even that talented – aside from having that chest, you might've noticed, which I think is what made her a fantastic screamer. But, she still has that actor mentality. Karen would have to *feel* the situation. First, she has to want to do it as a favor to me . . .'

'For putting her in your movies.'

'Yeah, and she lived with me too. Then, she has to have a certain attitude when she calls Michael, feel some of the old resentment. *He* walked out on *her*, so he owes her the courtesy of a positive response. You understand?'

'You and Karen lived together?'

'Three and a half beautiful years. So for old times' sake Karen lays a guilt trip on Michael and I get a free meeting with him.'

'Will she do it?'

'She's lying in bed at this moment thinking about it.'

'It sounds like a long way around to get there,' Chili said, taking his time. He couldn't see Karen living with this guy, even if he wasn't fat then. He could see her with Michael Weir. He said to Harry, 'Well, if she doesn't want to help you for some reason, maybe I could talk to Michael, get you your meeting.'

Harry said, 'How? Threaten him?'

'I'm serious,' Chili said. 'I think I could get next to him, talk about that movie he was in, *The Cyclone*.'

'How would you do that?'

'You want to discuss Michael Weir or Leo the dry-cleaner? All that dough he's carrying around? Came here with four hundred and fifty thousand . . .'

Harry wasn't saying a word now.

'You're thinking,' Chili said, 'what if I was to put you next to the drycleaner. Ask him what he'd rather do, invest his dough in a movie or give it back to the airline and do some time.'

Harry squirmed around in his chair saying, 'It did cross my mind.'

He reached for the pack of cigarettes and tore it open to get at the last one.

'Except I know it would bother you,' Chili said, 'the idea of using money Leo got the way he did.'

Harry said, 'Well, you take my investors, if you want to get technical,' tapping the cigarette on the table, fooling with it, 'or any investors. You don't ask where their money comes from.'

'Which brings us to the limo guys,' Chili said. 'You want 'em to leave you alone, be patient. The time comes to do the *Freaks* movie, okay, you'll give 'em a call. But right now you're into something doesn't concern them.'

Harry looked like he was afraid to move, hanging on every word.

'See, what I could do is talk to the limo guys along those

71

lines,' Chili said, 'make the point in a way they'd understand it.'

He reached over to take the cigarette from Harry's fingers.

'You gonna smoke this?'

'No, it's yours.'

Harry struck a match to light it.

'What would you say?'

'I'd tell 'em it's in their best interest, till you're ready for 'em, to stay the fuck off your back. Isn't that what you want?'

'You don't know these guys.'

'It's up to you, Harry.'

Chili watched Harry's gaze follow a stream of smoke. Harry the producer, with his forty-nine horror movies and his frizzy hair, looking at the offer. His gaze came back to Chili, his expression tired but hopeful.

'What do you get out of this?'

'Let's see how we get along,' Chili said. 'I'll let you know.' He thought of something that had been on his mind and said to Harry, 'The seven-hundred-pound broad that seduces guys in her trailer – what exactly does she do?'

Karen felt the bed move beneath Harry's weight. Lying on her side she opened her eyes to see digital numbers in the dark, 4:12 in pale green. Behind her Harry continued to move, settling in. She watched the numbers change to 4:13.

'Harry.'

'Oh, you awake?'

'What's going on?'

'It's late – I felt you wouldn't mind if he stayed over.'

'Harry, this isn't your house.'

'Just tonight. I put him in the maid's room.'

'I don't have a maid's room.'

'The one back by the kitchen?'

72

There was a silence.

'I don't get it.'

'What?'

'This guy – what're you doing?'

'He's got some ideas, gonna help me out.'

'Harry, the guy's a crook.'

'So? This town he should fit right in.'

Harry rolled away from her, groaning in comfort.

' 'Night.'

There was a silence, the house quiet.

'Harry?'

'Yeah.'

'What's going on?'

'I told you.'

'You want me to call you a cab? You and your buddy?'

She felt Harry roll back toward her.

9

Chili asked Harry if he liked to sleep in. He said, 'If you're gonna sleep in and I have to sit around waiting, forget it. Anything I can't stand is waiting for people.'

Harry acted surprised. He said it was only ten after ten. 'I got back in bed and Karen wanted to talk.'

That stopped Chili.

He wanted to know if Harry was putting him on or what. He couldn't imagine Karen letting this fat guy get in bed with her. But there was no way to find out if it was true.

He said, 'Well, she was up, no problem. She dropped me off to get my car. I come back and have to sit here another hour.'

Harry said the limo guys never got to their office before ten-thirty eleven anyway. Then they'd discuss for about an hour where they were going to have lunch and take off. He said it didn't matter what time you went to see the limo guys, you always had to wait.

Chili said, 'Harry, we don't go see them. They come see us. You want to make the call or you want me to?'

Now they were in Harry's office: upstairs in a two-story building that was part of a block of white storefronts, on Sunset Boulevard near La Cienega. Harry turned on lights, wall sconces in the shape of candles against dark paneling, raised venetian blinds behind his big desk stacked with folders, magazines, scripts, papers, unopened mail, hotel ashtrays, a brass lamp, a clock, two telephones . . .

'Remember 77 *Sunset Strip* on TV? Edd Kookie Byrnes, the parking attendant always combing his hair?'

Harry nodded out the window.

'They used a place right across the street for exteriors. I used to stand here and watch 'em shoot. Efrem Zimbalist, Jr., and Roger Smith were the stars, but the one you remember is Kookie.'

'I wanted blond hair just like his, with the pompadour,' Chili said. 'I was about ten.' He watched Harry staring out the window. 'What about the script?'

'That's right,' Harry said, 'you haven't read it.'

'I don't even know what it's about.'

Going through the pile on his desk, Harry said he hadn't been in the office much lately and his girl, Kathleen, had left him to work for the guy that owned the building, a literary agent who'd been working in Hollywood over fifty years. Had lunch at Chasen's every day, or he'd call and have them deliver. Scallops and creamed spinach. Go down the hall right now – Harry bet that's what he'd be eating, scallops and spinach. 'I asked him one time what type of writing brought the most money and the agent says, "Ransom notes."'

'What about the script, Harry?'

The guy's mind was wandering all over the place. In the car on the way here, Harry had started talking about *Mr Lovejoy*, the story, but was barely into it when he said, 'The famous Trocadero once stood right there,' and the ride to the office became a tour of Sunset Strip, Harry pointing out mostly where places used to be. Schwab's drugstore. Ciro's, known for movie-star bar fights, now the Comedy Store. A restaurant that was once John Barrymore's guesthouse. The

Garden of Allah, where movie stars used to shack up, now a bank and a parking lot. The Chateau Marmont was still there – look at it – home on and off to Jean Harlow, Greta Garbo, Howard Hughes, where John Belushi checked out. Harry wide-awake, but off into Old Hollywood. Then telling what it was like when hippies took over the Strip, little broads in granny dresses, traffic bumper to bumper. 'By the time you got from Doheny to here, you were stoned on the marijuana fumes.' Chili reminded him the limo guys were coming at noon and Harry said, 'Oh . . . yeah.'

He poked through the clutter on his desk till he came to several *Mr Lovejoy* scripts. 'Here it is.'

Chili picked one up, the first time he'd ever held a movie script in his hands. He had no idea what it would look like. It wasn't as thick as he thought it would be, less than an inch of pages between red covers, *ZigZag Productions* printed in gold on the front with speedlines coming off the lettering, the way they showed cars moving in a comic strip. Chili opened the script about in the middle, studied the way the page was set up and began to read, not understanding the first word he saw but kept going.

INT. LOVEJOY'S VAN – DAY

Ilona sits behind the wheel watching the corner bar across the street. Behind her, Lovejoy is getting his video camera ready for action.

ILONA
How long's he been in there?

LOVEJOY
(glancing at his watch)
Seventeen and a half minutes.

ILONA

I wish he'd hurry up.

LOVEJOY
(focusing camera)
We have to be patient. But
sooner or later . . .

ILONA

There he is!

LOVEJOY
(quietly)
I see him.

EXT. CORNER BAR – CLOSE ON ROXY – DAY

Roxy hooks his thumbs in his belt, looks about idly.
Gradually his gaze moves to the van and holds.

INT. LOVEJOY'S VAN – DAY

Ilona reacts, hunching down behind the wheel.

ILONA

He sees us!

LOVEJOY

No, he's walking to the car. Ilona,
this could be it!!!

Chili looked up from the script. 'What's he doing, following
the guy?'

'Read it,' Harry said. 'It's a grabber.'

Chili closed the script, laid it on the desk where he stood
between a pair of fat red-leather chairs, old and cracked. He
said to Harry, 'We better get ready,' placing his hands on the
chairs. 'Make sure they sit here, not over on the sofa.' He saw

Harry tugging at the string to lower the Venetian blinds. 'Leave 'em up, we want the light in their eyes. I'll be at the desk . . . But don't introduce me, let it go, just start talking. You're gonna be here.' Chili stepped back from the chairs. 'Behind 'em when they sit down.'

'They'll be looking at you,' Harry said, 'They don't know who you are.'

'That's right, they're wondering, who's this guy? You don't tell 'em. You're on your feet the whole time. You say, "Well, I'm glad you assholes stopped by, so I can set you straight." '

'You're kidding, right?'

'It's up to you. You're talking, relaxed, you stroll around to where you are now – all you tell 'em is the movie's been postponed. Say, till next year, if you want. But don't tell 'em why or what you're doing.'

'They won't like it.'

'They don't have to. Just do what I tell you,' Chili said. 'Okay, now the two guys. The one in charge is Ronnie? . . .'

'Ronnie Wingate. That's the name of the company, Wingate Motor Cars Limited, on Santa Monica.'

Harry was poking around the desk again, straightening it up. Or nervous, feeling a need to be doing something.

'Ronnie, I think of as a rich kid who never grew up. He's from Santa Barbara, real estate money, came to Hollywood to be an actor but didn't make it. He thinks he knows the business because his grandfather was a producer at Metro at one time. Now he's after me to give him a part, wants to play one of the freaks.'

'Why's he scare you?'

'I don't trust him, he's unstable. He's close to forty, he acts like a burned-out teenager.'

'Maybe that's what he is.'

'He has a gun in his office. He'll take it out and start

aiming it around the room while he's talking to you. With one eye closed, going "Couuu," making that sound, you know, like he's shooting.'

'What kind of gun?'

'I don't know, an automatic.'

'And the other one, Bo Catlett?'

It was a familiar name. When Chili first heard it he thought of an all-star jazz drummer by the name of Catlett.

'He doesn't say much,' Harry said. 'The only time he opened up, I happened to mention I was raised in Detroit and started out there doing movies for the car companies. Catlett said, "Yeah? I went to high school in Detroit. Loved it, like home to me." I told him I couldn't get out of there fast enough. He said, "Then you don't know it." Other times he'd call me Mr De-troit. He might be Chicano or some kind of Latin, I'm not sure, but he has that look. Ronnie mentioned once Catlett had been a farm worker, a migrant, and a lot of them I know are Chicano. He's tall, dresses up . . . You see Ronnie, the boss, he looks like he's going out to cut the grass, Catlett will have a suit and tie on. In fact, almost always. Dresses strictly Rodeo Drive.'

'Bo Catlett,' Chili said. The one he was thinking of was Sid Catlett. Big Sid.

'Ronnie, sometimes he'll call him Cat. He'll say, "Hey, Cat, what do you think?" But you know Ronnie's already made up his mind.' Harry came away from the desk. 'I have to go down the hall.'

'You nervous, Harry?'

'I'm fine. I gotta go to the bathroom, that's all.'

He walked out and Chili moved around behind the desk to sit in the creaky swivel chair and look over Harry's office, his world, old and dusty, his shelves of books and scripts, his photos on the wall above the sofa: Harry with giant bugs, Harry shaking hands with mutants and

79

maniacs, Harry and a much younger Karen with blond hair, Harry holding her by the arm. He didn't look too bad in the pictures. It got Chili thinking about them in bed together. It didn't make sense. There was no way, with her looks, she could be that hard up. This morning when he walked in the kitchen . . .

Karen was having a cup of coffee, reading the paper. Dressed up, ready to leave. Purse and a movie script on the table. She said good morning and asked if he slept okay. Karen could be one of those people who acted more polite when they were pissed off. Chili poured a cup and sat down with her, saying he woke up and forgot where he was for a minute. Karen started reading the paper again and he felt stupid, wanting to start over. She had on a neat black suit, no blouse under it, pearl stud earrings in her dark hair, some eye makeup. Her eyes were brown. She had a nice clean look and smelled good, had some kind of perfume on.

'I'm sorry about walking in your house last night,' Chili said, thinking she'd pass it off and that would be it.

But she didn't. Karen put the paper down saying, 'What do you want me to tell you, it's okay? I'm glad you're here?'

Giving it back to him, but sounding like she was asking a simple question. She wasn't anything like most of the women he was used to talking to. They would've said it in a real sarcastic tone of voice.

'I have a hunch,' she said now, 'if the patio door was locked you would've broken in, one way or another.'

He kept looking at her mouth, done in a light shade of lipstick. She had small white teeth, nice ones. He said, 'I was never much into breaking and entering.'

Karen said, 'But you've always been a criminal, haven't

80

you?' With the cool look and quiet voice, daring him. That's what it seemed like.

So he took it to her saying he had pulled a few holdups when he was a kid and didn't know better, hijacked freight, truckloads of merchandise and hustled it for a living, associated with alleged members of organized crime, but never dealt narcotics; telling her he'd been arrested, held over at Rikers Island, but never convicted of anything and sent to prison. 'Okay, I was a loan shark up till recently and now I'm in the movie business,' Chili said. 'What're you doing these days?'

'I'm reading for a part,' Karen said.

She took her coffee cup to the sink, came back to the table and picked up her purse and the script. Chili asked if she could give him a lift down to Sunset – he'd left his car there, back of a store. Karen said come on.

It wasn't until they were in her BMW convertible, winding down the hill past million-dollar homes, she started to come out of herself and communicate. He asked where she was going. Karen said to Tower Studios. She said she hadn't worked in seven years, didn't have to, but the head of production at Tower had offered her a part. Chili asked if it was a horror movie. A mistake. Karen gave him a look saying she hadn't screamed since leaving ZigZag and was never going to scream again, even in real life. Chili had noticed the title on the cover of the script, *Beth's Room*.

'What's it about?'

This was what opened her up.

'It's about a mother-daughter relationship,' Karen said, already with more life in her tone, 'but different than the usual way it's handled. The daughter, Beth, leaves her yuppie husband after a terrific fight and comes home to live with her mom, Peggy.'

'Which one're you?'

81

'The mom. I was in high school when I had Beth and now she's twenty-one. I did get married but the guy, the father, took off right after. So for the next twenty years I devoted my life to raising Beth, working my tail off – but that's all in the back story, it's referred to. The picture opens, I'm finally living my own life. I own a successful art gallery, I have a boyfriend, an artist, who's a few years younger than I am . . . and along comes Beth, wanting to be mothered. Naturally I'm sympathetic, at first, this is my baby . . .'

'She act sick?'

'She has migraines.'

'I can hear her,' Chili said. ' "Mom, while you're up, would you get me my pills off the sink in the kitchen?" '

Karen was staring at him. She looked back at the road and had to crank the wheel to swerve around a parked car.

' "And bring me a glass of milk, please, and some cookies?" '

'Warm milk,' Karen said, 'with a half ounce of Scotch in it. Did you look at the script?'

'Never saw it before. The daughter, she have a whiney voice?'

'It could be played that way. It's a young Sandy Dennis part. You know who I mean?'

'Sandy Dennis, sure. The daughter blame the mom for her marriage going to hell?'

Karen gave him another look. 'She accuses me of talking her into getting married before she was ready. And that, of course, adds to my sense of guilt.'

'What'd you do you feel guilty about?'

'It's not anything I did. It's more . . . what right do I have to be happy when my daughter's miserable?'

'You know the kid's faking?'

'It's not that simple. You have to read it, see the way Beth works on me.'

82

'You got a problem.'

'Well, yeah, that's what the picture's about.'

'I mean feeling guilty. I think what you oughta do, either give little Beth a kick in the ass or tell her go see a doctor, get her head examined.'

'You don't get it,' Karen said. 'I'm her *mother*. I have to come to grips with my maternal feelings.'

Turning off Doheny, Karen shot through an amber light to swing into the traffic crawling along Sunset.

'People have guilt trips laid on them all the time and they accept it, the guilt. It doesn't have to make sense, it's the way people are.'

'Anywhere along here's fine,' Chili said, thinking of times he had been asked if he was guilty and not once ever having the urge to say he was. Real-life situations, even facing prison time, were never as emotional as movies. Cops got emotional in movies. He had never met an emotional cop in his life. He liked the way Karen side-slipped the BMW through a stream of cars to pull up at the curb. He thanked her, started to get out and said, 'What happens, the kid goes after your boyfriend and that's when you finally stand up to her?'

'You're close,' Karen said.

What he liked best, thinking about it, was not so much guessing the ending but the look Karen gave him when he did. The eye contact. For a moment there the two of them looking at each other in a different way than before. Like starting over. Karen broke the spell saying she had to run and he got out of her car.

Still looking at the photos on the wall he thought about taking a closer look at the ones Karen was in. Check out her eyes. See what they were like when she was a screamer with blond hair. Maybe later.

Right now Harry was saying, 'Here we are.'

Harry, in the doorway, stepping aside, the two limo guys coming into the office past him.

10

Chili stayed where he was, at the desk. The one he took to be Ronnie Wingate – and had been thinking of as the rich kid – glanced at him, that's all, then looked around the office saying, 'Harry, what year is it, man?' with a lazy rich-kid way of talking. 'We enter a time warp? I feel like I'm back in the Hollywood of yesteryear.' He was wearing a suede jacket so thin it was like a second shirt, with jeans and running shoes, sunglasses resting in his rich-kid hair he hadn't bothered to comb.

The other one, Bo Catlett, was an opposite type, tall next to Ronnie and put together in a tan outfit, suit, shirt and tie all light tan, a shade lighter than his skin. But what was he? From across the room he looked like the kind of guy who came from some island in the Pacific Ocean you never heard of. Ronnie kept moving as he looked at the photos over the sofa, his motor running on some chemical. Now Harry was waving his arm, inviting them to sit in the red chairs facing the desk.

Chili watched Catlett coming first, saw the mustache now and the tuft of hair beneath the lower lip and wondered what was wrong with Harry. The guy wasn't Latin or even from some unknown island out in the ocean. Up close he was colored. Colored and something else, but still colored.

Sitting down he said, 'How you doing?'

That's what he was and what the other Catlett, the jazz

drummer, was too. Chili said to him, 'You any relation to Sid Catlett?'

It brought a smile, not much, but enough to make his eyes dreamy. 'Big Sid, huh? No, I'm from another tribe. Tell me what brings you here.'

'The movies,' Chili said.

And Catlett said, 'Ah, the movies, yeah.'

Ronnie was seated now, one leg hooked over the chair arm, the leg swinging up and down on some kind of energy, his head moving too, as if plugged in to a Walkman. Behind them Harry said, 'This is my associate, Chili Palmer, who'll be working with me.'

Harry already forgetting his instructions.

The limo guys nodded and Chili gave them a nod back. 'I want to make sure there's no misunderstanding here,' Harry said. He told them that despite rumors they might have heard, their investment in *Freaks* was as sound as the day they signed their participation agreement.

'Harry, are you making a speech?' Ronnie had his face raised to the ceiling. 'I can hear you, but where the fuck are you, man?'

'What I been wondering,' Catlett said in a quiet voice, looking at Chili, 'is where he's been.'

Ronnie said, 'Yeah, where've you been? You called us once, Harry, in three months.'

Harry came around from behind them to stand at one side of the desk, his back to the window, saying he'd been off scouting locations and interviewing actors in New York and his secretary had left without his knowledge to work for an agent, for Christ sake, Harry saying that was the kind of help you had to rely on these days, walked out, didn't even tell him.

Chili listened, not believing he was hearing all this.

Ronnie said, 'Let's get the man a girl. Harry, you want one with big hooters or one that can type?'

Chili's gaze moved from Ronnie the fool to Bo Catlett the dude, the man composed, elbows on the chair arms, his fingertips touching to form a tan-skinned church, a ruby ring for a stained-glass window.

'The main thing I want to tell you,' Harry said, 'the start date for *Freaks* is being pushed back a little, a few months. We should be in production before the end of the year . . . Unless because of unforeseen complications we decide it would be better to shoot next spring.'

Chili watched Ronnie's leg, hanging over the chair arm, bounce to a stop.

'What're you telling us, Harry?'

'We have to put the start date off, that's all.'

'Yeah, but why? Next spring, that's a whole year away.'

'We'll need the prep time.'

Ronnie said, 'Hey, Harry? Bullshit. We have an agreement with you, man.'

Chili raised his hand toward Harry.

'Wait a minute, okay? What we're talking about here – Harry, you're gonna make the movie, right. *Freaks?*'

Harry said, 'Yeah,' sounding surprised.

'Tell him.'

'I just did.'

'Tell him again.'

'We're gonna make the picture,' Harry said. He paused and said, 'I've got another project to do first, that's all. One I promised this guy years ago.'

Chili wondered if there was a way to shut Harry up without punching him in the mouth.

He saw Catlett watching him over the tips of his fingers while Ronnie fooled with his sunglasses, Harry telling them he'd be starting the other project any time now, a quickie, and as soon as it wrapped *Freaks* would go before the cameras.

There was a silence until Ronnie got up straighter in his chair and said, 'I think what happened, you put our bucks in some deal that blew up in your face and now you're trying to buy time. I want to see your books, Harry. Show me where it is, a two with five zeroes after it in black and white, man. I want to see your books and your bank statements.'

Chili said to the rich kid, 'Hey, Ronnie? Look at me.'

It caught him by surprise. Ronnie looked over. So did Bo Catlett.

Chili said, 'You have a piece of a movie, Ronnie. That's all. You don't have a piece of Harry. You don't tell him what you want to see that has to do with his business, that's private. You understand what I'm saying? Harry told you we're doing another movie first, before we come along and do *Freaks*. And that's the way it's gonna be.'

'Excuse me,' Ronnie said, 'but who the fuck are you?'

'I'm the one telling you how it is,' Chili said. 'That's not too hard, is it, figure that out?'

He watched Ronnie turn to Catlett, who hadn't moved or changed his expression much. Ronnie said, 'Cat? . . .'

Chili watched Catlett now. He still couldn't understand how Harry missed seeing the guy was colored. He was light-skinned and his hair was fairly straight, combed over to one side, but that didn't mean anything. The color itself didn't mean anything either, Chili thinking the guy wasn't any darker than he was. Colored, but could you call him black? The guy was taking his time, giving the situation some thought.

When he spoke it was to Harry, Catlett asking, 'What's this movie you're doing first?'

A simple enough question.

Chili said, 'Harry, let me answer that.'

88

He saw Catlett looking at him again.

'But first, I want to know who I'm talking to. Am I talking to you, or am I talking to him?' Meaning Ronnie.

He saw Catlett's expression change, not much, but something in the eyes, with that dreamy kind of half-smile, that told Chili the man understood. The man saying now, 'You can talk to me.'

'That's what I thought,' Chili said. 'So let me put it this way. Outside of *Freaks*, it's not any of your fuckin business what we do.'

Now it was between them, Chili giving the guy time but that's all, no way out for him except straight ahead or back off and the guy knew it too, looking at it and not moving a muscle, making up his mind . . .

Christ, when Harry stepped in, Harry reaching over the desk to pick up the script, Harry telling them, 'This is the project, *Mr Lovejoy*. I'm not trying to pull anything on you guys. This is it, right here.' Harry blowing the setup and there wasn't a thing Chili could do about it.

He eased back in the chair and saw Catlett watching him with that dreamy half-smile again.

Ronnie was saying, '*Mr Loveboy*?' reaching for the script. 'What is it, Harry, a porno flick?'

Harry saying, 'Love*joy*,' backing away, holding the script to his chest.

'Okay, but what's it about?'

'It's fluff, it's one I got involved in as a favor to a writer friend of mine. The guy's terminally ill and I owe it to him. Believe me, it's nothing you'd be interested in.'

Ronnie said, 'You think we go see the shit you turn out? Cat says he's seen better film on teeth.' He looked at Catlett and said, 'Right? I bet it's porno. Harry's lying to us.'

Chili watched Catlett, the guy taking it all in, Harry telling them now the script was unreadable – holding it with both hands against his body – it needed all kinds of work. Catlett pushed out of the chair, in no hurry, and Chili had to look up to see his face, with that bebop tuft under his lip.

'I got an idea,' Bo Catlett said to Harry. 'Take our twenty points out of *Freaks* and put 'em in this other one, *Mr Loverboy*. What's the difference.'

'I can't do it,' Harry said.

'You positive about that?'

'It's a different kind of deal.'

'Okay.' Catlett paused. 'Then be good enough to hand us our money back.'

'Why?' Harry said. 'We have a deal, a signed agreement to do a picture I guarantee you is gonna get made.'

'Take some time, think about our going into this other one,' Catlett said. 'Will you do that?'

'Okay, I'll think about it,' Harry said. 'I will.'

'That's all we need to know. Harry. Till next time.'

Chili watched Catlett look over before he turned – not long enough to be in each other's face, just a look – and walked out, Ronnie following after him.

Now they were in Harry's Mercedes, Chili not saying much for the time being: getting his thoughts together, deciding what kind of attitude he should have if he was going to stay in this deal: take it seriously or just go along and see what happens. So when Harry said, 'That's where Lew Wasserman lives,' Chili didn't ask who Lew Wasserman was. When Harry said, 'There's where Frank Sinatra lives,' Chili did look up, caught a glimpse of the house, but saw mostly Frank Sinatra's bushes, nice ones.

'You want to look at a star's home you can't even tell it's there,' Harry said, 'I'll take you past Bob Hope's place, over in Toluca Lake. You want to get a look at actual homes you can see, I'll show you where two of the Three Stooges used to

90

live, also Joan Crawford, George Hamilton . . . Who else? The house Elvis Presley lived in when he was out here. It's in Bel Air. You know he made over thirty pictures and the only one I saw was *Stay Away Joe*? A wonderful book they completely fucked up.'

Chili kept thinking about right after the limo guys left saying to Harry, 'What's wrong with you? What'd you tell 'em all your business for? Whyn't you do like I told you?'

Harry said, 'What?' Acting surprised and then offended. 'I had to tell 'em *some*thing.'

'What'd we talk about, Harry, before? The way to handle it, you weren't gonna tell 'em shit. Isn't that right?'

'It didn't work out that way.'

'No, 'cause you wouldn't shut up. You want these guys off your back, I tell you okay, here's how we do it. Next thing I know you're saying yeah, maybe they can have a piece of *Mr Lovejoy*. I couldn't believe my fuckin ears.'

'I said I'd think about it. What does that mean? In this business, nothing. I was buying time. All I have to do is hold 'em off till I make a deal at a studio.'

'That's the difference between me and you,' Chili said. 'I don't leave things hanging. If I wanted Karen to talk to Michael I'd say, "Karen, how about talking to Michael for me?" I told the limo guys it wasn't any of their fuckin business, period. They don't like it, that's too bad. What's the guy gonna do, Catlett, take a swing at me? He might've wanted to, but he had to consider first, who is this guy? He don't know me. All he knows is I'm looking at him like if he wants to try me I'll fuckin take him apart. Does he wanta go for it, get his suit messed up? I mean even if he's good he can see it would be work.'

'He could've had a gun,' Harry said.

'It wasn't a gun kind of situation. You don't pack, Harry,

less you're gonna use it. You say Ronnie plays with his in the office. That told me something right there. Then, soon as I saw the colored guy, I knew he was the one in charge. I asked him – you heard me – he goes yeah, without coming right out and saying it. Ronnie's sitting there, he don't even know what I'm talking about.'

'What colored guy?'

'Who do you think? Catlett. I don't know how you could've missed that. He lets the rich kid think he's the boss, but Catlett's pulling his strings. You don't see that?'

Harry said, 'You think he's a black guy?' Sounding surprised again.

'I know he is. Harry, I've lived in Brooklyn, I've lived in Miami, I've seen all different shades and mixtures of people and listened to 'em talk and Catlett's a black guy with light-colored skin, that's all. Take my word.'

'He doesn't talk like a black guy.'

'What do you want him to say, Yazza, boss? He might be part South American,' Chili said, 'have some other kind of blood in him too, but I know he's colored.'

They left the office talking about Catlett and the rich kid. Now they were in the car heading for Michael Weir's house. Chili wanting to get a good look at it, maybe let Harry drop him off and he'd stroll by. Harry said, 'You see anybody out strolling? Not in this part of Beverly Hills. It's against the law to be seen on the street.'

'The one on the left,' Harry said, 'that's where Dean Martin used to live.' Chili looked at the house without saying anything. 'The one coming up – see the gate? Kenny Rogers rented that while he was having his new home built. You know what he paid a month? Fifty thousand.'

'Jesus Christ,' Chili said.

'Okay, right around the bend on the left, the one that

looks like the place they signed the Declaration of Independence, that's Michael's house.'

Coming up and now passing it: red brick with white trim behind a vine-covered brick wall and a closed iron gate. Through the bars Chili could see the drive curving up to the front door. He wondered if Michael Weir was in there at this moment.

'Why don't we ring the bell, see if he's home?'

'You don't get to see him that way, believe me.'

'Go by again.'

Harry nosed the Mercedes into a drive, backed around and came past the house saying, 'Worth around twenty million, easy.'

'It doesn't look that big.'

'Compared to what, the Beverly Hills Hotel? It's twelve thousand square feet plus a tennis court, pool, cabana guesthouse and orange trees on three acres.'

'Jesus Christ,' Chili said. He could see the upper windows as they crept past the wall, the top part of a satellite dish in the side yard.

'There's no way you could sit in your car and watch the house,' Harry said, 'without attracting the police inside of two minutes. If you're thinking of waiting for him to come out.'

'What's he do for fun?'

'His girlfriend lives with him. When he's not here, he's in New York. Has a place on Central Park West.'

'I'd like to find out more about him,' Chili said, 'where he goes, so maybe I can run into him.'

'Then what?'

'Don't worry about it. I got an idea.'

'There was a piece on him, a cover story,' Harry said, 'fairly recently in one of the magazines. About his career, his life. I remember there's a shot of him with his girlfriend.

She was in entertainment, I think a singer with a rock-and-roll group when he met her. I wouldn't be surprised Karen has the magazine. I know she gets the trades, has stacks of 'em she keeps – I don't know why.'

'I have to go back there anyway,' Chili said, 'pick up my car.'

For a minute or so he was quiet, catching glimpses of the big homes through the trees and manicured shrubs, all the places so clean and neat and not a soul around, nobody outside. Not like Meridian Avenue, South Miami Beach. Not anything like Bay Ridge, Jesus, you had to go all the way over past the Veterans Hospital to Dyker Beach Park to find trees of any size.

He said to Harry, 'You know the one Michael Weir was in, *The Cyclone*? When I saw it I recognized places on Bayview, Neptune Avenue, Cropsey. That's all close to my old neighborhood. I was in Miami then, but I heard some guys I know actually met him.'

'Sure, every picture Michael's in,' Harry said, 'he researches the part, finds out exactly how he's supposed to play it. That's why he's so good. *The Cyclone*, he makes you believe he's a Mafia character.'

'Well, basically, yeah, he sounded okay,' Chili said. 'What I couldn't believe, they would've let him in, the kind of simple asshole he was. Or let him get away after, a snitch? He would've ended up with his dick in his mouth. I don't mean to say there aren't assholes in those different crews, they're full of assholes. I just mean the particular kind of asshole he was in the movie.'

'If he played a Mafia character,' Harry said, 'then I guarantee you he talked to some of them.'

'Tommy would know,' Chili said. 'Tommy Carlo. I could call him and double-check.'

'For what?'

'I'd like to know. Me and Tommy were both in Miami when they were making the movie, but he'd remember it. It was at the time we were running the club for Momo. Tommy was the one booked the different groups'd come in. Made him feel he was in the entertainment world.'

'Well, if you want,' Harry said, 'call him from Karen's.'

'What if she's not home? We just walk in?'

'It didn't bother you before.'

'That was different. I'm not gonna bust in.'

'If the patio door was open last night,' Harry said, 'it's still open. Karen's never been good at locking doors, closing windows when it rains, putting her top up . . .'

'When you were living together?'

'Anytime. She'd come in, forget to shut off the alarm system. Then the company that put it in calls and you have to give them an identifying code, three digits, that's all. But Karen could never remember the numbers. Pretty soon the cops pull up in the drive . . .'

'Harry, if Karen sets up Michael for you, what does she get?'

'She already got it.' Harry said, 'Me. I made her a movie star. She wasn't too bad, for that kind of picture. There aren't any lines that run more than ten words. Now she's reading for a part . . . Hasn't worked in seven years, she wants to get back in it. I don't know why – Michael set her up for life.'

'*Beth's Room*,' Chili said.

'What?'

'*Beth's Room*. That's the name of the movie she's gonna be in.'

Harry gave him a quick glance. Looking at the road again he said, 'I'll bet you a hundred bucks she doesn't get the part.'

11

Bo Catlett liked to change his clothes two or three times a day, get to wear different outfits. In less than two hours he was meeting friends at Mateo's in Westwood, so he had dressed for dinner before driving out to the airport.

Seated now in the Delta terminal, across the aisle from the gate where the mule from Miami would arrive by way of Atlanta, Catlett had on his dove-gray double-breasted Armani with the nice long roll lapel. He had on a light-blue shirt with a pearl-gray necktie and pearl cuff links. He had on light-blue hose and dark-brown Cole-Haan loafers, spit-shined. The loafers matched the attaché case next to him on the row of seats. Resting on the attaché case was a Delta ticket envelope, boarding pass showing – for anyone who might think he was sitting here with some other purpose in mind. Anyone who might think they recognized him from times before. Like that casual young dude wearing the plaid wool shirt over his white T-shirt, with the jeans and black Nikes.

Catlett liked to watch people going by, all the different shapes and sizes in all different kinds of clothes, wondering, when they got up in the morning if they gave two seconds to what they were going to wear, or they just got dressed, took it off a chair or reached in the closet and put it on. He could pick out the ones who had given it some thought. They weren't necessarily the ones all dressed up, either.

96

The young dude in the jeans and the wool shirt hanging out, he'd given that outfit some thought. A friendly young dude, said hi to the ladies behind the airline counter and they said hi back like they knew him.

Catlett wondered if the Bear had noticed that.

The Bear, having shown himself once, like reporting in, was around someplace: the Bear in a green and red Hawaiian shirt today with his baby girl.

Ninety-nine percent of the people in LA did not know shit about how to dress or seem to care. Nobody wore a necktie. They'd wear a suit and leave the shirt open. Or the thing now, they'd button the shirt collar, wearing it with a suit but no tie, and look like they'd just come off the fucking reservation. Ronnie Wingate, not knowing shit either, said, 'Why wear a tie if you don't have to?' Like not wearing it was getting away with something. He had told Ronnie one time, 'I use to dress just like you when I was a child and didn't know better.' Living in migrant camps, moving from Florida to Texas to Colorado to Michigan, out here to California, the whole family doing stoop labor in hand-me-down clothes.

He said to Ronnie Wingate, 'You know what changed my whole life?' Ronnie said what and he told him, 'Finding out at age fourteen, not till then, I was part black.'

Asshole Ronnie saying, 'Negro?'

'Black. And if you're part, man, you're all.'

Finding it out in a photograph the time he and his mother and three sisters went to visit his grandmother about to die; drove all the way to Benson, Arizona, from Bakersfield and his grandma got out her old pictures in an album to show them. The first ones, her own grandparents in separate brownish photos. An Indian woman in a blanket. (He had been told about having some Warm Springs Apache Indian blood, so this fat woman in the blanket came as no surprise.) It was the next photo that knocked him out. A black guy in the picture, no doubt about it. But not just any black guy. This one had a fucking sword, man, and sergeant stripes on his uniform. He was a US Cavalryman, had served twenty-four years in the Army and fought in the Civil War when he was fifteen years old and was wounded at a place called Honey Springs in Missouri. Across the bottom of the photo it said: *Sgt. Bo Catlett of the 10th, Fort Huachuca, Arizona Territory, June 16, 1887.* And was signed by a man named *C.S. Fly*.

He asked could he have the photo and his grandma gave it to him.

'I think it was the sword did it,' Catlett said to Ronnie that time. 'I kept thinking about it a year until now *I* was fifteen. You understand the significance of what I'm saying? I changed my name from Antonio to Bo Catlett, left the camps for good and took off for Detroit to learn how to be black.'

Asshole Ronnie didn't get it. 'Detroit?' Even sucking on his base pipe didn't get it or ever would, 'cause the man would always be from Santa Barbara and never know shit about Detroit, about Motown, about Marvin Gaye . . .

Catlett spotted the Bear in his Hawaiian shirt, the Bear coming along carrying his three-year-old baby, cute little girl licking an ice-cream cone, dripping it on the Bear's shirt. The Bear looked this way without making eye contact, turned his head toward the young dude in the wool shirt and back this way again, wiping his little girl's mouth with a paper napkin, the Bear playing he was big and dumb but a nice daddy.

A voice just then announced the Atlanta flight was on the ground and would be at the gate in a few minutes.

Catlett got his mind ready. He'd been told the mule coming with the product this trip was a Colombian dude he had met one time before by the name of Yayo. Like so many of those people a mean little Colombian dude, but no size on him to speak of, going maybe one-thirty. They saw that movie *Scarface* and turned into a bunch of Al Pacinos doing Tony Montana. Only they didn't know how. They maintained a level of boring meanness that was like an act they put on. It made him think of the man sitting at Harry Zimm's desk, Chili Palmer, in his black jacket zipped up, not looking like any kind of movie producer or sounding like them either, full of shit. Chili Palmer maybe could be a mule, except he was bigger than any Colombian and looked at you different. Didn't put it on so heavy. Chili Palmer was quiet about it but came right at you, wanting to get it done. Catlett was thinking he could put the Bear in front of Mr Chili Palmer, see if the man behaved the same way, gave the Bear that look . . .

The Bear and his baby girl were among the people by the gate now. Passengers were coming out of the ramp from the plane. The way it was set up, Yayo would have his ticket envelope in his hand, the envelope with a baggage claim check stapled inside. He'd lay the envelope on the trash container right there, not stick it down in, and keep coming. The Bear would step over, pick up the envelope and take off with his little girl to the baggage claim area. There it was happening . . .

And now Yayo was looking straight ahead coming through the people waiting – Catlett seeing them from behind moving aside to give this ignorant bean picker who looked like he'd never been in an airport before the right of way. That's what he reminded Catlett of, a migrant picker dressed for Saturday night in a clean starched shirt and khakis too big for him. Ignorant man, didn't know shit. Look at him being cool looking this way, coming over now.

As Yayo reached him Catlett said, 'Don't say nothing to me. Turn around and act like you're waiting for somebody suppose to meet you.'

'The *fock* you talking about?' Yayo hitting the word hard,

the way Tony Montana did. 'They nobody know me here, man. Give me the focking case.'

'Ain't in the case. Now turn around and be *looking*,' Catlett said. 'You got eyes on you. Man over to your right in the blue wool shirt hanging out . . . The other way, *derecho*.'

Catlett hunched over to rest his arms on his thighs, the seat of Yayo's khakis hanging slack before him, Yayo between him and the dude in the wool shirt now.

'That's a federal officer of some kind, most likely DEA. He moves his leg look for the bulge. You savvy bulge? Something stuck to his ankle, underneath his pants. His backup piece . . . *Hey*. Try it without looking right at him if you can.'

Come out here you should always take some pills first, keep your blood pressure cool.

'You know he's there, now forget about him. While you wondering where your relatives are, suppose to meet you, I'm getting up. Gonna leave you and walk over to the cocktail lounge. After I'm gone, you sit down in this same seat I'm in. You feel something under your ass it's the key to a locker where your money is. But before you go open the locker you look around good now, understand? You don't want any guys have bulges on their ankles watching you. Take your time, go have a snack first. You know what a snack is?'

Yayo turned his head to one side. 'You suppose to give me the focking money yourself.'

Catlett got up, adjusted his dove-gray double-breasted jacket, smoothing the long roll lapel. He said, 'Try to be cool, Yahoo,' turning to pick up the ticket envelope and attaché case. 'I was to hand you this fulla money we'd be speed-cuffed before we saw it happen. Do it how I told you and have a safe trip home. Or as you all say, *vaya con Dios*, motherfocker.'

Down in Baggage Claim, Catlett stood away from the Bear

and his little girl waiting at one of the carousels, the Bear looking at the numbers on the claim check that told him which bag coming out of the chute would have ten keys of cocaine in it. Seventeen thousand a key this month, a hundred and seventy grand waiting in the locker, the money plus some product they were returning: a whole key stepped on so many times it was baby food. No problem if Yayo was careful, looked around before he opened the locker. The trouble with this business, you had to rely on other people; you couldn't do it alone. Same thing in the movie business, from what Catlett had seen, studying how it worked. The difference was, in the movie business you didn't worry about somebody getting turned to save their ass and pointing at you in court. You could get fucked over in the movie business all kinds of ways, but you didn't get sent to a correctional facility when you lost out. The movie business, you could come right out and tell people what you did, make a name. Instead of hanging out on the edge, supplying highs for dumbass movie stars, you could get to where you hire the ones you want and tell 'em what to do; they don't like it, fire their ass. It didn't make sense to live here if you weren't in the movie business. High up in it.

The Bear came away from the carousel carrying his little girl and a Black Watch plaid suitcase. Catlett followed them outside, through the traffic in the covered roadway that was like an underpass to one of the islands where people were waiting for shuttles in daylight. The little girl said, 'Hi, Bo,' to Catlett coming up to them.

Catlett, smiling, said, 'Hey, Farrah. Hah you, little honey bunny? You come see the big airplanes?'

'I been on airplanes,' Farrah said. 'My daddy takes me to Acapulco with him.'

'I know he does, honey bunny. Your daddy's good to you, huh?'

Little Farrah started to nod and the Bear nuzzled her clean little face with his beard saying, 'This here's my baby sweetheart. Yes her is. Arn'cha, huh? Arn'cha my baby sweetheart?'

'Man, you gonna smother the child.' Catlett raised the little girl's chin with the tips of his fingers. She seemed tiny enough to get lost in that shaggy beard, one tiny hand hanging on to it now, her tiny body perched on the Bear's arm. The Bear was going to fat but had taught bodybuilding at one time, worked as a movie stuntman and had choreographed fight scenes. Catlett thought of the Bear as his handyman.

'You know that place they use to shoot *77 Sunset Strip*?'

'Yeah, up by La Cienega.'

'Harry Zimm's office is right across the street, white building, you see Venetian blinds upstairs. I need to get in there, pick up a movie script. If you could meet me there tonight, open the door . . .'

'You want, Bo, I'll go in and get it.'

'No, you do the B part and I do the E.'

'I know that,' Farrah said in her tiny voice. 'A, B, E, C, D.'

Catlett was smiling again. 'Hey, you a smart little honey bunny, ain'cha?'

'Yes her is,' the Bear said.

12

Chili reached Tommy Carlo at the barbershop but didn't get a chance to talk about *The Cyclone* and Michael Weir.

Tommy said, 'I been wanting to call you, but you didn't gimme a number. Ray Bones is looking for you. He's got some kind of bug up his ass, can't sit still. He kept after Jimmy Cap about he wants to go to LA till Jimmy tells him to go ahead and fuckin go, he's tired hearing about it.'

Chili was at the desk in Karen's study, the chair swiveled so that his back was to Harry, across the room. Harry was sitting on the floor; he had the cabinet in the bookcase open and was going through magazines.

Chili said, 'You hang out with Jimmy Cap now?' keeping his voice low.

'I happen to be by there when they're talking, I notice Bones, how he's acting.'

'You pay him the eight yet?'

'Fuck no, he'll get it when he gets it. Chil, it doesn't have nothing to do with money, you know that. I hate to say I fuckin told you, but I did. I told you, don't start nothing with him that time.'

'You said don't say nothing, and I didn't.'

'No, you broke his fuckin nose instead.'

Talking about something that had happened twelve years ago, still hanging over him. 'The guy only has room in his brain for one thing,' Chili said, 'that's the problem, he's a fuckin idiot.'

'He don't like the way you talk to him. You ever showed him any kind of respect at all, he wouldn't be on your ass.'

'I should've hit him a half-inch lower that time, with the thirty-eight. You think he's coming out, uh?'

'I know he is. He asked me where you're staying. I told him I didn't know. I still don't.'

'When's he coming?'

'He never said, but I think the next couple days.'

Getting into the kid stuff again and sounding stupid, hearing himself, Jesus, like he was reverting, talking like those hard-ons sitting around their social clubs.

'Wait a minute,' Chili said. 'How's he know I'm here?'

'I told him you went out to Vegas on a collection job and they sent you to LA.'

'What'd you tell him that for?'

'He already knew it. I don't know how unless – did you talk to the drycleaner's wife since you're out there? What's her name, Leo's wife? I know Bones went to see her and maybe she mentioned it. This was yesterday.'

'Tommy? What makes you think I told Fay I was going to Vegas?'

'I don't know – it musta been something Bones said. I just assumed.'

'I'll call you back,' Chili said, hung up and dialed information to get the number of Paris Cleaners in North Miami. Fay answered the phone. Chili asked her how she was doing. He was going to take his time, ease into it, but Fay started talking right away, sounding anxious to tell him.

'A man came to see me said he was a friend of yours? He asked had I spoken to you since Leo was killed and I said yes, I had. He asked what it was we talked about. I said oh, nothing in particular, and he hit me with his fist. I have a

104

black eye and my jaw hurts something awful, I try to eat on that side? It might be broken. When I get off I think I'll go the doctor's and see about it.'

'Fay? You told him what we talked about?'

'He asked had I given you any money and then, yeah, he made me tell him. If I didn't he was all set to beat me up.'

'I mean, you told him Leo was alive?'

'I had to.'

'And about the money, the settlement?'

'He went through my things and found the letter from the airline the check come in.'

'Fay, what else did you tell him?'

'That's all.'

'What about the woman Leo knows out here, Hi-Tone Cleaners?'

'Oh. Yeah, I might've mentioned her, I forget.'

That meant she did. Chili was pretty sure.

'I was kinda groggy from him hitting me.'

'There was nothing you could do, Fay.'

She said, 'I guess now everybody's gonna know about Leo, what he did.'

'No, I think just us three,' Chili said. 'The guy won't tell anybody. I think what he'll do is try and find Leo, get the money for himself.'

Fay said, 'Well, how are you doing otherwise? Are you coming back here sometime?'

Chili gave her Karen's number, hung up and called Tommy Carlo at the barbershop.

'Tommy, did Bones say anything to Jimmy Cap about Leo?'

'Not that I heard. Why?'

'Only that he was gonna come looking for me?'

'That's what he said.'

'He didn't tell you anything, I mean about Leo?'

105

'Like what?'

'Nothing,' Chili said. 'Listen . . .' and asked about Michael Weir and the time he was in Brooklyn making the movie.

Tommy said yeah, he knew guys talked to him personally, had Michael Weir to their club, one on 15th corner of Neptune, another place on 86th Street. Yeah, they shot scenes in Bensonhurst, Carroll Gardens, on the bridge, the Bush Terminal docks, the amusement park . . . 'That movie, you know, was from a book called *Coney Island*, but Michael Weir had it changed, he didn't like the title. He said to call it *The Cyclone* and they did.'

'The Cyclone,' Chili said, 'the roller coaster.'

'Yeah, the roller coaster. You remember the movie? Michael Weir, he's Joey Corio, he's running the fuckin roller coaster in the beginning part, before he gets in with the guys and he's made. So the guys call him Cyclone. 'Hey, Cyc, how you doing?' You don't remember that?'

Chili looked up to see Harry coming to the desk with a stack of magazines. 'I'll talk to you later,' Chili said, paused, lowered his voice then as he said, 'Tommy? Find out when's he coming out. I'll call you,' and hung up.

'Michael's in every one of these,' Harry said, dropping the magazines on the desk. 'Recent ones in *American Film* and *Vanity Fair*, about the picture he just finished, called *Elba*. This one, there's a cover story. Everything you ever wanted to know about him. There's a picture of Karen in there and also his present live-in.'

Chili picked up the magazine, *Premiere*, to see Michael Weir full face, almost life-size, grinning at him. The guy had to be up in his late forties but looked about thirty-five. Not bad-looking, thick dark hair he wore fairly long, kind of a big nose. There was that Michael Weir twinkle in his eyes, Michael telling his many fans he was basically a nice guy and didn't put on any airs. It said next to the picture in big

106

letters, MICHAEL WEIR, and under it, smaller, WILL THE REAL ONE PLEASE STAND UP?

'He's got a big nose,' Chili said. 'I never noticed that before.'

'Prominent,' Harry said.

'It's big,' Chili said, opening the magazine to the cover story, a full-page color shot of Michael in a faded work shirt and scruffy jeans, wearing black socks with his Reeboks. See? Just a regular guy who happened to make seven million every time he did a movie. Chili started to tell Harry his observation in a dry tone of voice, but caught himself in time.

What was he putting Michael Weir down for? He didn't even know the guy.

He had that fuckin Ray Bones on his mind now, that was the problem, and he was taking it out on this actor who happened to have a big nose and liked scruffy jeans.

The beginning of the article, on the opposite page, had for a title over it, WEIR(D) TALES. On the next two pages were more pictures of Michael, Michael in different movies, Michael in *The Cyclone* holding a gun and looking desperate, Michael with Karen – there she was – still a blonde.

Chili turned the page, looked at more pictures, still thinking about Ray Bones, realizing Bones would check out the woman at Hi-Tone Cleaners and if he didn't find her he'd use his connections, talk to the lawyers that ate raw fish, and next he'd be coming this way to check out Harry Zimm. That fuckin Bones, all he did was mess things up.

'Here's the one he's living with now,' Harry said over Chili's shoulder as he turned the page. 'Nicki. She's a cutie, except for all that hair, a rock-and-roller. They met at Gazzarri's, on the Strip. Nicki was performing with some group.'

'You know what?' Chili said, looking at a color shot of

107

Michael and Nicki by a limo, both in black leather jackets. 'I think I know her. There was a girl with a group we used quite a few times at Memo's . . . Only her name was Nicole.'

'That's close,' Harry said. He ran his finger down a column of the story. 'Here. She's twenty-seven, born in Miami. Performed with different groups . . . she's a singer.'

'So's Nicole,' Chili said, 'but her hair's a lot blonder and she's older.' He picked up the phone and dialed the back room of the barbershop.

Tommy said, 'I talk to you more in LA 'n when you're here.'

'There was a group we had at Memo's about seven eight years ago, the girl singer's name was Nicole?'

'Sure, Nicole. Man, I wanted to jump her so bad.'

'She had blond hair, almost white?'

'Yeah, but not necessarily. I meant to tell you,' Tommy said, 'we talking about Michael Weir? Nicole lives with him. Only now she's Nicki.'

'You sure it's the same one?'

'I just read about her, putting together a group. She was out of music for a while.'

'How old would Nicole be, thirties?'

'Around there, thirty-four.'

'This one's twenty-seven.'

'Hey, Chil, it's the same broad, take my word.'

'What's the name of the group?'

'Prob'ly "Nicki." I'll check, see what I can find out.'

Chili gave him Karen's number and hung up. He said to Harry, 'I was right, I know her.'

Harry said, 'Yeah, but does she know you?'

Now they were having a drink while they looked at magazines. Chili learning facts about Michael Weir: that he had three homes, three cars, three ex-wives, a dirt bike he rode in the desert, liked to play the piano, cook, didn't smoke, drank moderately . . . That he had appeared in seventeen features he was willing to talk about . . . That while grips and gaffers loved him, directors and writers 'were not that enchanted by Michael's tendency to trample indifferently on their prerogatives; but since he was arguably a genius . . .'

Karen walked in on them in her neat black suit, looking good, calm, but maybe putting it on, and Chili learned a little more about her and about the movie business. Karen said, 'Nothing's changed in ten years – you know it?' Harry raised his glass saying, 'And it never will. Let me guess what happened. No, first tell me who was there.' Chili, at the desk, became the audience, looking from one to the other.

Karen: 'You know Warren Hurst?'

Harry: 'Never heard of him.'

Karen, looking at their drinks: 'He's one of the production v.p.'s, a new guy. I don't think he'll last.'

Harry, as Karen picked up Chili's drink, took a big sip and handed him the glass: 'Who else?'

Karen: 'Elaine Levin . . .'

Harry: 'No – what's she doing at Tower?'

Karen: 'Harry, she runs production. Don't you read?'

Harry: 'What, the trades? I've missed a few lately.' To Chili: 'This's good. Elaine Levin, a few years ago was selling cosmetics . . .'

Karen, lighting a cigarette: 'She was at UA and then Metro nine years.'

Harry: 'Okay, but before that she was at an ad agency in New York, right? Elaine comes up with an idea for a cosmetic she calls "Bedroom Eyes" – you put it on you increase your chances of getting laid. The head of a major studio says to her, "Honey, if you can sell that shit you can sell movies." Next thing you know she's a vice-president of production.'

Karen: 'Elaine started in marketing.'

Harry: 'And how long was she there? That's what I'm talking about, before they moved her into production, this broad that sold eye makeup?'

Karen: 'Harry, everybody used to do something else. What about when you were Harry Simmons making slide films, *How to Load a Truck*? To Chili: 'Did you know Zimm wasn't his real name?'

Harry: 'The only thing I wasn't sure of, should Zimm have one *m* or two? Hey, but I was always a filmmaker, behind the camera. These people that run the studios, they're lawyers, former agents. They're strictly money guys.'

Karen: 'What are you, Harry?'

Harry: 'They wouldn't even *see* movies, I'm convinced, they didn't have a screening room on the lot. That's why with few exceptions I've remained independent. You know that song Old Blue Eyes does, "I did it my way"? . . .'

Karen: 'But now you're going to a studio.'

Harry: 'I have no choice. But you know which one? Tower, I just decided. Play the power game with Bedroom Eyes, see if she's any good. Get in there and compete with all the ass kissers and bottom feeders, all the no-talent schmucks that constellate around the studio execs who don't know what they're doing either. All trying to figure out what the public wants to see. How about teenagers from outer space?'

Karen: 'It's been done.'

Harry: 'Well, I got a property I *know* is gonna go into release. We open on a thousand screens we'll do over ten mil the first weekend. You oughta read it, see what I'm talking about. Why Michael would be the perfect Lovejoy. Karen? One phone call, I'm in business.'

Chili watched her stub the cigarette out in the ashtray, maybe giving herself time to think. Harry said, 'I'm gonna be optimistic, okay?' Karen didn't answer and Harry, after a moment, brought it back to where they had started.

110

'You haven't told us what happened at the meeting.'

'I thought you wanted to guess.'

'Okay. They liked what you did and'll let you know.'

'I didn't read. I turned down the part.'

'I thought you wanted to do it.'

'I changed my mind,' Karen said, and walked out.

'You know what happened,' Harry said to Chili. 'They told her don't call us, we'll call you, and she won't admit it.' Harry paused to sip his drink. 'I'm serious about going to Tower.' He paused again. 'I'll wait'll Karen's in a better mood and lay the script on her.'

'I thought,' Chili said, 'I was gonna read it.'

'What'd you bring, one copy?'

Chili thought about it and said, 'I'm going back to the motel, get cleaned up and check out, find someplace over here to stay. Lemme have the key to your office, I could stop on the way back, pick up a script for myself. How would that be?'

Karen, still in the neat black suit, was at the kitchen table pouring a Coke. Chili watched her from the doorway – where she had stood last night in the Lakers T-shirt.

'Can I ask you a question?' She looked up at him and he said, 'Why'd you change your mind?'

'About the part? I can't say I was dying to do it.'

Karen looked down to pour some more Coke in the glass, careful that it didn't foam over. Chili got ready to say well, maybe he'd be seeing her sometime, when she looked up at him again.

'I probably would've taken it though. But during the meeting I got into what we were talking about this morning, my feeling guilty? You know . . .'

Chili said, 'Why you let the daughter walk all over you.'

'Yeah, I questioned that, and the answer I got, it's what

111

the audience expects, it's what they want to see. I said, but if I'm not stupid, if I realize in the end I'm being used, why don't I realize it right away? Warren goes, "But if you did, Karen, we wouldn't have a movie, would we?" In this tone. You know, like I'm an idiot. It really pissed me off. I said well, if that's the way you want to do it, I'll see you.'

'They try to talk you into it?'

'Elaine did, in a way. I got the feeling the studio forced the script on her and she has to go with it. She said, well, the story isn't exactly a great idea – she knows – but it's involving, reflective, has resonance, a certain texture – those are all story department words. I said, "Yeah, and lines no one would say except in a movie." Warren goes, "But that's what it is, Karen, a movie." Elaine stared at him without saying a word, like she was thinking, Where did I get this guy? You have to understand, there are movie lines and there are movie lines that work. Bette Davis comes out of a cabin, walks up to a guy on the porch, gives him a flirty look and says, "I'd kiss you but I just washed my hair." I love it, because it tells you who she is and you have to like her. But some of the stupid lines I've had to deliver . . .'

Chili said, 'You want to get back into it, don't you?'

'I know I'm better than what I used to do. In Harry's movies I was always the bimbo. I walked around in a tank top and those fuck-me pumps with stiletto heels till it was time to scream. Harry kills me, he says don't ever take this business seriously, and he's the most serious guy I know. He puts studio people down – the main reason, because he'd love to run a major studio.' Karen nodded saying, 'If he ever did, he might not be bad. The cheapskate, I know he'd save them money.' She started to smile, just a little, saying, 'Another one of my favorite Bette Davis lines: "He tried to make love to me and I shot him."'

Chili smiled with her. He said, 'I was thinking, you know

what you could do? Make a deal with Harry. You'll call Michael if he'll give you a part in the movie, a good one.'

Karen said, 'You're kidding,' but kept staring at him until finally she said, 'In the first place Michael will never do the picture—'

'Harry told me he loves it, he flipped.'

'Michael is known for his flipping. He flips over a script, and then when the time comes to make a deal, he flips out. But what I started to say, Michael would never make the picture with Harry, he doesn't have the track record. It would not only have to be a big-name producer, Michael would also demand script, director and cast approval, and he'd get it.'

Chili watched her finish pouring the Coke.

'You haven't answered my question.'

'Which one?'

'You want to get back into it, don't you?'

'I'm thinking about it,' Karen said. 'I'll let you know.'

13

Chili wondered if Leo was attracted to sweaty women in sundresses. Across the counter from him in Hi-Tone Cleaners on Ventura, Studio City, Annette looked kind of damp, clammy. She was on the heavy side, needed to fix her blond hair, but wasn't too bad-looking. It was seven P.M. The help had left and Annette was closing up when Chili walked in, timing it to be the last customer. He gave his name, Palmer.

Annette stood looking through an alphabetical file on a turntable. 'You don't have your receipt?'

'No, I don't,' Chili said. He didn't have a pair of pants here, either, but that's what he told Annette he'd brought in. 'They're light gray.'

She said, 'Are you sure? I don't see no Palmer in the file.' She said *fahl* with the same kind of accent Fay had. Chili wondered what Leo gained trading for this one. Outside of about twenty-five pounds and those big round jugs in her brown-print sundress. He told her he'd brought the pants in yesterday and needed them since he was leaving tomorrow for Miami. Annette said, 'Taking a vacation?' Chili told her no, it was where he lived. She said, 'Oh?' showing a certain amount of interest.

Chili had on his dark-blue muted pinstripe, a blue shirt with a tab collar and rust-colored tie. He appeared reasonable about his pants, not too concerned; he told her if she couldn't find them it was no big deal, and smiled, easy to get along with.

'Well, if you're sure,' Annette said, nice about it because he was, 'I can check, see if there's a pair of pants without a ticket on them.' She stepped over to the conveyor loaded with clothes hanging in clear plastic covers, reached up and pressed a button. The conveyor started moving, bringing the clothes past her before it circled and returned them to the back part of the shop. Annette said, 'I think you're gonna have to help me out here.'

Chili walked around behind the counter to stand next to her. He looked at clothes going past for a minute before saying, 'I've seen you someplace . . . You weren't by any chance in Vegas last week.'

Annette had her hand raised to the button, so she could stop the conveyor if they saw his pants. She looked past her bare shoulder at him and he could tell she was smiling, even though he couldn't see her mouth. She said, 'No, but I was in Reno. How about that?'

'Getting a divorce?' Kidding with her.

'I took care of that 'fore I come out here. Got rid of excess baggage. No, this fella I was with took me.'

'I hope your luck was better than mine. I dropped a bundle and it wasn't my laundry,' Chili said, getting into it, showing Annette what a nice simple guy he was.

She told him she only played the slots and did okay. 'But would you believe the fella I was with lost over a hundred thousand dollars and it didn't even bother him?'

'Jesus,' Chili said, looking from the cleaning going by to Annette. 'Guy must be loaded, drop that much and not worry about it.'

'His philosophy is you win some, lose some.'

'I guess that's as good a way to look at it as any.'

'He's from Miami, Florida, too, originally.'

'Yeah, what's his name?'

'I doubt you'd know him.'

'He move out here?'

'I'm trying to get him to. He spends the whole day out to Santa'nita, loves the racetrack.'

'You don't lose it as fast betting the horses.'

'Oh, he wins, don't worry about that. You know the state lottery in Florida?'

'Yeah? He won that?'

'He won, I mean, big. But soon as his wife found out . . . His wife – listen to this. She's divorcing him at the time, but then when she finds out about the money she wants half as part of the settlement. He said the hell with that noise and took off.'

'I don't blame him,' Chili said.

'Changed his name, too. The wife never even played the lottery herself. But soon as he won, oh, now she wants in on it. Larry said he'd burn the money before he'd give her any.'

'I imagine he's doing what he never dreamed of in his life,' Chili said. 'Right up there on top.' He turned his head to look at Annette's bare shoulder and blond hair, dark strands of it combed up from her neck and held with a plastic comb. He said, 'Your friend knows how to pick winners,' waited for Annette to look at him and gave her a nice smile. 'Why don't you shut this place down and we'll go have a drink.'

'What about your pants?'

'I got other pants. Come on, let's do it.'

'Gee, I'd like to,' Annette said, 'but I have to get cleaned up and meet my fella. He gets back from Santa'nita we meet at his hotel, have a drink in the Polo Lounge and go on out for dinner.'

'Sounds good.'

'You been there, haven't you?'

'Where's that?'

116

'The Polo Lounge, in the Beverly Hills Hotel? It's late now – the best time's around six, you see all kinds of celebrities in there.'

'Is that right?'

'I've seen movie stars right at the next table.'

'You have? Like who?'

Annette said, 'Let's see,' and thought about it staring at the clothes going by. She pressed the button to stop the conveyor. 'I can never think of their names, after. There was one, he played in a western use to be on TV. What was his name? . . . They give you, with your drinks they give you corn chips with that guacamole dip? No charge. You see men, they have a phone brought to their table and you actually hear them talking about movies they're gonna make and what stars'll be in them. It's exciting to hear it, movie stars being mentioned like they're just, you know, regular people.'

'I'll have to stop by there,' Chili said, 'maybe next time I come out. The Beverly Hills Hotel, that's where your friend stays, huh?'

'He has a suite costs him four hundred a night. Living room, bedroom, a balcony you can sit out on . . .'

'Sounds good. Listen, I was thinking,' Chili said, 'your friend's wife, she could have somebody looking for him, hire somebody.' He watched Annette giving it some thought. 'In case anybody comes by asking about him . . .'

'I'll just say I never heard of him.'

'Yeah, except if the person happens to know you're an old friend maybe.'

'I see what you mean,' Annette said, giving it some more thought. 'Just say he hasn't been here then.'

Chili moved back around the counter telling her not to worry about his pants, he said those things happened. He was anxious to get going, stop and have a bite to eat before

117

taking that canyon road, full of hairpin turns, back over the mountain to Beverly Hills. For a moment he wondered what the mountain was called and thought of asking Annette, but changed his mind and was almost to the door when she said, 'I remember who it was now, the movie star? Doug McClure.'

Chili paused to say, 'Oh,' nodding.

'He was so close,' Annette said, 'I could've touched him.'

He wondered if maybe the lights outside the Sunset Marquis had been left over from Christmas: little pinpoint lights in the trees along the front, on both sides of the canopy that came out from the entrance. It was a slick place, only three stories hidden away in a lot of foliage down the hill from Sunset Boulevard – outdoor dining and the pool right in the middle, in a courtyard. Harry had recommended it and made the reservations, saying it used to be popular with rock groups and guys whose wives had kicked them out of the house for one reason or another. What Chili had in 325 was a two-hundred-buck suite with windows facing apartment balconies about fifty feet away; but that was okay, he wouldn't be looking out much. There was a phone in the bedroom, another one on the counter separating the living room from the kitchenette. Chili got the number of the Beverly Hills Hotel. When he asked for Larry Paris, the operator said just a moment, she'd connect him, Chili wondering how the little drycleaner had ever come this far as dumb as he was, going to the track every day and living in a four-hundred-dollar suite Chili would bet couldn't be any nicer than this one. It had an oriental look to it, maroon lamps shaped like pagodas. He let it ring till the operator came back on to say Mr Paris's room was not answering. Chili had no intention of speaking to him anyway. He hung up and phoned Tommy Carlo at home, six P.M. in Miami.

'How about Nicole?'

'You mean Nicki,' Tommy said. 'I got hold of the guy use to be her manager through the booking service. You remember him? Marty, little guy with hair down to his ass?'

'Yeah, sorta.'

'He's the A and R guy for a record company in Los Angeles, scouts new talent. He says Nicki's getting ready for a gig at Raji's on Hollywood Boulevard. She's been rehearsing there, putting a new band together and that's prob'ly where you'll find her. Raji's on Hollywood Boulevard. I think Marty said east of Vine, you got it?'

Chili was making notes on the Sunset Marquis pad by the phone. 'Yeah. What about Bones? When's he coming?'

'I don't know any more'n I told you already.'

'You find out anything, call me, okay?'

Chili gave him the number and said, 'I'll see you.'

'When?' Tommy said.

It stopped him.

Chili said, 'I don't know, I may be going into the movie business, see what it's like.'

Now it sounded like Tommy was stopped. 'What're you talking about? You wanta be a movie star?'

'I'm no actor. I'm talking about producing.'

'How you gonna do that? You don't know shit about making movies.'

'I don't think the producer has to do much,' Chili said. 'The way it is here, this town, it goes out in all directions with all kinds of shit happening. You know what I mean? Like there's no special look to the place. Brooklyn, you got streets of houses are all exactly the same. Or Brooklyn in general, you know, has a bummed-out look, it's old, it's dirty . . . Miami has a look you think of stucco, right? Or high-rises on the beach. Here, wherever you look it's something different. There homes'll knock your eyes out, but there's a lot of cheap shit, too. You know what I mean? Like Times Square. I think the movie business is the same way. There aren't any rules – you know, anybody saying this's how you have to do it. What're movies about? They're all different, except the ones that're just like other movies that made money. You know what I'm saying? The movie business, you can do any fuckin thing you want 'cause there's nobody in charge.'

Tommy said, 'Hey, Chil, you know what I think?'

'What?'

'You're fulla shit.'

He sat down on the sofa to relax for a while in his new surroundings with the oriental look, turned on the TV and punched remote control buttons to see what they had out here. . . . As many Spanish programs as Miami . . . The Lakers playing Golden State . . . *Shane*. He hadn't seen *Shane* in years. Chili got low in the sofa, his feet on the glass coffee table, and watched from the part where Shane beats the shit out of Ben Johnson for calling him sody pop to where he shoots Jack Wilson, practically blows him through the wall. It was almost real the way the guns went off in that movie, loud, but still not as loud as you heard it in a room, shooting a guy in the head just a little too high, and now the guy was coming out here.

Chili left his rented Toyota in the hotel garage, hiked up Alta Loma the half block to Sunset and had to stop and catch his breath from the climb, out of shape, before walking along Sunset till he was opposite white storefronts across the street. It was dark, a stream of headlights going by. He stood waiting for a break in the traffic, his gaze on the white building, and began to wonder why a light was on in Harry's office. He was pretty sure it was Harry's, the wide window with the Venetian blinds. Maybe the cleaning woman was in there.

Chili jogged across the wide street, let himself in and climbed the stairs to ZigZag Productions, dark except for a light at the end of the hall. It was Harry's office, but not a cleaning woman who looked up from the desk as Chili entered.

It was the colored limo guy, Bo Catlett, wearing glasses and with a movie script open in front of him.

Catlett said, 'This ain't bad, you know it? This *Mr Lovejoy*. The title's for shit, but the story, man, it takes hold of you.'

14

Chili walked toward the desk thinking he'd better nail the guy right away, not say a word, hit him with the phone, wrap the cord around his neck and drag him out. Except the guy had not busted the door, jimmied the lock, he wasn't robbing the place, he was sitting there with his glasses on reading a script. The guy telling him now, 'I started reading, I couldn't put it down. I'm at the part – let's see, about fifteen pages to go – Lovejoy's coming out of court with his sister, can't believe what's happened to him.' Chili reached the red leather chairs facing the desk, the guy saying, 'I want to know how it ends, but don't tell me.' Saying, 'Yeah, I can see why Harry's dying to do it.'

The guy talking about the script, but saying to Chili at the same time, Let's see how cool you are.

Chili sat down in one of the red leather chairs. He unbuttoned the jacket of his pinstripe suit to get comfortable and said, 'I don't like the title either.'

For a moment he saw that dreamy look in the man's eyes, almost a smile.

'You understand I knew Harry was lying,' Catlett said. 'I'm talking about his saying this wasn't any good, but holding on to it, man, like you have to break his fingers to get it from him.' Catlett paused. 'I'm explaining to you what I'm doing here. Case you think I come to rob the place, rip off any this dusty old shit the man has.'

Chili said, 'No, I'd never make you as a burglar, not with that suit you have on. It tells me what you do – when you're not taking people for rides in your limo.'

'It's funny, I was thinking along the same line,' Catlett said. 'Guys in your business you don't see dressed up much anymore, but you have a nice suit of clothes on.'

'You mean the movie business,' Chili said.

There was that little slow gleam in Catlett's eyes again, showing understanding, maybe appreciation.

'Movie people don't dress up either, 'cept the agents. You see an agent duded up it means he's taking a serious meeting someplace, at a studio or a network. Or he wants you to think it's what he's doing. Or the older crowd at Chasen's, in the front room, they dress up. But I'm talking about your *main* business, working for the Italians.'

'Yeah? How you know that?'

'Man, listen to you. You street, same as me, only we from different sides of it,' Catlett said. 'See, the first thing I wonder about I see you, I ask myself. What's this man Chili Palmer doing here? Is he'n investor? Harry called you his associate, but what does that mean? I never heard your name spoken in the business or read it in *Variety* or *The Reporter* or anyplace. I kept thinking till it came to me. It's wiseguy money financing *Lovejoy* and Frank DePhillips, the man, put you here to look out for Harry, see he doesn't mess up or keep people like myself from bothering him.'

'You're part right,' Chili said.

'Part or mostly?'

'You know DePhillips?'

'Enough about him.'

'Then you oughta know if I worked for a guy like DePhillips,' Chili said, 'we wouldn't be talking. I would've thrown you out that window by now. I don't work for him and I don't work for Harry, either. It's what he said, I'm his associate.'

Catlett slipped his glasses off. 'You must bring something heavy to the deal.'

'That's right, me,' Chili said, and watched the man's smile come all the way, showing goldwork on his teeth.

Catlett said, 'But no special talent, huh? Walk in off the street and become a film producer. You the financial or the creative side?'

'Don't worry about it.'

'Can I ask you – how 'bout your lead? Who you see for Lovejoy?'

'We're getting Michael Weir.'

'Hey, shit, come on. How you gonna do that?'

'I put a gun right here,' Chili said, touching the side of his head, 'and I tell him, "Sign the paper, Mikey, or you're fuckin dead." Like that.'

'I wonder,' Catlett said, 'would that work. Man, it would simplify dealing with movie stars. They get temper'mental on you, lay the piece alongside their head. "Get back to work, motherfucker." Yeah, Michael Weir, he'd be good. You got anybody else?'

'We're working on it.'

'You know who I see for Al Roxy? Harvey Kei-tel. The man could do it with his eyes closed. But you know who else? Morgan Freeman. You know who I mean?'

Chili said, 'Yeah, Morgan Freeman. But he's a colored guy.'

'Where's it say in the script he's white? Color is what the part needs, man, somebody to do it has some style. The way it is now Ronnie could do it, play himself, a cracked-out asshole. You also what you need is a good woman part, get some love in it. The only women you have now, you have

Lovejoy's sister, on his ass all the time, and you have that whore friend of Roxy's, but she's only in two scenes.'

Chili was trying to think of the name of the girl in the one page of the script he'd read. Not Irene . . .

'You know what I'm saying? A good juicy woman part.'

Chili gave him a nod, still trying to think of the girl's name.

'You have Lovejoy smelling his flowers, right. So what you need is a woman different than he is to come along and help him out. Like, say, Theresa Russell, man. Or the one, what's her name? Greta something . . .'

'Greta Scacchi,' Chili said.

'That's the one. That's how you pronounce it, huh, Skacky? I never knew that. I heard Scotchy, I never heard Skacky.'

'You're hearing it now,' Chili said.

'Sexy woman. You can go either way, Greta or Theresa Russell,' Catlett said. 'Take Roxy's friend the whore and make her more important. You understand? Like he beats up on her, so she goes to Lovejoy, tells him something important will help him out, just about the time he's thinking of giving up.'

Chili remembered the girl's name in the script. 'There's Ilona.'

'What about her?'

'Get something going there.'

'With I*lona*? You know how old Ilona is?'

Chili got out a cigarette and lit it. He felt the guy watching him. 'Yeah, she's young.'

'She's sixteen,' Catlett said, 'same age as Lovejoy's kid, Bernard, she calls Bernie.'

'I was thinking you could make her older.'

The guy kept staring at him.

'You do that, you lose her telling things to Lovejoy about

125

his own son he don't know about, when he thought he was so close to the boy.' Catlett paused a moment and said, 'Have you *read* this?'

'Part of it, yeah.'

'*Part* of it?' Catlett said, sitting back in Harry's creaky chair. 'You know what it's about?'

'I know Lovejoy's following this other guy . . .'

There was a silence, not long, Chili and Catlett looking at each other until Catlett said, 'Al Roxy, the one he's following around, killed his kid.'

'Killed him – how?'

'Ran over him with his car. On his way home drunk, hits the kid crossing the street and keeps going. It's right in front of Lovejoy's flower shop. He sees it happen and almost goes to pieces right there, his boy laying dead. Before this we know Lovejoy's wife left him and all he has is this boy. The boy and his flower business, that's his whole life.'

Chili didn't say anything.

He hadn't read the script, so the guy was telling him about it and it seemed okay. Why not? Saying now there was a witness who got the license number . . .

'So the cops pick up Roxy, he says he didn't know he hit anybody. It's the next day, so there's no way to tell he was drinking, but they have evidence, find some blood on his car matches up . . . Anyway, Roxy's lawyer does a job on the court and all the man gets is his license suspended, can't drive a car for six months. Lovejoy, he's at the court hearing, can't believe it. That's *all*? The motherfucker kills my kid and that's all he gets? That's what he's thinking, but see, the man is too . . . well, he's too timid to come out and say anything. After it's over Roxy says to Lovejoy, "Tough break. But the kid shouldn't have run out in the street." Or, "The kid should have watched where he was going." Something like that.'

'What's Roxy do?' Chili said. 'I mean, what kind of work?'

'He runs a body shop. You know, bump and paint. Does good too. This is in Detroit it takes place, Harry's hometown, though he don't have a fondness for the city like I do. I lived there nine years.'

A question popped into Chili's mind.

'You ever do time?'

The guy started to smile, then let it go.

'I been bound over, but no jail time, no.'

'So what happens?'

'Lovejoy gets it into his head Roxy, sooner or later, is gonna drive his car, this Cadillac. So what Lovejoy does, he takes his florist delivery van and changes it over. Paints out the name, has peepholes cut in the sides and gets in there with a video camera. He's gonna stay on Roxy every time the man shows himself. The minute he ever drives off in a car, Lovejoy is gonna have it on tape and show it to the cops.'

'Ilona helps him out?'

'She drives him after school and they talk about Bernard, the kid. See, but now he's letting his business go to hell and his sister gets on him. Her and her husband, this big asshole that's always giving Lovejoy a hard time. It's good the way it starts out, but then it gets slow in the middle. You see Roxy, what he's doing. Likes to drink, likes to gamble, but you don't see him do anything so bad you get the idea the man's dangerous. You know what I'm saying? Like if Lovejoy gets too close and Roxy sees what he's doing, Lovejoy could get taken out. What I was thinking was if Lovejoy finds out the man's got some kind of crooked deal going.'

'Using his place as a chop shop,' Chili said. 'Buys hot cars, cuts 'em up and sells the parts.'

'Yeah, that's the kind of thing. Then get the woman in it, she's the one tells Lovejoy what the setup is.'

'He catch the guy driving or not?'

127

'Yeah, he catches him, videos the man driving down the road. Catches him the last day he's gonna do this.'

'The guy doesn't see him?'

'Never suspects a thing. So Lovejoy puts it on him, shows his tape to the cops. They pick up Roxy, there's a court hearing and what you suppose he gets? His license taken away again, this time for a year. Lovejoy is right back where he started only worse. He gets sued by Roxy for annoying him, invading his privacy, different other legal shit and the court decides in favor of Roxy. Lovejoy has to pay him a hundred thousand in damages. Coming out of court his sister is calling him a fool, saying now you have to sell your business and you got nothing. That's where I ended off.' Catlett picked up the script. 'With, yeah, fifteen pages to go.'

Chili said, 'You don't know how it ends? Take a look.'

'I don't cheat, look at the end when I read something. But it's good, huh? What would you do,' Catlett said, 'you were Lovejoy?'

'I know guys,' Chili said, 'would cut Roxy in half with a chainsaw.'

'Yeah, but what would you do?'

'I'd have to think about it.'

'I'd shoot the man in the head,' Catlett said. 'Set him up and do it.'

'You like to think you would,' Chili said. 'Take a look, find out.' Chili reached over, picked up one of the red-covered scripts from the desk and opened it. 'What page you on?'

Catlett was looking at his script. 'Ninety-two. They come out of the courthouse, his sister's on his ass. Then the brother-in-law, Stanley, gets on him.'

Chili found the page, began to read:

128

EXT. COURTHOUSE – DAY

ANGLE ON Lovejoy's van pulling up in front. Ilona gets out, her expression distraught as she looks up and sees:

REVERSE – ILONA'S POV

Lovejoy and Helen coming out of the courthouse followed closely by Stanley. Helen is already speaking as they pause at the top of the stairs.

ANGLE ON LOVEJOY, HELEN AND STANLEY

Lovejoy sees Ilona, a wistful smile touches his face.

> HELEN
> You're so smart, aren't you? Now you have nothing, and you brought it all on yourself.

> STANLEY
> If you're thinking of coming to us for help, forget it.

Lovejoy turns to Stanley with a level gaze.

> LOVEJOY
> I wouldn't dream of it, Stanley. Besides, you both have your own problems.

> STANLEY
> (scowling)
> What're you talking about?

> LOVEJOY
> Being married to each other.
> (starts down the stairs)
> Have a nice day.

ANGLE ON ILONA, WATCHING

129

As Lovejoy approaches and we hear Stanley CALL after him.

STANLEY (O.S.)
No more Sunday dinner at our house, Roger!

Lovejoy gives Ilona a wry grin.

LOVEJOY
At least some good has come of this.

They get in the van and drive off.

Chili looked at Catlett turning pages, skimming through the script. 'I think when Stanley opens his mouth Lovejoy oughta pop him and walk away, not say a fuckin word.'

'That's 'cause you don't know the man,' Catlett said, turning another page. 'Next, you see him alone in his flower shop watering some plants, thinking what he should do. The man likes working here and now he's gonna lose it. Next, you see him in the van again, going by Roxy's place.'

Chili turned pages to catch up, came to a scene, Roxy – it looked like Roxy was having a party.

'Inside the office there,' Catlett said, 'Roxy's celebrating his putting it to Lovejoy, having drinks with his friends . . . Now you see Lovejoy in the van parked across the street, waiting, but we don't know what for. Looking like he's doing some more thinking . . . Back to Roxy, he's getting drunk, say he wants everybody to come out to his place on the lake . . . Now Lovejoy is listening to symphony music on the radio, still in the van . . . Roxy, inside the office, is now getting ugly, has a fight with the woman wants to take him home.'

Chili turned some more pages. 'What's I-N-T?'

'Interior,' Catlett said. 'Inside. Roxy goes out . . .'

'What's P-O-V?'

'Point of view. Lovejoy's P-O-V, like he's seeing it when

130

Roxy comes out and gets in his Cadillac. Drives off – now we looking at the Cadillac through Lovejoy's windshield, following him.'

Both Chili and Catlett turned a page.

'He's got the video camera with him,' Chili said. 'He's gonna get Roxy driving again.'

'That's what he's doing,' Catlett said.

'Roxy spots him.'

'I could see that coming.'

'He makes a sudden U-turn.'

For several moments they both read in silence.

'I knew it,' Catlett said. 'He's on Lovejoy's ass now.'

Chili kept quiet, reading the scene:

EXT. CITY STREETS – NIGHT

ANGLES ON the Cadillac chasing the van through traffic, squealing around corners, narrowly missing cars at intersections, the Cadillac sideswiping a parked car.

INTERCUT

Roxy at the wheel of the Cadillac, recklessly determined.

Lovejoy in the van, glancing at mirror apprehensively.

EXT. INTERSECTION – NIGHT

Quiet, little traffic, then none. Until suddenly the van comes around the corner and ducks into an alley. We SEE the rear lights go off. Now the Cadillac takes the corner and flies past the alley. After SEVERAL BEATS the van backs out, proceeds at a normal pace.

EXT. LOVEJOY'S FLOWER SHOP – NIGHT

The van arrives and parks at the curb across the street.

Lovejoy gets out slowly, exhausted. As he starts across the street:

HEADLIGHTS POP ON

down the block. We hear an engine ROAR. And now a car, the Cadillac, is hurtling toward Lovejoy in the middle of the street, frozen in the highbeam of the headlights, *in the exact spot where his son was killed*.

Catlett said, 'Hmmmm,' sitting back, finished.
Chili said, 'Wait,' still reading, 'don't say nothing.' He was on the second to last page of the script.

INTERCUT

Roxy hunched over the steering wheel, wild-eyed.

Roxy's POV – to see Lovejoy through windshield.

CLOSE ON Lovejoy standing in the street.

REVERSE – Lovejoy's POV-car hurtling toward him.

Roxy's POV as Lovejoy suddenly bolts for the flower shop.

EXT. FLOWER SHOP – NIGHT

AN ANGLE – on the Cadillac swerving after Lovejoy, who dives out of the way just in time.

INT. CADILLAC – CLOSE ON ROXY

His look of horror as he sees:

THROUGH THE WINDSHIELD

The plate-glass front of the flower shop suddenly in front of him.

INT. FLOWER SHOP (SLOW-MOTION SEQ.) – NIGHT

The Cadillac crashes through the plate glass, plows across the store interior to smash into the refrigerated showcase and come to a dead stop.

INT. FLOWER SHOP – ANOTHER ANGLE – NIGHT

Lovejoy enters, cautiously approaches the Cadillac, looks in to see:

ROXY IN CADILLAC

His bloody countenance among flowers, plants, the man obviously dead.

Chili turned to the last page. Now the cops are there, lot of activity. Medics come out with Roxy in a body bag. Lovejoy watches, depressed, looks up. There's Ilona. Ilona takes him aside and 'with wisdom beyond her years' tells him it's over and a few other things about flowers, saying, 'Besides, making things grow is your life.' *Besides* – they used that word all the time in movies, but you hardly ever heard it in real life.

Catlett said, 'Well?'

Chili looked up, closing the script.

Catlett said, 'Didn't shoot him, like he should have.'

'He didn't do anything,' Chili said. 'The guy gets killed, yeah, but what's Lovejoy do?'

Catlett came up in the chair to lean on the desk.

'He makes it happen.'

'What, he planned it? He dives out of the way to save his ass, that's all.'

'What you don't understand,' Catlett said, 'is what the movie is saying. You live clean, the shit gets taken care of somehow or other. That's what the movie's about.'

'You believe that?'

'In movies, yeah. Movies haven't got nothing to do with real life.'

Chili was about to argue with him, but changed his mind and said, 'I don't like the ending.'

Catlett eased back again. 'You want to change it?'

Chili didn't answer, looking at the ZigZag script cover, opening it then and looking at the title page.

MR LOVEJOY

An Original Screenplay

by

MURRAY SAFFRIN

The title was the first thing that ought to be changed. And the guy's name. Murray Saffrin was better than Lovejoy.

'You don't care for the ending,' Catlett said, 'and I don't like the middle part. I'm thinking what we could do is fix it. You hear what I'm saying? Get some heat in it. Make the people's hands sweat watching it You and me, we could do it. It's our kind of shit we talking about here. Like the action Roxy's into you mentioned, doing stolen cars.'

'Fix up the girl's part,' Chili said. An idea came to him and he said, 'We might even be able to get Karen Flores.'

Catlett looked up at him. 'Karen Flores . . .'

'She's been out of movies a few years, but she's good.'

Catlett said, 'Karen Flores, I know that name . . .'

'Change the ending,' Chili said, 'so Lovejoy's the one makes it happen, he isn't just standing there.'

'We could do all that,' Catlett said, 'you and me, sit down and write the script over where it needs it.'

Chili opened the script again, flipped through a few pages looking at the format. 'You know how to write one of these?'

'You asking me,' Catlett said, 'do I know how to write down words on a piece of paper? That's what you do, man, you put down one word after the other as it comes in your head. It isn't like having to learn how to play the piano, like you have to learn notes. You already learned in school how to write, didn't you? I *hope* so. You have the idea and you put down what you want to say. Then you get somebody to add in the commas and shit where they belong, if you aren't positive yourself. Maybe fix up the spelling where you have some tricky words. There people do that for you. Some, I've even seen scripts where I *know* words weren't spelled right and there was hardly any commas in it. So I don't think it's too important. You come to the last page you write in 'Fade out' and that's the end, you're done.'

Chili said, 'That's all there is to it?'

'That's all.'

Chili said, 'Then what do I need you for?'

He heard the elevator as he was opening the door to 325, looked down the hotel hallway and saw Karen coming toward him, Karen in a loose-fitting white shirt and gray slacks. Chili pushed the door open and waited, two copies of *Lovejoy* under his arm.

'I was in the bar when you came in,' Karen said. 'I thought you saw me.' He shook his head saying no, but was glad to see her now, motioning Karen to go in. She said, 'Well, I read it.' He followed her into the living room, the pagoda lamps still on, and dropped the scripts on the counter. A light on the phone was blinking on and off.

'You want to check your messages?'

'I can do it later,' Chili said. 'Sit down, make yourself comfortable. I want to hear what you think.'

He took off his suitcoat as Karen went over to a fat chair next to the sofa.

'You read the script . . .'

'I could play the sister,' Karen said, 'and wear sensible shoes. That would be a switch.'

135

Chili moved to the sofa, folding his suitcoat.

'I don't see you doing that one, the sister.'

He laid the coat next to him as he sat down.

'But there isn't anything else, as it stands, you'd want to do.'

'I wasn't really looking for a part.'

'There could be a good one though. I got some ideas.'

Karen said, 'You do, huh?'

Looking at Karen he could see the phone on the counter above her, the message light blinking on and off. It would have to be Tommy, something about Bones maybe, or Nicki. He began telling Karen how he thought the script needed to be fixed, change the whore to make it a bigger part: how she helps Lovejoy out and pretty soon they have something going.

'The hooker and the florist,' Karen said.

'You wouldn't have to be a hooker exactly.'

'Mousse my hair and chew gum? Why don't you check your messages?'

'I can wait.'

'You've read the script?'

'Not all of it, but I know what it's about.'

'You and Harry'll make a great team. Has he read it?'

'He bought it, he must've.'

'You sure? Harry used to have someone else read for him. Then he'd skim it if he thought he was going into production.'

'He told me he read it twice.'

'This one he might've. You like the idea?'

'Basically, yeah, except what I mentioned. The part I read, the ending, I didn't like 'cause it's a letdown. You know what I mean? Lovejoy's just standing there.'

'What do you think he should do?'

'Well, if he's the star he's the one ought to make it

136

happen. Get some action going that's his idea.' She kept looking at him and he said, 'I don't like the title either.'

'Harry thinks he needs you,' Karen said, 'but he can't pay you anything, he's broke.'

Chili said, 'I know exactly how much he doesn't have.'

'So what do you get out of it?'

'You came here to ask me that?'

She said, 'I want to know,' staring at him the way she did last night. It wasn't the old dead-eyed look exactly, but it wasn't bad.

'I like movies,' Chili said. 'I help Harry make one, I'll find out what you have to do outside of have an idea and raise the money. That doesn't sound too hard. I was in the money business and I get ideas all the time.'

She looked so serious he had to smile at her.

'Then I'll do one, make a movie and put you in it.'

He glanced at the message light on the phone flashing on and off.

Karen was still watching him.

She said, 'I took your advice and made a deal with Harry. Not to act in it. The way I see it, if I save Harry a half million by setting him up with Michael, I should have a piece of the action. I told him I want co-producer.'

'What'd Harry say?'

'Harry would agree to anything. But I said I'd only do it if he can get a studio to put *Lovejoy* into development. So the first thing he has to do is sell the idea to Tower. That's where he wants to take it. He thinks he can handle Elaine Levin.'

'What do you think?'

'If Elaine doesn't like the idea, Harry's not going to sell her on it. If she likes it, it could get made, with or without Michael.'

Chili said, 'The script still needs to be fixed.'

137

'You know that,' Karen said, 'and you haven't even read it.'

He watched her lean over to push out of the chair, then pause and toss her head as she looked at him again, her hair falling away from her eyes – and remembered Karen doing it with blond hair, giving the guy in the movie the same look.

She said, 'This might work. You never know.'

He asked the operator for his messages. She said, 'Just a minute.' He waited. She came back on saying, 'A Karen Flores called. She didn't leave a message.' The operator sounded Latin. 'A Mr Zimm called. He'll talk to you tomorrow.' That was it.

Later on, watching *Taxi Driver* on TV, Chili kept thinking of the way Karen had looked at him and wondered if she was telling him something and if he should've asked her to stay and have a drink. But then when Robert De Niro shaved his hair into a Mohawk, Chili started thinking of Ray Bones, even though Ray Bones didn't have a Mohawk or look anything like Robert De Niro. Maybe it was all those guns De Niro had, wanting to shoot somebody.

15

Catlett lived way up in the Hollywood hills where you could see the lights of LA spread out in kind of a grid and hear coyotes yipping in the dark. Here were all these modern homes built on stilts hanging over the sides of cliffs and there were still wild animals running around free. Catlett, barefoot, wearing a white silk bathrobe, stood at the rail of his deck, nothing below it for about twelve stories to where faint voices were coming from a lit-up swimming pool, a bright little square of light blue down there in the night, a girl laughing now, a nice sound . . . while the Bear told about the Colombian mule, Yayo the yoyo, dumb son of a bitch, still out at the airport.

'Thinks they have him spotted.'

'He call you?' Catlett said, his voice quiet. 'How'd he know to do that?'

'He called Miami and they gave him our service number,' the Bear said. 'The service calls me and I call the yoyo at LAX. He says the focking guy you told him was a fed left, but two more focking guys just like him took his place. With those focking gones on their legs.'

'Irritable, huh?'

'Making sounds like he's coming loose on us.'

'Yeah, that's how those people are.'

'He makes a run at the locker they'll grab him. Then you

139

have to think,' the Bear said, 'pissed as he is, he could give us up too.'

'Out of meanness,' Catlett said, 'or making a plea deal. You suppose you could go get him?'

'That's what I was thinking. Tell him the airport's too hot right now.'

'I appreciate it,' Catlett said.

'You want me to take him anyplace special?'

'I don't care, long as you get him out.'

'I could take him home.'

'Yeah, but don't let him go near Farrah, hear? How's the child?'

'Cute as a bug.'

Catlett said, 'Bear? Something else that's pressing. This man Chili Palmer, staying at the Sunset Marquis. I wonder you could do a read on him for me.'

'Chili Palmer,' the Bear said.

'Thinks he's mean. I wouldn't mind you ran into him. See if he's real.'

'I could do that.'

Catlett said, 'Shit, everything at once. I also need to know where Harry Zimm's been hanging out. Put a limo on him' – Catlett starting to grin – 'tail the motherfucker in a white stretch.'

The Bear said, 'I best take care of Yayo first,' and left.

It was cool out on the deck, Catlett wearing just the thin robe, but felt good, some stars out and that clear sound of voices in the dark, the girl laughing again. People with style knowing how to live. It looked like they might be skinny-dipping down there, couple of pink shapes in the blue-lit square. Coyotes watching them from the bushes . . . Young coyote asks his daddy, What's that looks like a pussy over there? And his daddy says. It's what it is, boy. They might even be movie people, work either side of the camera, it didn't make any difference. They were the kind of people he wanted to associate with in his life, not have to fool with fools like Yayo anymore. Even if you had to watch your step in the movie business, keep from getting fucked over, at least the ones doing it had some style. Chili Palmer had it in his own way, something, but it was hard to put your finger on it. Chili Palmer looked like a mob guy and talked like one – not a movie mob guy, a real one – though he could maybe play one in a movie. He had the bullshit to make it work, if the camera didn't scare him. Ask him what did he bring to Harry's deal and he says, 'Me.' Catlett had to smile, by himself out on his deck and starting to shiver with cold, he had to smile at the man's bullshit. 'Me.' Or was it confidence he had in himself? Either way, it could work for him. And then saying what he did, if writing a script was so easy, saying, 'What do I need you for?' He did know a few things about movies, who Morgan Freeman was and how to say Greta Scacchi's name, without looking like he'd know such things. He let you think he'd read the script but didn't get sassy when he got caught – no, he listened to it told, wanting to know. That showed confidence, too, didn't it? The man out in the open with himself. Maybe less bullshit about him than you think. Even though he looked and talked like a mob guy and those guys would bullshit you to death.

Catlett felt himself close to something here and said it out loud to hear it. 'You close. You know it? You close.' Thinking, Chili Palmer might know something about movies. Then saying out loud, 'But you know more.'

Time to quit thinking and start doing. Yeah.

Not let anything stand in the way. No.

Not Chili Palmer, not anybody.

Ronnie said, 'I have to make all the decisions around here? Why don't you decide for a change. It's not that hard, Cat.

You want to go to Mateo's? The Ivy? You want to go to Fennel? Drive out to Santa Monica? Or we can run across the street to the Palm, I don't give a shit. But we have to eat, right?'

'I don't know,' Catlett said, 'do we?'

Give him a hard one like that, mess up his head.

'You have anything has to be done around here?'

There wasn't much that looked like business on Ronnie's desk. It stayed neat, his girl Marcella in the other office doing the scheduling and billing.

Ronnie said, 'Not that I know of.'

Catlett didn't have a desk. He sat across from Ronnie looking at Ronnie's cowboy boots up on the desk, ankles crossed, Ronnie low in his big chair, down behind there somewhere.

'Well, I know you got three cars out working. You got to pick up the producer coming in from New York, and later on the rock group that likes the white stretch. I know that much,' Catlett said, 'and I barely work here.'

Ronnie said, 'You know that, but you can't tell me where you want to have lunch. Hey, how about Chinois? The curried oysters with salmon pearls, mmmmm.'

Catlett said, 'How about Spago?' acting innocent, knowing they didn't serve lunch, and got a mean look from Ronnie. The last time they went there the woman tried to seat them over on the other side of the open kitchen and Ronnie went berserk, told her, 'My fucking Rolls is in the front row outside and you want to put us in *back*?' The man had a point. You sat at the right tables if you expected to be recognized in this town. Ronnie's trouble was nobody remembered him.

Next, Catlett heard Ronnie's desk drawer open and saw Ronnie's automatic come edging out of the V between his crossed cowboy boots and heard Ronnie making gunfire sounds, *couuu, couuu*, the little guy playing with his Hardballer .45, a pistol ten inches long. *Couuu*, pretending he was shooting that lady maître d' at Spago.

'Put it away.'

'I'm not pointing it at you.'

'Ronnie?'

'Shit.'

'In the drawer.'

'I wouldn't mind somebody trying to rip us off,' Ronnie said. 'You know what this would do to a guy?'

'I know I'm not ever having lunch with you no more you don't put that thing away.' Catlett waited, hearing the drawer slide open and close. 'You have a delivery to make, don't you? Down to Palm Desert?'

'You want to take it?'

'They your friends, not mine.'

Four years of this shit, being the buddy of an idiot Earlier, when Catlett came in, he told Ronnie they were having trouble with Yayo and Ronnie said, 'Which one's Yayo?' Four years retained on the books as Marketing Consultant, which meant sitting here with Ronnie deciding where to eat. Then having the martini lunches and watching him get shitfaced on those see-throughs. It meant going to Ronnie's parties with all the glitter twits. Watching Ronnie have his nose bleeds about every day. Put up with all that shit, it was still better than running a dope house or sitting in a boiler room selling fake bonds over the phone. Better than managing a string of bitchy ladies, better than thinking up the everyday kinds of hustles to get by . . . But not better than being in the movie business. He hadn't mentioned to Ronnie he'd read *Mr Lovejoy* or said anything about it since their meeting with Harry. From now on it wouldn't be any of Ronnie's business.

'Hey, Cat? How about Le Dome? We haven't been there in a while.'

They got a nice table on the aisle in that middle section and Catlett waited for Ronnie to relax with his extra-dry martini before telling him he should take a rest. 'You going down to Palm Desert anyway, why don't you stay awhile, take a month off, man, and ease out, share your toot with some nice young lady. You been working too hard.'

Get the motherfucker out of his hair while he set up making his move.

Back in the office of Wingate Motor Cars Limited, past closing time and the help gone, Catlett sitting at Ronnie's desk starting to make plans, he got a call from the Bear.

'This guy's driving me nuts.'

'Where you at?'

'Home. We were out at Universal – you know the studio tour? It's like Disneyland.'

'You took Yayo?'

'I forgot I promised Farrah. Yeah, so I brought the yoyo along. All the guy does is bitch and say fock, in front of my little girl. I gotta dump him somewhere.'

'Bring him by,' Catlett said, 'I'll talk to him.'

Standing at the window Catlett watched the Bear's blue Dodge van come off Santa Monica, out of traffic and into the drive. By the time Catlett made his way through the offices and the reception room to the garage, the steel overhead door was coming down to seal off street sounds, Yayo was out of the van and the Bear, his Hawaiian shirt today full of blue and yellow flowers, was coming around the front end. There was one limo parked in the garage, the white stretch reserved for the rock group, and Catlett's car, a black Porsche 911.

He was in his shirtsleeves, a striped shirt with a tab collar, tie in place – had put it on thinking of Chili's shirt last night; it had looked pretty sharp.

Yayo could use a clean shirt and a shave, comb his hair, Yayo giving him the Tony Montana look with the lip curl. A man that didn't know how dumb he was.

'You have a nice time, Yayo?'

The little Colombian mule started out in Spanish before switching over to English, saying, 'I tell this guy I want my focking money or you in trouble, man, believe me.'

'There's no pleasing him,' the Bear said, fooling with his beard. 'I took his picture standing with this cutout of *Magnum PI*? Tom Selleck, looks real as can be. All he does is bitch.'

Yayo turned enough to tell the Bear, 'You think you funny. Is that it?'

'I took him to the *Miami Vice* Action Spectacular . . .'

'Man, it was shit.'

'It opens,' the Bear said, 'here come Crockett and Tubbs on jet skis. It's like a movie set. You know, some shacks at the edge of the water, we're in the grandstand watching. The voice-over says, "They have ruffled some feathers in flamingo land and the band of smugglers have a dynamite surprise waiting for them." It's all low-grade special effects, but the tourists eat it up.'

'It was all shit,' Yayo told Catlett.

'He kept talking like that,' the Bear said, 'saying fock in front of my little girl.'

Catlett frowned, a pained look. 'He did?'

'Man wouldn't shut his mouth.'

'Listen to me,' Yayo said. 'I wan' to leave this place, go home. Wha' you have to do, get the money and give it to me. Or give me some other money.'

'I gave you the key,' Catlett said. 'That's all you need, and some patience.'

Yayo had that lip curled saying, 'I don't wan' no focking key. I wan' the money.'

Catlett stood with his fingers shoved into his pockets. He shrugged saying, 'Give it some time, pretty soon there won't be nobody watching you.'

Yayo pointed a finger at him. He said, 'Okay, man, I tell you something. I go the airport and open that focking locker. They bus' me, I tell them I come to get something for *you*, tha's all I know.'

Catlett said, 'Tha's all you know, huh? Wait here a minute, Yayo, I be back directly.'

He left them: went back to Ronnie's office and got Ronnie's big AMT Hardballer .45 auto out of the center desk drawer and racked the slide, knowing Ronnie kept the piece loaded. Catlett walked through offices and the reception room to the garage, closed the door behind him and extended the Hardballer's long barrel at Yayo, walking up to within ten feet of the man. Yayo didn't move. The Bear didn't either.

Yayo cocked his head then and put his hands on his hips, giving Catlett a Tony Montana pose.

'The fock you doing with that?'

Catlett said, 'I'm taking you out, Yayo,' and shot him in the chest, the gun going off loud – man, it was loud – but didn't buck as much as Catlett expected. No, looking down at Yayo on the cement floor now among oil stains, arms flung out, eyes stuck wide open, he'd put that hole right where he'd aimed.

'Dead focking center, man.'

'I get the feeling,' the Bear said, 'you done this before.'

'Not in a while,' Catlett said.

16

The way Chili found out Leo the drycleaner's room number at the Beverly Hills Hotel, he wrote *Larry Paris* on an envelope, handed it to the girl at the front desk and watched her stick the envelope in the mail slot for 207. It looked like 207, but he wasn't sure. So he used a house phone, around the corner by the entrance to the famous Polo Lounge, and asked for 207. The operator tried it, came back to say she was sorry, Mr Paris wasn't answering. Chili, friendly because he was getting somewhere, told the operator Mr Paris was probably still out at the track giving his money away. Ha ha. To double-check, Chili stepped into the Polo Lounge and ordered a Scotch at the bar.

He didn't see Leo or Leo's friend Annette waiting or Doug McClure or any faces he recognized from the silver screen. The room was crowded, six P.M., people at booths and little round tables, most of them probably tourists looking for movie stars. Harry said if anybody here even halfway resembled a star the rest of the tourists would say, 'There's one. Isn't that, you know, he was in . . .' and some guy from out of town would have a few minutes of fame he'd never know about. Harry said there were guys in the picture business had their secretaries call them here; they get paged, everybody sees the phone brought to the table and then watch the schmuck talking to his secretary like he was making a deal and knew personally all the names he

147

was dropping. Harry said the trouble with Hollywood, the schemeballs worked just as hard as the legit filmmakers.

The limo guy, Catlett, struck Chili as that type wanted to be seen. Looked good in his threads, sounded like he knew what he was talking about – the type of guy if he wasn't dealing drugs would be into some other kind of hustle. There were guys like him Chili knew by name in Miami, all five boroughs of New York and parts of Jersey. They gave you that stuff about having something in common, being from the street but different sides of it. You had to watch your back with guys like Catlett. Keep him away from Harry.

Earlier today Harry had called from his apartment on Franklin to say he'd come home to change but would be going right back to Karen's. 'You know what I did? Asked her to come on the project as associate producer and she jumped at it.' Chili was learning a little more about Harry every time the guy opened his mouth. 'Karen dropped off the script at Tower and we're waiting to hear when Elaine can see us. Miss Bedroom Eyes. Listen to this. Elaine doesn't even take pitch meetings, but she'll do it for Karen. I'm telling you, bringing my old screamer aboard was a stroke of genius.' Chili asked him, shouldn't the script be rewritten first, fixed up? Harry said, 'What's wrong with it?' Chili told him point by point what he thought and Harry said, 'Yeah, Karen mentioned that. It needs a polish, that's all. I'll cover that at the meeting. Don't worry about it.'

Okay, for the time being he'd forget about *Lovejoy* and concentrate on Leo the drycleaner, find him and get him out of town before Ray Bones showed up. Chili watched a waiter serving a tray of drinks, thinking he could sit here and get smashed and never even see Leo. Leo gets back, cleans up and goes out again without ever coming in here. It was watching the waiter with the drink order that gave Chili an idea, a way to get into Leo's suite.

He ordered a bottle of champagne, paid his tab and told the bartender he wanted the champagne put in room 207 right away, before his buddy got back, so it would be a surprise. The bartender acted like this was done all the time. Chili finished his drink and took the stairway to the second floor. Room 207 was right there, at an open center point where halls went off in three different directions, the wallpaper in the halls big green plants, or they might be palm-tree branches. About ten minutes later a room service waiter arrived with the champagne in a bucket and two glasses on a tray. Chili hung back by the stairway till the waiter had the door open, then moved fast to walk in right behind him saying, 'Hey, I'm just in time,' and handed the guy a ten-dollar bill.

Three cigarettes and a couple glasses of champagne later, he heard the key in the lock and watched the door open.

Leo came in wearing a sporty little plaid hat cocked on the side of his head. Leo still playing the high roller, not even dragging after all day at the track, not looking over this way either, going straight for the Chivas on the desk and having one out of the bottle, ahhh, before pulling a fat wad of cash out of his jacket, tossing it on the desk like it was change from the cab fare and then taking the jacket off, the shirt too, it was coming off, Leo getting down to his undershirt hanging on bony shoulders, but not touching the hat, the sporty hat stayed, Leo thinking he must look good in it or the hat brought him luck, Leo in his four-bills-a-day hotel suite having another swig from the bottle.

'You got no class.'

The poor guy didn't move.

Not till Chili said, 'Look at me, Leo.'

Watching him now reminded Chili of the time in Vegas, Leo pinned to the roulette table, no escape, and finally coming around to say, 'How much you want?' Leo the loser, no matter how much he won. Leo came around this time with the same hopeless look, but didn't say anything.

He was taking in the scene. Chili in his pinstripe, on the sofa. The champagne on the coffee table. But what caught Leo's eye and held his attention was sitting next to the champagne. His briefcase. The same one the bodyguard had carried for him in Vegas.

'I wouldn't think you're that dumb,' Chili said, 'leave over three hunnerd grand in the closet, underneath the extra blanket, but I guess you are.'

For a second there Leo looked surprised. 'I didn't know where else to keep it. Where would you?'

The guy was serious.

'You're here a while, what's wrong with a bank?'

'They report it to the IRS.'

'You don't open an account, Leo, you put it in a deposit box. Dip in whenever you want.'

He watched Leo nodding in his sporty hat and undershirt, thinking it over, what to do the next time he scammed an airline. Jesus, he was dumb.

'You been losing huh?'

'I'm up twelve grand today.'

'From when? You left Vegas with four-fifty.'

'Who told you that?'

'Now you're down to three-ten in the briefcase. You must've cooled off quite a bit in Reno.'

'Who says I was in Reno?'

The poor guy kept trying.

'Your friend Annette,' Chili said.

Leo narrowed his eyes and stared, trying hard to fake who he was. He raised his preshaped plaid hat and recocked it, see if that would help. No, there was nothing dumber than a

150

dumb guy who thought he was a hotshot. You did have to feel a little sorry for him . . .

Till he said, 'It was Fay, wasn't it, told you about Annette. She tell you my whole life history, for Christ sake?'

'I wouldn't let her if she tried,' Chili said. 'Why I'm here, Leo, basically, is to save your ass.'

'How? By taking my money?'

'You can keep what you won today. That's yours.'

'It's *all* mine,' Leo said. 'You don't have any right to it.' Starting to whine. 'You're some friend.'

'No, I'm not your friend, Leo.'

'I'll say you aren't. Come in and ruin my life. Why are you doing this to me? I paid you what I owed.'

'Sit down, Leo.'

Leo had to think about it, but he did. Went to the deep chair facing the coffee table, sat down and stared at his briefcase.

Chili said, 'I don't know how you stayed in business, Leo, you're so fuckin dumb. Or how you ever got this far. But now you're through. I'm gonna explain to you why and I hope you're not too dumb you don't understand what I'm saying. Okay?'

So Chili laid it out, told how Ray Bones was now in the picture and the kind of guy Bones was, the reason Leo and Annette would have to disappear or else risk serious injury. That seemed simple enough, a no-option kind of situation.

Leo thought about it a minute and said, 'Well, I'm not going home.'

Look how his mind worked.

'I don't care where you go, Leo.'

'I mean back to Fay.'

'That's up to you.'

'After what she did to me?'

'You aren't only dumb, Leo, you're crazy.'

151

Leo thought about it another minute and said, 'I don't see any difference who takes the money, you or this other guy. Either way I'm cleaned out.'

'Yeah, but there different ways of getting cleaned out,' Chili said. 'Ray Bones'll take everything you have—'

'What – you won't?'

'Leo, listen to me. When I say everything, I mean even that sporty hat if he wants it. Your watch, that pinkie you have on . . . and then he'll hit you with some kind of heavy object if he doesn't shoot you, so you won't tell on him. I won't do that,' Chili said, 'take your jewelry or hurt you. You have three-ten in the case, right? I'm gonna take the three hundred you scammed off the airline, but the rest of it, the ten grand? I'm gonna borrow that and pay you back sometime.'

He knew Leo wouldn't understand what he meant, Leo squinting at him now.

'You take all my money, but you're borrowing part of it?'

'At eighteen percent, okay? And don't ask me no more questions, I'm leaving,' Chili said.

He picked up the briefcase as he rose from the sofa and Leo came up out of his chair.

'You're saying you want me to *loan* you the ten grand?'

'I'm not asking you, Leo. What I'm saying is I'm gonna pay you back.'

'I don't understand.'

'You don't have to. Let's leave it at that.'

'Yeah, but how're you gonna pay me?'

Chili was moving toward the door. 'Don't worry about it.'

'I mean you won't know where I am. I don't even know where I'll be.'

'I'll find you, Leo. You leave a trail like a fuckin caterpillar.' Chili reached the door and opened it.

Leo saying now, 'Wait a minute. What's this eighteen-percent-a-year shit? You want to borrow ten, the vig's three

152

bills a week. You hear me?' Chili crossing the hall toward the stairway, shaking his head, Leo yelling after him, 'Fifteen for the vig plus the ten, that's twenty-five big ones you go a whole year, buddy! You hear me?'

Chili stopped. He turned around. As he started back he saw Leo's scared look just before he slammed the door shut. Jesus, he was dumb.

17

He thought Raji's would be a cocktail lounge with entertainment, a Hollywood nightspot. It turned out to be a bar with pinball machines and video games making a racket, also a counter where you could buy Raji's T-shirts, in case you wanted to show you had actually come in here. Sometimes it was hard to keep an open mind. Chili, in his pinstripe suit, nice tie, wondered if any regular people came here or just these kids trying to look like heroin addicts. He said to one of them, 'How come there's no sign out in front?'

The kid said, 'There isn't?'

He said to the kid, 'I see they have Yul Brynner in the sidewalk outside.'

Part of Hollywood's famous Walk of Fame, the names of 1,800 show-biz celebrities inlaid in stars.

The kid said, 'Who's Yul Brynner?'

Chili said to the bartender, a young guy who looked normal, 'How come there's no sign out in front?' The bartender said it was down temporarily while they reinforced the building against earthquakes. Chili asked him how come there weren't any barstools? The bartender said it was a stand-up kind of place: A and R guys from the record companies didn't like to sit down, they'd catch a group and then come back upstairs to have their conversation, where you could hear yourself think. He told Chili Guns N' Roses had been signed out of here. Chili said no shit and asked if Nicki

154

was around. There were 'Nicki' posters by the entrance. The bartender said she was downstairs but wouldn't be on for a couple hours yet.

'You in records?'

'Movies,' Chili said.

He had never made it with Nicki or even tried, but she still ought to remember him. The idea, get her to ask him to drop by the house, say hello to Michael and he'd take it from there. Get next to him. *Look at me, Michael* See what happens.

Chili went downstairs to an empty room with a bar and a few tables, hearing a band tuning up, hitting chords. It reminded him of bands at Memo's cranking up, doing sound checks, setting those dials just right, then blasting off loud enough to blow out the windows and he'd wonder what all that precision adjusting was for. Maybe they said they were reinforcing the place against earthquakes, but it was to keep the rockers from shaking the walls down, and that's why they played in the basement here: the bandstand through an archway in a separate room that was like a cave in there and maybe would hold a hundred people standing up.

There were four guys, three with guitars and a guy on the drums. He didn't see Nicki anywhere, just these four skinny guys, typical rock-and-roll assholes with all the hair, bare arms tricked out with tattoos and metal bracelets, all of them with that typical bored way they had. Looking over at him now standing in the archway, but too cool to show any interest. Some dickhead in a suit. Chili stared back at them thinking, Oh, is that right? Any you assholes want to be in the movies? No chance. They were turned toward each other now, one of them, with wild blond hair sticking out in every direction, talking as the others listened. Now the blond-haired one was looking over this way again, saying, 'Chil?' The middle one.

Christ, it was Nicole, Nicki. They all looked like girls – that's why he thought she was a guy.

'Nicki? How you doing?'

He should've spotted her, the skinny white arms, no tattoos. Nicki handed her guitar that had a big bull's-eye painted on it to one of the guys and was coming over now, Nicki in black jeans that were like tights on her and, Christ, big work boots, smiling at him. Chili put his arms out as she raised hers, high, and saw dark hair under there in the sleeveless T-shirt, Nicki saying, 'Chili, Jesus!' glad to see him and it was a nice surprise, knowing she meant it. Now she was in his arms, that slender body tight against him, arms around his neck giving him a hug, hanging on, while he kept thinking of her armpits, the dark tufts under there like a guy's, though she certainly felt like a girl. Nicki let go but kept grinning at him, saying, 'I don't believe this.' Then saying over her shoulder to the guys, 'I was right, it's Chili, from Miami. He's a fucking gangster!'

The way they were looking at him now – he didn't mind her saying it.

'That's your new band, huh? They as good as the one you used to have?'

Nicki said, 'What, at Momo's? Come on, that was techno-disco pussy rock. These guys *play*.' She took him by the arm over to a table, telling how she met them in the parking lot of the Guitar Center, standing there with their Marshall stacks, and couldn't believe her luck 'cause these kids could play speed riffs as good as – 'You know the kind Van Halen did on "Eruption" and every metal freak in the world copied? . . . No, you don't. What am I talking about? Eight years ago you were still into Dion and the Belmonts, all that doo-wop shit.'

' "I'm just a lonely teenager," ' Chili said.

'Right, and "I Wonder Why." Who do you listen to now?'

'Guns N' Roses, different ones.' He had to think fast. 'Aerosmith, Led Zeppelin . . .'

'You're lying. Aerosmith, that's who I was listening to in Miami, way back when. I'll bet you're a Deadhead, you dig that California acid Muzak.'

'Let's have a cigarette,' Chili said, sitting at the table with her now. 'I wasn't sure you'd recognize me.'

'You kidding? You're the only guy at Memo's didn't try to jump me.'

'It crossed my mind a few times.'

'Yeah, but you didn't make a big deal about it, like Tommy. I had to beat him off with a stick.' She reached across the table to put her hand on his. 'What're you *doing* here anyway?'

I'm making a movie.'

'Come on—'

'And you live with a movie star.'

'Michael, yeah.' She didn't sound too happy about it. She didn't sound unhappy either. Glancing at her watch, Nicki said, 'He's gonna stop by. You want to meet him?'

Just like that.

'Yeah, I wouldn't mind.'

'Michael won't stay for the performance, too many people. Crowds scare the shit out of him, like he's afraid he'll get mobbed.'

'Sure, the guy's a star. Not only that, he can act.'

'I know,' Nicki said, 'he's incredible. His new one, *Elba*? It isn't out yet – I caught some of the dailies when they were shooting. You see Michael, he *is* Napoleon. He doesn't play him, I mean he *is* this fucking military genius, man, this little guy . . .' She drew on her cigarette looking toward the bandstand. 'I have to get back.'

'How'd you meet him?'

'At a performance. I was with a metal group, Roadkill?

157

They're still around. They try to sound like Metallica, straight-ahead rock with a lot of head banging. I had to fucking sing and throw my hair at the same time, only it was shorter then so I had to wear extensions. I remember thinking – this was about a year and a half ago – if only I was a light-skinned black chick I could make it on my voice, not have to do this shit.'

'Michael saw you perform . . .'

'I guess he was in a particular mode at the time.' Nicki tapped her cigarette over the ashtray, maybe giving it some thought. 'Sees me up there thrashing, this chick in geek-wear, shitkickers, hair under my arms . . . He still won't let me shave. I guess I fill some need. He works, I work and in between we kick back. We do drugs, but not all the time. I wouldn't call either of us toxic. We play tennis, we have a screening room, a satellite dish, twelve TV sets, seventeen phones, a houseman, maids, a laundress, gardeners, a guy who comes twice a week to check out the cars . . . But where am I really? Down in a basement with a sticky floor and three guys barely out of Hollywood High. I feel like I'm their mother.'

'Why don't you get married?'

'You mean to Michael? I don't think I would even if he asked me.'

'Why not?'

'What's the point? It's not like, wow, I'd be making it, something I've always wanted. You get married, then what? All it does is fuck up your life, especially marrying an actor. Look at Madonna . . . No, don't. I don't have all that underwear going for me. I'm a rock-and-roll singer and that's it, man, nothing else.' She looked off toward the bandstand. 'Listen, I have to go. But when Michael comes, I'll introduce you.'

'Yeah, I wouldn't mind talking to him, he has time.'

158

'You want him to do a movie?'

'We're thinking about it.'

'Good luck.' Nicki stubbed out her cigarette before looking up at him again. 'We're gonna open tonight, play around with the Stones' "Street Fighting Man." What do you think?'

With that innocent straight face, putting him on.

It took Chili four seconds to find the album cover and the title in his mind from twenty years ago, the concert recorded live at the Garden and Tommy playing the record over and over, Tommy at the time stoned on the Stones.

Chili said, straight-faced back to her, 'From *Get Yer Ya-Ya's Out*, huh? That one?'

It got Nicki smiling at him, looking good, those nice blue eyes shining. She said, 'You're a cool guy, Chil, without even trying.'

They'd start a number, race into it and stop and Nicki would play part of it over on her bull's-eye guitar, slower, smoother, and then one of the guitar players would pick it up, imitating, give a nod and the drummer would kick them off again. They might be good – Chili couldn't tell. Hearing a line of music by itself, when Nicki showed them how, it sounded okay, but all of them playing together came out as noise and was irritating.

Thinking of that album cover again, he seemed to recall a guy in an Uncle Sam hat jumping up in the air with a guitar in each hand. He liked the Rolling Stones then, back in the hippie days, all the flakes running around making peace signs. It made him think of the time they grabbed this hippie, dragged him into Tommy Carlo's cousin's barbershop and zipped all his fuckin hair off with the clippers. He thought of that and started thinking of Ray Bones again and Leo the drycleaner, his calling Leo dumb for leaving three hundred grand in a hotel-room closet, and where was it now? Under his bed at the Sunset Marquis. He'd check, make sure Leo and Annette had taken off, just to be on the safe side. Later tonight he'd call Fay, tell her to look for three hundred big ones coming by Express Mail. Put it in one of those containers they gave you at the post office. He'd hang on to the extra ten grand. Maybe pay off Ray Bones, get that out of the way, or maybe not. But the three hundred, basically, was Fay's. Let her do whatever she wanted with it. Two to one she'd tell a friend of hers about it and pretty soon the suits would come by, knock on the door, flash their I.D.'s . . .

He wondered what would've happened if he'd brought Fay with him to Vegas . . .

And realized he was thinking of it as a movie again, the way he had told it to Harry and Karen, but seeing new possibilities, getting the woman, Fay, into the story more, looking at it the same way he had looked at *Lovejoy* and saw what was needed. Fay comes to LA with him . . .

Except it wouldn't be *him*, it would be an actor, Jesus, like Robert De Niro playing the shylock. And for Fay . . .

Karen. Why not? Karen even had kind of a you-all accent, though it wasn't as downhome as the way Fay talked. Okay, now, by the time they get to LA they realize they're hot for each other and aren't even sure they want to find her husband. Leo, except he's got all that fuckin dough. Do they want it? They know somebody who does, Ray Bones, he's coming after them and he'll kill for that money.

It didn't sound too bad.

You have Leo pulling the scam on the airline in the opening . . .

Or, no, you start with the shylock and Fay waiting for Leo to come home from the track, while actually he's out at the airport getting smashed and the jet takes off without him and goes down in the swamp, blows up.

So you have the shylock, basically a good guy, a former shylock, played by Bobby De Niro. You have Karen Flores making her successful comeback as Fay . . . She wouldn't have a sweaty job, she could be something else, an entertainer, a singer. You have Leo . . . You wouldn't have Harry in it or the limo guys – it wasn't a movie about making a movie – but you'd have Ray Bones in it. Leo would be a tough one to cast. Get an actor who could play a good sleazeball . . . It took Chili a moment to realize the room was quiet. Nicki and her guys were looking this way, but not at him. He looked over . . .

And saw Michael Weir.

It was, it was Michael Weir crossing the room from the stairs, giving Nicki a wave, the other hand in his pants pocket, baggy gray pants too long for him. Chili saw that as part of the whole picture, his first look at Michael Weir in person, white Reeboks too. But what caught and held his attention was Michael Weir's jacket. It was like the one left at Vesuvio's twelve years ago, that worn-out World War Two flight jacket nobody wanted. It was exactly like it. On a guy that made seven million bucks a movie.

Now Michael Weir had his hand raised to the band. Chili heard him say, 'Hey, guys,' and it was his voice, Chili recognized it from movies. Michael Weir was good at accents, but you could still tell his voice, kind of nasal. The cockrockers gave him a nod, not too impressed, these young dropouts with their hair and their guitars. Now it looked like Michael was joking around with them, doing the moonwalk and pretending he was strumming a guitar. He was good, but the guys still didn't seem impressed. Michael turned to Nicki and right away she grabbed his arm and Chili saw them coming this way, Nicki doing the talking, Michael Weir

161

looking up and then Nicki looking up as she said, 'Chil? I'd like you to meet Michael.'

Chili got to his feet, ready to shake hands with a superstar. What surprised him now was how short the guy was in real life.

18

It took Chili a couple of minutes to figure Michael Weir out. He wanted people to think he was a regular guy, but was too used to being who he was to pull it off.

The two of them sitting at the table now, Chili asked him if he wanted a drink. Michael, watching Nicki and her band through the archway, said yeah, that sounded like a good idea. Chili asked him what he wanted. Michael said oh, anything. Did he want Scotch, bourbon, a beer? Michael said oh, and stopped and said no, he'd like a Perrier. Still watching Nicki and the band. They hadn't started to play. Chili looked over at the bar, not open yet, thinking he'd have to go all the way upstairs to get the movie star his soda water. Right then Michael said, 'They're a tough audience.'

Chili noticed the movie star's expression, eyebrows raised, like he'd just heard some bad news but was more surprised than hurt.

'My Michael Jackson went right by them.'

Oh – meaning his moonwalk routine. Chili said, 'It looked good to me.' It did.

'To do it right you put on a touch of eye makeup, white socks, the glove . . . I was a little off on the voice too, the baby-doll whisper?'

Chili said, 'I couldn't hear that part.'

'But I can understand it, guys like that, their attitude. It has to do with territorial imperative.'

Chili said, 'That must be it,' feeling more at ease with the movie star, knowing a bullshitter when he met one. It didn't mean the guy wasn't good.

'I'm not certain why,' Michael said, 'but it reminds me of the one, the third-rate actor doing Hamlet?' Michael smiling with his eyes now. 'He's so bad that before long the audience becomes vocally abusive, yelling at him to get off the stage. They keep it up until the actor, finally, unable to take any more, stops the soliloquy and says to the audience, "Hey, what're you blaming me for? I didn't write this shit." '

Now they were both smiling, Michael still doing his with his eyes, saying, 'I could tell those kids I didn't invent Michael Jackson . . . someone else did.' Chili wondering, if it doesn't bother him, why didn't he just drop it? Chili looking for the right moment to bring up *Mr Lovejoy*.'

He was ready to get into it, said, 'Oh, by the way . . .' and Nicki's band kicked off, filling the room with their sound, and Michael turned his chair to face the bandstand through the archway. They were loud at first, but then settled down and it wasn't too bad, more like rhythm and blues than rock and roll. The beat got the tips of Chili's fingers brushing the table. Michael sat with his hands folded in his lap, his legs in the baggy pants stretched out in front of him, ankles crossed, the laces of one of his Reeboks loose, coming untied. He looked more like in his thirties than forty-seven. Not a bad-looking guy, even with the nose, Chili studying his profile. There was no way to tell if Michael liked the beat or not. Chili thought of asking him, but had the feeling people waited for the movie star to speak first, give his opinion and then everybody would say yeah, that's right, always agreeing. Like with Momo, the few times Chili saw him in the social club years ago, noticing the way the guys hung on to whatever Momo said. It was like you had to put kneepads on to talk to this man who never worked in his life.

Chili leaned into the table saying, 'You might not remember, but we met one time before.'

He gave the movie star time to look over.

'In Brooklyn, when you were making *The Cyclone*, that movie.'

Michael said, 'You know, I had a feeling we'd met. I couldn't quite put my finger on it, the occasion. Chil, is it?'

'Chili Palmer. We met, it was at a club on 86th Street, Bensonhurst. You dropped by, you wanted to talk to some of the guys.'

'Sure, I remember it very well,' Michael said, turning his chair around to the table.

'You were, I guess you were seeing what it was like to be one of us,' Chili said, locking his eyes on the movie star's the way he looked at a slow pay, a guy a week or two behind.

'Yeah, to listen more than anything else.'

'Is that right?'

'Pick up your rhythms of speech.'

'We talk different?'

'Well, different in that the way you speak is based on an attitude,' the movie star said, leaning in with an elbow on the table and running his hand through his hair. Chili could see him doing it on the screen, acting natural. 'It's like ya tone a voice,' the movie star said, putting on an accent, 'says weah ya comin' from.' Then back to his normal voice, that had a touch of New York in it anyway, saying, 'I don't mean where you're from geographically, I'm referring to attitude. Your tone, your speech patterns demonstrate a certain confidence in yourselves, in your opinions, your indifference to conventional views.'

'Like we don't give a shit.'

'More than that. It's a laid-back attitude, but with an intimidating edge. Cut-and-dried, no bullshit. Your way is the only way it's going to be.'

'Well, you had it down cold,' Chili said. 'Watching you in the movie, if I didn't know better I'd have to believe you were a made guy and not acting. I mean you be*came* that fuckin guy. Even the fink part,' Chili said, laying it on now. 'I never met a fink and I hope to God I never do, but how you did it must be the way finks act.'

The movie star liked that, starting to nod, saying, 'It was a beautiful part. All I had to do was find the character's center, the stem I'd use to wind him up and he'd play, man, he'd play.' The movie star nodding with Nicki's beat now, eyes half closed, like he was showing how to change into somebody else, saying, 'Once I have the authentic sounds of speech, the rhythms, man, the patois, I can actually begin to think the way those guys do, get inside their heads.'

Like telling how he studied this tribe of natives in the jungles of Brooklyn. That's how it sounded to Chili.

He said, 'Okay, I'm one of those guys you mention. What am I thinking?'

The movie star put on an innocent look first, surprised. What? Did I say something? The look gradually becoming a nice-guy smile. He ran both hands through his hair this time.

'Don't get me wrong, I'm not saying an actual metamorphosis takes place, I become one of you. That wouldn't be acting. I had the opportunity one time, years ago, to ask Dame Edith Evans how she approached her parts and she said, "I pretend, dear boy, I pretend." Well, I'll get involved in a certain life, observe all I can, because I want that feeling of realism, verisimilitude. But ultimately what I do is practice my craft, I act, I pretend to be someone else.'

'So you don't know what I'm thinking,' Chili said, staying with it.

It got another smile, a tired one. 'No, I don't. Though I have to say, I'm curious.'

'So, you want to know?'

'If you'd like to tell me, yeah.'

'I'm thinking about a movie.'

'One of mine?'

'One we're producing and we want you to be in,' Chili said, seeing the movie star's eyebrows go up, and one of the arms in the worn-out leather jacket, raising his hand as Chili tried to tell him, 'It's one you already know about, you read.'

But Michael wasn't listening, he was saying, 'Wait. Time out, okay?' before lowering his arm and settling back. 'I don't want to come off sounding rude, because I appreciate your interest and I'm flattered, really, that you'd think of me for a part. But, and here's the problem. My agent won't let me go anywhere near an independently financed production, I'm sorry.'

Chili got to say, 'It isn't that kind—' and the hand shot up again.

'My manager along with my agent, the business heads, they've made it our policy. Otherwise, I'm sure you can understand, I'd have pitches coming at me from independents day and night.' The movie star shrugged, helpless, his gaze moving off to the band.

'You think I'm talking about wiseguy money,' Chili said. 'No way. This one's gonna be made at a studio.'

It brought the movie star partway back.

'I'm not connected to those people anymore. Not since I walked out of a loan-shark operation in Miami.'

That brought the movie star all the way back with questions in his eyes, sitting up, interested in the real stuff.

'What happened? The pressure got to you?'

'Pressure? I'm the one applied the pressure.'

'That's what I mean, the effect that must've had on you. What you had to do sometimes to collect.'

'Like have some asshole's legs broken?'

'That, yeah, or some form of intimidation?'

'Whatever it takes,' Chili said. 'You're an actor, you like to pretend. Imagine you're the shylock. A guy owes you fifteen grand and he skips, leaves town.'

'Yeah?'

'What do you do?'

Chili watched the movie star hunch over, narrowing his shoulders. For a few moments he held his hands together in front of him, getting a shifty look in his eyes. Then gave it up, shaking his head.

'I'm doing Shylock instead of *a* shylock. Okay, what's my motivation? The acquisition of money. To collect. Inflict pain if I have to.' Michael half-closed his eyes. 'My father used to beat me for no reason . . . Take the money I earned on my paper route, that I kept in a cigar box . . .'

'Hold it,' Chili said. 'I was a shylock – what do I look like?'

'That's right, yeah,' Michael said, staring at Chili, his expression gradually becoming deadpan, sleepy.

'You the shylock now?'

'Guy owes me fifteen large and takes off, I go after him,' the movie star said. 'The fuck you think I do?'

'Try it again,' Chili said. 'Look at me.'

'I'm looking at you.'

'No, I want you to look at me the way I'm looking at you. Put it in your eyes, "You're mine, asshole," without saying it.'

'Like this?'

'What're you telling me, you're tired? You wanta go to bed?'

'Wait. How about this?'

'You're squinting, like you're trying to look mean or you need glasses. Look at me. I'm thinking, You're mine, I fuckin own you. What I'm *not* doing is feeling anything about it one way or the other. You understand? You're not a person to

168

me, you're a name in my collection book, a guy owes me money, that's all.'

'The idea then,' the movie star said, 'I show complete indifference, until I'm crossed.'

'Not even then. It's nothing personal, it's business. The guy misses, he knows what's gonna happen.'

'How about this?' the movie star said, giving Chili a nice dead-eyed look.

'That's not bad.'

'This's what I think of you, asshole. Nothing.'

'I believe it,' Chili said.

'I turn it on when I confront the guy.'

'Yeah, but you haven't found him yet.'

Chili watched the movie star wondering what he was supposed to do next, giving him a strange look, Chili wondering himself exactly what he was doing, except he could see it right there in his mind so he kept going.

'The guy took off for Las Vegas.'

'How do I know that?' The movie star picking up on it.

'The guy's wife tells you.'

Chili paused, the movie star waiting.

'Yeah?'

'The wife wants to go with you on account of her husband skipped with all her money . . . three hundred grand,' Chili said, starting to roll and not seeing anywhere to stop, 'they conned off an airline after this jet crashed the guy was supposed to be on but wasn't and everybody was killed.'

The movie star was looking at him funny again.

'If the guy wasn't on the plane . . .'

'He was, but he got off just before it left and blew up. So his bag's on the plane, his name's on the passenger list . . .'

'The wife sues the airline,' the movie star said, nodding. 'This is a gutsy babe.'

'Good-looking too.'

'The husband takes off with the money, plus he still owes me the fifteen large,' Michael the shylock said, 'and the wife and I take off after him. Go on. When do I meet up with the guy and give him the look?'

Chili had to think about it. Tell Michael what actually happened or what he thought would sound better?

'It's not that simple,' Chili said. 'You have to be careful. Leo, the husband, isn't much to worry about, outside of he could try and nail you from behind if you get close. But there's another guy that comes along, a hard-on you happen to owe money to. A mob guy. He knows about the three hundred grand and would like to take you out anyway, on account of a past situation.'

This time when Chili paused, wondering how to get back to where this thing had started, the movie star said, 'This actually happened, didn't it? It's a true story.'

'Basically,' Chili said.

'You're the shylock.'

'I was at one time.'

'So, did you find the guy? What's his name, Leo?'

'I found him,' Chili said, 'yeah.'

That was a fact. But now he didn't know what else to say, or how he actually got this far into' it.

'You understand, you're pretending you're a shylock.'

'Yeah? Go on.'

'I mean that's all we're doing. You wanted to see if you can think like a shylock, get in his head. So I gave you a situation, that's all.'

'You're not going to tell me the rest?'

'At this point, basically, that has to be it.'

Michael was giving him a strange look again: not so confused this time, more like he was figuring something out. He said, 'Well, if you won't, you won't,' and started to grin. 'I don't know how long you've been in the business, but that was the most ingenious pitch I've ever had thrown at me, and I mean in my entire career. You got me playing the guy, the shylock, before I even realized it was a pitch. So now I have to read the script to find out what happens. Beautiful. Really, that was artfully done.'

Chili said, 'Well, actually . . .' The movie star had his head turned and was watching Nicki and her group wailing away. 'Actually, what I started to mention, the movie we want you to be in is *Mr Lovejoy*. We understand you read the script and like it . . . a lot.'

Now he had to wait for this to make sense, give the movie star time to think about it Michael said, '*Lovejoy*,' looking over again. 'That's the one, the florist sees his boy run over?'

'And goes after the guy, to catch him driving his car.'

'What production company was that?'

'ZigZag, Harry Zimm.'

'That's right, the slime-people guy. I read for Harry when I first started working in features. I didn't get the part.'

Chili said, 'He turned you down? Come on.'

'I wasn't Michael Weir then,' Michael said.

He wasn't kidding either. It sounded strange.

'Anyway, we're going to Tower Studios with it,' Chili said, and that got a smile from Michael.

He said, 'You know what they say about Elaine Levin. She fucked her Rolodex to get where she is. But I'll tell you something, she didn't have to if she did. Elaine knows what she's doing. She made an awful lot of money for Metro up to the time they forced that disaster on her. Did you see it, *San Juan Hill*?'

'I liked it,' Chili said.

'It wasn't a bad picture,' Michael said. 'It had the facts right for once, the black troops saving Teddy Roosevelt's ass, but that didn't sell tickets and it was way overproduced. The picture cost more than the actual war, which hadn't been

171

done to my knowledge since *A Message to Garcia* with John Boles. I remember a script called *Siboney*, the same war, I thought very seriously about doing. That was a fascinating period, the US emerging as a world power, the enactment of the Monroe Doctrine, eminent domain . . . I might look at that script again, *Siboney*. That was where our troops landed in Cuba.'

'Sounds good,' Chili said, not having any idea what the guy was talking about. He tried to get back to *Lovejoy* with, 'Listen, what we're thinking—'

But Michael was already saying. 'The title does have a nice sound. Build the score around the song. Si-bo-ney, da da *da* da . . .'

Christ, now he was singing it, against the rock beat in the background.

'Da da *da* da, Si-bo-ney . . . It's an old piece but has all kinds of dramatic riffs in it. It can be stirring, romantic, militaristic. Someone like John Williams could score the ass off that picture.'

Chili said, 'What I wanted to mention . . .' and paused. The room was quiet again, the band finished with their number. 'We're definitely gonna produce the movie at a studio.'

Michael Weir nodded. But now he was getting up, looking over at Nicki raising her guitar strap over her head. He said, 'I guess we're taking off. It was nice talking to you.'

'You have to go, huh?'

'Nicki's waiting. We're going to duck out . . .'

'But you like *Lovejoy*?'

'I like the character, the guy, he has possibilities. But the way the plot develops it turns into a B movie by the time you're into the second act. Take a look at *The Cyclone* again, the way a visual fabric is maintained even while the metaphor plays on different levels, with the priest, with the

172

mother . . . so that you never lose sight of the picture's thematic intent.'

Chili said, 'Yeah, well, we're already making changes. Getting a girl in it, fixing up the ending . . .'

'Sounds good.'

'Can we talk about it, you get a chance?'

'Anytime,' Michael Weir said, moving away. 'Call Buddy and we'll set something up.'

'Buddy?'

'My agent,' the movie star said. 'Harry knows him.'

Chili opened the door to 325 to see the message light on the phone blinking on and off. He lit a cigarette before dialing the operator.

She said, 'Just a minute.' The one with maybe a Latin accent. She came back on saying, 'A Mr Zimm called. You have a meeting tomorrow, three P.M. at Tower Studios. He'll call you in the morning. Let's see. And a Mr Carlo called. He said he was going out for the evening and to tell you . . . Mr Barboni will arrive tomorrow on Delta Flight Eighty-nine at twelve-oh-five. You like me to repeat that?'

Chili told her thanks anyway.

19

Catlett was thinking maybe the best way would be if Lovejoy did have a gun and shot Roxy with it to get his satisfaction.

He was dressed casual today, white linen jacket over French blue India cotton, sitting in Ronnie's chair in Ronnie's office waiting for the Bear to come in and report, Marcella's radio playing Top 40 hits in the other office. There was no reason for her to come in here; Marcella was the kind you said hi to and bye to, you didn't chat with her.

The audience would like it: see Lovejoy open this old trunk of his, take out a big revolver and load it. Be dramatic, that part, except this was movies and the kind of good guy Lovejoy was couldn't just go out and shoot the bad guy – like you drive past a man's house was edging into your business and shoot him off his front steps. Or another time the man was sitting in his car, pull up next to him, *bam*. The way it was done in real life. The way soon as Yayo threatened him, bye-bye, Yayo, the mean little Colombian now two feet under the desert somewhere off US 10. The Bear had said, 'Never again. I don't clean up after, become an accessory.' The Bear due here any minute now. Yayo's people in Miami had called asking where he was and Catlett told them, 'I saw him take the bag from the locker. He never came back? You have any friends down in Old Mexico could look into it? Check out Acapulco? Ixtapa?' Something you could pull on those people one time only. Losing a hundred and seventy grand and a mule was worth a phone call; it ever happened again, they'd be out. Man, but that money and the stepped-on bag of product in the locker could come in handy for something else now, the way Catlett was looking at his future: his mind going from Lovejoy to Chili Palmer, but most of the time stuck on Chili Palmer and the need to get the man out of the picture.

The Bear brought Farrah and a video game they plugged into the TV, something to occupy the child while the Bear made his report.

'One, according to the plane ticket on his dresser he's C. Palmer. Flew here from Vegas and has an open return to Miami. Two, also on the dresser, an Express Mail receipt for a package he sent to a person by the name of Fay Devoe in Miami. Three, the label in his suit and a couple of sport coats are all a men's store in Miami. So what does that tell you?'

Catlett was watching the little girl playing Top Gun, three years old in a jet fighter, zapping bandits out of the sky. He said, 'Look at that child.'

'I mean what else does it tell you,' the Bear said, 'outside of he's from Miami?'

'Not what you're thinking,' Catlett said. 'That he's connected to Yayo? Uh-unh. He was here before Yayo, has nothing to do with product, or he'd have made some mention of it or let it slip. What else have you got to tell me?'

'The man has ten grand in casino bank straps, all hundreds.'

'That's interesting.'

'Laid out in the bottom of his suitcase.'

'You take it?'

'I almost did.'

'Anybody see you go in his room?'

'Come on.'

'Just checking. What about Harry? You put somebody on him?'

'Harry showed up at his apartment yesterday afternoon, stayed about an hour and came out carrying a hanging bag. He drove to an address on La Collina in Beverly Hills, top of the street. I went over there later and spoke to a neighbor's maid walking the dog. For ten bucks, she says, "Oh, that's a movie star lives there, Karen Flores." '

'Man, I been trying to place that name. Sure, Karen Flores,' Catlett said. 'Was in some of Harry Zimm's pictures and some others after that, but never made it. That's where he's been hanging out?'

'It's where he was last night.'

'That old man – I believe he's casting. Gonna get himself some of that. Say he'll give her a part in *Lovejoy* if she'll play Great Balls of Fire with him.'

'What's Great Balls of Fire?'

'You never played it? You light your dick and the woman quick has to blow it out.'

The Bear didn't say anything.

'Man, you don't ever smile, do you?'

'If I hear something funny.'

'So – Karen Flores, yeah. The way she was built she could play the whore, except she be too old now. Less they want to do the part as an old whore. That wouldn't hurt nothing. Get Theresa or Greta for the new female lead.' Catlett paused. He said, 'Wait a minute,' getting up straighter in Ronnie's cushy chair. 'Karen Flores, she was married one time to Michael Weir. And Michael Weir's suppose to be in the movie.'

He saw the Bear watching Farrah shooting down jets with that electronic wapping-zapping sound, hitting every one of them as they popped on the screen, the Bear urging her now, saying, 'Get it, honey. Get that son of a bitch.'

'You hear what I'm saying?' Catlett said. 'Karen Flores,

Michael Weir, and Harry's over at her house . . . The man wasn't lying, Harry's doing the picture with Michael Weir and, man, it's gonna be *big*. I had the feeling, you know it, ever since I noticed the way Harry was hanging on to that script. Like it was made of gold and you'd have to kill him to get it. I knew it without even reading it. Then when I did . . .'

The Bear was grinning, watching his little girl.

'There was two copies of the script and Chili Palmer took 'em both. Wouldn't even consider us getting together on it, the perfect team. Dumbass, hadn't even read it. And Harry took him as his associate? Bear, this is *my* chance. Chili Palmer's gonna have to wait on his, get in line. You listening to me?'

Not only listening the Bear was a jump ahead, saying, 'I'm not taking any more trips to the desert. I told you that. Stick my neck out to help your career. You want to be a producer there's all kinds of deals in this town you can buy into.'

Catlett said, 'Not with Michael Weir on a twenty-million-plus production. This is a big big one. No mutated bugs, no bloodsucking geeks or kung-fu kind of Rambo assholes kicking the shit out of dress-extras, uh-unh. This's the big movie I've been looking to get in on.'

'They all sound big,' the Bear said, 'at the talking stage.'

Catlett said, 'Bear, I drive limos now and then.'

'I know that.'

'Why – 'cause I like to listen, hear all about the deals and shit happening. Hear who's hot and who's not. What names you can take to the bank this month. Learn what studio head is on his way out 'cause he pissed on a big producer's script. Learn who the hot agents are, what they're packaging, who's getting two hundred phone calls a day. Hear the agent tell the actor he's gonna pull out the guns, kill to make the deal, gonna take no fucking prisoners. Weekends, some of the agents and producers and studio execs, they're up in the Malibu hills playing war games with these CO_2 guns. Running around in the woods shooting paint bullets at each other. You hear what I'm saying? They talk about how they're gonna kill to make a deal. Then they go out and play with toy guns.' Catlett grinned. 'Shit, huh? You think I can't manage with people like that? Man, I've done it for real.'

'I've played that game,' the Bear said. 'It's fun.'

'And you've fallen off buildings and rolled cars and been in five hundred fights – in the movies. But you don't know what the real thing is like, do you? The ultimate deed. Shoot a man.'

'How many have you?' the Bear said, not watching Farrah now, Farrah on her own.

'What's the difference, one or five, or ten? One and you're blooded,' Catlett said, leaning on Ronnie's desk. 'My first time, I was eighteen years old and had gone to Bakersfield to see my mother. Got out of school, picked up an Olds Cutlass, maroon, and drove there from Detroit. This day we're out for a ride, we stop at a gas station, my mother wanting to use the ladies' room. The gas station man told her no migrants could use it. Then he changed his mind, said okay. She's in there, he comes in and starts messing with her. She told me in the car, after. I drove back there, I said to the man, "You disrespected my mother. I'd like you to apologize to her." He started laughing and told us to get out. My mother was crying the whole time . . . I went back later on to have a talk with the man. He got ugly and I shot him.'

'Eighteen years old,' the Bear said. 'Where'd you get the gun?'

'I had it. Brought it with me.'

'But why'd you have it?'

'I was out of school, starting to look over career

possibilities.' Catlett smiled. 'Way before I knew I wanted to be in the movie business.'

'You killed a man 'cause he showed your mother disrespect?'

'He dissed me too. Said I must be one of those mother-fuckers he'd heard about. I did him, got on the interstate and went back to Detroit. Oh, and I took his cash. I sent it to my mother.'

'Show her,' the Bear said, 'what a sweet boy you are.'

'I see her. She's living in Delano now, has friends there she doesn't want to leave. I bought her a house.'

'I imagine,' the Bear said, 'not knowing any better, she's proud of you.'

Catlett watched the Bear, rubbing his beard, look over toward the wapping-zapping sound of his child knocking jets out of the sky. A daddy proud of his little girl. It would be fun to have one of those of his own. Pick a good-looking woman with nice features and have one. Pick a woman wasn't a tighthead. He used to say he didn't deal in coal when he was running around with white women, but had changed his mind about that, since meeting some fine little sisters out here.

He said, 'Bear? This man Chili Palmer, what you suppose he does?'

'Ten grand in his suitcase,' the Bear said, 'what do you think, he's a bank messenger?'

'He scored it at a casino, didn't he?'

'Whether he did or not,' the Bear said, 'the guy's into some kind of hustle.'

'How do you know that?'

'I've done desk reads in this business,' the Bear said, looking over, 'where somebody wants to know, say, what this executive is up to. Like if he's about to leave with a property he hasn't told the studio about. They want to know

179

if he might be negotiating someplace. I look at the man's telephone notes, play his recorder, see who's on his Rolodex, get to know him. This guy C. Palmer has got nothing that puts him with anybody or tells what he might be doing. He's too clean. The only thing he had written down on his note pad was "Raji's, Hollywood Blvd. near Vine." '

Catlett frowned. '*Ra*ji's? Man, that's a hard rock joint. You can tell looking at Chili Palmer he ain't into that metal shit. I might have to look into that one.'

'I'll tell you one thing,' the Bear said. 'You shoot him, you'll never see me again.'

Catlett started frowning again. 'No, man, I don't want that on my conscience. Focking Yayo, that was different, he could've hurt us. And I mean both of us, right? You buried that monkey chaser you were protecting your own ass as much as mine. No, what I'm thinking . . . Bear, you listening?'

'I can hear you.'

'We got the cash out the airport and the stepped-on bag that ain't worth shit. What I'm thinking, what if Chili Palmer went out there to pick it up?'

Catlett waited for the Bear to turn his head this way, the Bear nodding, seeing the picture.

'Yeah?'

'We even call the feds. Make that anonymous kind of phone-in tip they love to get. What would happen?'

'You'd be out a hundred and seventy grand.'

'When they bust him, haul his ass off to jail.'

'You don't care about the money?'

'We got stuff for it, didn't we? We're not out nothing.'

'He'll tell the feds he was set up.'

'I 'magine he will, but how's he gonna put it on *me*? I don't even know the man and there isn't anybody seen us together.'

'Harry has.'

'I can talk to Harry,' Catlett said. 'No, the trick will be getting Mr Chili Palmer to go out to the airport and open that locker.'

Find some way to work that or do it clean and quick, the way Farrah was zapping jets out of the sky.

Catlett said, 'Man, she's gooood.'

The Bear said, 'That's my little ace.'

Ray Bones came off the Delta flight to find a young guy with more hair and gold jewelry than he needed holding a square of laundry cardboard that said MR BARBONE in black Magic Marker. The young guy's shirt was open halfway down, his sleeves turned up twice. He said, 'Mr Barbone? Welcome to LA. I'm Bobby, your driver. Mr DePhillips asked me to extend you his best and be of help any way I can. You have a good flight?'

Bones said, 'I hope you drive better than you fuckin spell. My name's Barboni, not Bar-bone.'

Northbound from the airport on 405, Bones rode in the backseat of the Cadillac enclosed in dark glass. He commented on the traffic. 'Shit, this isn't bad. Miami, we got bumper to bumper all day long.' He asked Bobby the driver, 'What's that over there?'

'Oil wells,' Bobby said.

'They're ugly fuckin things. You got oil wells and freeways. You got smog . . .'

'You ever wanta go to the beach,' Bobby said, 'here's the freeway you take, we're coming to.'

'I live in Miami Beach,' Bones said, 'and you want to show me a fuckin beach? The sun ever come out here, or you have this smog all the time? Jesus. Where's downtown at? I don't see it.'

Four-oh-five to Santa Monica Boulevard to the Beverly

Hilton, Bobby telling Bones it was the home of Trader Vic's, if he liked Chinese. Bones said he hated it. They pulled up to the hotel entrance and got out.

'What do you have for me?'

Bobby opened the trunk, brought out Bones's luggage, one bag, went back in and came out with a black leather attaché case. 'Compliments of Mr DePhillips. The names and phone numbers are in here. The same ones that were given to your friend Mr Palmer.'

'What else?'

'It's in there too. Beretta three-eighty, a nice one.'

'Gimme the car keys.'

'I'm suppose to drive you.'

'Frank DePhillips said extend me his best wishes and help me out any way I want, right?'

'Yeah . . .'

'So gimme the fuckin keys.'

Bones handed the kid five bucks and told him to get a haircut.

20

In the car on the way over, Harry told Chili and Karen what to expect. 'We'll sit down and start schmoozing about the business. Who got fired, divorced, had an abortion, entered a treatment center, moved back to New York, died of AIDS, came out of the closet . . . We'll get offered something to drink like Evian water or decaffeinated coffee and Elaine will ask if *Lovejoy* was inspired by a true story reported in the media – since you don't see that many original ideas that are original and weren't stolen from a book or a picture made forty years ago – and that's when I begin to ease into the pitch. I say, "You know why you ask that, Elaine? Because *Lovejoy* is about life, about universal feelings of sorrow and hope. It's about redemption and retribution, the little guy's triumph over the system . . ."'

Karen said, 'Harry, you're full of shit.'

He said, 'If I'm wrong then I haven't made something like three hundred pitches in my career. You're talking to a distributor or studio execs, it's the same thing.'

Karen said, 'You haven't met Elaine Levin.'

Chili had his dark pinstripe suit on, striped shirt and conservative dark tie, walking into Elaine's office in the Hyman Tower Building on the Tower Studios lot, Hollywood, California. It wasn't like an office; it was like a big old-fashioned living room with a dining L, but unfinished, or as if all this furniture was in the wrong room. A dark-haired woman in her forties, wearing glasses down on her nose was sitting at a dining-room table talking on the phone. She covered it with her hand as they came in and said, 'Hi, I'll be right there. You want a soda, mineral water, some coffee?' She was from New York, no question. Karen gave her a wave saying thanks, but they just had lunch. Harry said to Chili, 'What'd I tell you?' They sat down in the living room part, Chili next to Karen on a dull-green sofa that looked like an antique and felt like one, the seat round and hard. Harry was moving his butt around in a chair with a carved wood back and arms, trying to get comfortable. The floor and the walls were bare, no carpeting, no pictures or anything. As Chili was looking around Karen said, 'Elaine's redecorating. All this stuff goes.' Harry said, 'Studio office, one week it's Old English, the next week art deco moderne. You know who makes out in this town, the interior designers. On account of turnover.' Harry started pushing himself up and now Karen got up, so Chili did too as Elaine came over to them, her hand out.

She was smaller than Chili thought she'd be, maybe five-two in her stocking feet, which was the way she actually was, wearing a beige suit with the sleeves pushed up but no shoes. She wasn't bad-looking though, even with that mop of hair all over the place, like she hadn't combed it in a week. Shaking Harry's hand she said, 'Harry, I feel as if I know you. I've been a fan of yours ever since *Slime Creatures*. They remind me of so many people I know in the industry.' Harry told Elaine he'd been following her career with interest ever since she broke in. Elaine turned to Chili and gave his hand a good grip as Karen introduced them and Elaine said, 'My word, both the gentlemen in suits, I'm flattered. You should see the way most of them come in, like they do yard work and I guess some of them do, the writers, if they're not parking cars.' Still holding on to his hand she said, 'Chili

184

Palmer, hmmmm,' in the slow way she spoke. It surprised him, this offhand manner she had about her, talking a lot but in no hurry. Maybe her mind somewhere else. Not what he'd heard about dynamic women executives. Elaine sat down, now the four of them around a coffee table where there was a big ashtray loaded with butts. She brought a pack of cigarettes and a lighter out of her jacket saying, '*Mr Lovejoy* . . .' and Chili got ready to take his first meeting at a movie studio.

Harry: 'What hooked me, Elaine, is the theme. Redemption and retribution, the little guy's triumph over the system.'

Elaine: 'Yeah . . . well, I'm as turned on by redemption and retribution, Harry, as anyone; but what's the system he triumphs over?'

Harry: 'The legal system.'

Elaine: 'I don't see the ending exactly as a triumph. The man who killed his boy is dead, but Lovejoy would still owe – what is it, a hundred thousand to somebody, the guy's heirs?'

Harry: 'We're revising the ending . . .'

Elaine: 'Good.'

Harry: 'Roxy has brought Lovejoy to court, but the case is still pending when Roxy is killed. So Lovejoy keeps his flower shop, doesn't have to pay anything.'

Elaine: 'Uh-huh, yeah . . . But what about motivation? Why he goes after the guy with a video camera.'

Harry: '*Why?* To see justice done.'

Elaine: 'But it isn't. The guy gets his license revoked again – so what?'

Harry: 'What we plan to do as part of revising the ending, is have Lovejoy do something to cause Roxy's death. I don't mean murder him, but not have Lovejoy just standing there either.'

Elaine: 'That gets us back to his motivation. I can't see this mingy florist becoming so vindictive.'

Harry: 'Who, Lovejoy?'

Elaine: 'Even his name.'

Harry: 'We're thinking of changing it. No, but the idea – here's a guy you think is a schlub, right? But beneath that quiet exterior he's passionate, impulsive and extremely likable. Once you get to know him.'

Elaine: 'He's passionate? Who does he fuck?'

Harry: 'You mean in the script?'

Elaine: 'In his life. His wife left him – who does he sleep with. He's quiet, low-key, yeah, but does that mean he doesn't fuck?'

Chili couldn't believe he was hearing her say that. There were all kinds of movies where nobody got laid in them. Unless she meant it as something the guy did that you never saw. Like people in movies never went to the bathroom even though you know they would have to.

There was a pause, a silence right after Elaine spoke. And then Karen got into it.

Karen: 'What he needs – what the story needs is for somebody to give him a kick in the ass, get him going. I'm thinking about a woman who's been abused by Roxy, knows his life, his habits, that he's into something illegal. And she also knows he's *driving* – that's it, when he's not supposed to. Otherwise where does Lovejoy get the idea to catch him at it? She goes to Lovejoy and lays it out. Let's get this son of a bitch. Catch him driving. What's the girl's name in the script, the hooker?'

Harry: 'Lola.'

Karen: 'Lovejoy, Ilona, *Lola* – come on. Call her – I don't know – Peggy. Working class but bright. From a big family she's had to help support. Worked all her life . . . Roxy's hobby is making porno films he shows to his friends. He gets

Peggy stoned and shoots nude footage of her. She discovers it, burns the tape and he beats her up . . . This is the *kind* of situation I mean, not necessarily what will work best. But get her personally involved. Where does the video camera come from? It's Roxy's. She rips it off . . . You see what I'm getting at?'

Elaine: 'You're on the right track.'

Harry: 'But then it's not Lovejoy's story, it's the girl's.'

Karen: 'It's a subplot. We're looking for motivation, what gets Lovejoy started.'

Harry: 'And I'm looking at a properly, as it *is*, Michael Weir wants to do.'

Elaine: 'Oh, God. Michael.'

Chili watched Elaine look over at Karen.

Harry: 'Elaine, Michael read it and flipped. Why? Because it's about life. It's cosmic, it's about universal feelings and values. But he won't touch it if it isn't his story. You know that. Michael is bigger than the idea.'

Elaine: 'Mr Indecisive, won't be pressured into making a commitment. I love him, but he's worse than Hoffman and Redford put together, and his price isn't even as high as theirs. You know what he does, don't you? He puts his writer on it and every few months or so they show up with a different version of the story. Then he'll bring a director, some guy who's in awe of Michael and if the picture's ever shot he'll make the mistake of allowing Michael in the cutting room. You go over budget, miss release dates and post-production goes on forever while Michael fine-tunes.'

Harry: 'And if you can get him, it's worth it.'

Elaine: 'Why don't you bring me a nice sci-fi/horror idea? Something original. No pissed-off teenagers or comic-book characters. Drama, if it's offbeat, quirky but real. I want to discover new actors, do something different.'

Chili saw her looking at him over her glasses. She blew out a stream of cigarette smoke.

Elaine: 'Mr Palmer, what do you think of Michael Weir?'

'I think he's a great actor,' Chili said, 'and I think you could get him to do it. When I was talking to him last night he said he likes the character a lot.' That got their attention. 'He also likes the idea of putting a girl in it and fixing the ending, but he thinks it turns into a B movie in the second act.'

Elaine: 'He means whenever you cut away from him.'

'I think he was talking mostly,' Chili said, 'about the visual fabric of the movie and the theme, what you're doing here, so it doesn't start to look like something else.'

Elaine: 'You know Michael?'

'I know the girl lives with him, Nicki. She introduced me.' Harry was looking at him from across the coffee table, staring. Karen, on the sofa next to him, had her head turned to look right at him. 'Speaking of the ending,' Chili said, 'I think if Lovejoy runs the guy over with his van the audience in the theater would get up and cheer.'

Elaine: 'The direct approach.'

'Say he wants to do it,' Chili said. 'He starts out with every intention and then changes his mind. But it happens anyway, he runs the guy over and kills him and you don't know for sure if he meant it or it was an accident.' He watched Elaine take her glasses off. She kept looking at him without saying anything.

Karen: 'I kind of like that. Keep it ambiguous till the very end. Say he tells Peggy it was an accident and she believes him . . .'

Elaine: 'But the audience still isn't sure.'

Karen: 'That's what I was thinking. Give them something to talk about after they walk out.'

Elaine: 'You mean leave the theater.'

Karen, smiling: 'Right.' Still smiling: 'Warren's idea – did he tell you?'

Chili placed the name, the studio exec Karen had mentioned who sounded like an asshole.

Elaine: 'We talked about it briefly.'

Karen: 'Lovejoy videotapes a couple of robberies and becomes a surveillance expert?'

Elaine: 'With Mel Gibson. We do sequels or sell it to a network for a series.'

Harry: 'So, the next step—'

Karen: 'I thought he'd be here.'

Elaine: 'Warren's no longer with us. He's in Publicity.'

Karen: 'Oh.'

Harry: 'So, we know the script needs a little work, no problem. I'll give Murray our comments.'

Elaine: 'Which Murray is that?'

Harry: 'Murray Saffrin, my writer.'

Elaine: 'Oh . . . Well, I'll tell you right now, I wouldn't have a chance with Murray Saffrin. Karen could take the script upstairs bareass and not sell Murray Saffrin.'

Harry: 'So I'll get somebody else.'

Elaine: 'It's your decision. I can give you a few names, writers I know would be acceptable, like . . .'

Chili listened to the names, not surprised he'd never heard of any of them. How many people knew who wrote the movies they saw?

Harry: 'So we're talking development?'

Elaine: 'Not till I have at least a treatment I know I can sell. It's still your project, Harry. Your decision, if you want to see how far we can run with it.'

Harry: 'You're saying I pay the writer. Any of the guys you mentioned, what's a rewrite gonna cost me?'

Elaine: 'Depending on who you get, I would say anywhere

from one-fifty to four, and a few points. Call their agents, see who's available and might want to do it.'

Harry: 'I love talking to agents, right next to having a case of hives. You don't think bringing Michael Weir deserves a development deal?'

Elaine: 'Michael Weir signed, gagged and chained to a wall till you start shooting, I can take upstairs. I tell them Michael Weir likes the part . . . Yeah? What else is new? Harry, it's your decision, think it over. Karen, I wonder if you'd stay a few minutes. If the gentlemen wouldn't mind waiting . . .'

Chili got up with Harry. They started out.

Elaine: 'Harry? What about romance among less than attractive people?'

Harry: '*Marty?*'

Elaine: 'Beyond *Marty*.'

Harry: 'The seven-hundred-pound broad who crushes her lovers to death when she climaxes?'

Elaine: 'Call me, Harry, okay?'

'They waited for Karen in Harry's car, parked next to a sound stage as big as a hangar, up the street from the Hyman Tower Building and the front gate. Chili half expected to see extras walking around in period costumes and military uniforms, the way you saw them in movies about movies, but there didn't seem to be anything going on. Harry, coming out of the building, kept asking about Michael Weir. And then what did he say? He really seemed interested? How was it left? Why didn't you call me last night? Why'd you wait till in the meeting? You trying to make points? All that. Chili said, 'I think you ought to listen to what Elaine says about the guy. He doesn't sound too reliable.' Getting in the car, the front seat. Chili said, 'Last night I noticed he's a lot shorter than I thought.'

Next, Harry started bitching about how studio people never come right out and say yes or no, they string you along. They put you in a high-risk position you can't afford to be in and say it's up to you.

It was hot in the car. Chili rolled down his window. 'What'd she say a writer would cost?'

'Between one-fifty and four hundred thousand.'

'Jesus Christ,' Chili said, 'just to fix it? That's what I thought she meant, but I wasn't sure. The writers do okay, huh?'

'It's the fucking agents ruining the business. Agents and the unions. But you know what? If I had the dough I'd hire one of those guys. That's how sure I am of this one.'

Chili, not at all sure, didn't say anything.

'With a little luck, say if you were to run into your pal the drycleaner,' Harry said, 'and could negotiate me a quick loan . . .'

Chili watched two young ladies walking up the middle of the studio street: long blond hair, miniskirts, a couple of Miss Californias.

'I found him, Harry.'

Harry said, 'Where?' jumping on it, twisting around in that tight space between the seat and the steering wheel.

'What's the difference where? I took the money off him and sent it to his wife.'

'You didn't.'

'Three hunnerd grand. I kept ten for Bones, if I decide to pay him.'

'You had the money in your *hand*?'

'Take it easy, Harry.' The guy looked like he might go berserk. 'I didn't have to tell you, 'cause it isn't any your business, is it? But I did. Okay, so forget it.'

'Three hundred thousand.' Now he was shaking his head,

still not looking too stable. 'I don't know what good you're doing me.'

'I don't raise money for you, Harry, that was never in the deal.'

'What deal? I'd like to know what you do for me.'

'You telling me you'd use Leo's money? Take a chance of him getting picked up – 'cause he will, I know it. The first thing he'd do then is try and lay it on us, the whole con, and throw his wife in too.'

Harry, staring straight ahead now, didn't say anything. He looked uncomfortable, his suit too tight for him.

Chili got out and held the door open as Karen approached the car. He couldn't tell anything by her expression. When she got close to him, before ducking inside, she said, 'The visual fabric of the theme? You might just make it, Chil.'

He got in back. Harry started the car but didn't move, looking at Karen. 'You want to tell me what that was about?'

'Elaine's going to call Michael,' Karen said. 'If he shows enough interest and you have the script revised, she'll put it into development.'

'Fucking studios,' Harry said, 'they can't give you a simple yes or no, they have to intrigue it up. Why'd she tell you that and not me?'

'That wasn't why she asked me to stay,' Karen said, and paused and said in a quieter tone, 'Elaine offered me a job.'

Harry squinted at her. 'As what?'

'Production exec. Maybe vice-president in a year.'

Harry said, 'Jesus Christ, I don't believe it.'

Chili reached over the seat to touch Karen's shoulder. He said, 'Nice going,' and just for a second she laid her cheek against his hand.

21

'The last person Catlett would ever imagine having a tender feeling toward was Marcella, the woman that kept the limo service going. But he had one today. Walked in from the garage through the working office where Marcella looked up from her computer to say, 'Mr Zimm has been trying to get hold of you,' and Bo Catlett wanted to hug her.

He said, 'You don't mean to tell me.'

'He didn't leave a message. He'll call back.'

'When?'

'I don't know, but he sure called a buncha times,' this big doll in her pink outfit and pink-frame glasses said. Just then the phone rang on Marcella's desk. He watched her pick it up and say, 'Wingate Motors Limited,' dainty for a woman her size, the way she moved, the way she held her fifty-year-old head of golden hair. He had never noticed this before. Marcella said, 'Yes, Mr Catlett's here. Just a moment, please.' Looked at him and nodded and this time he wanted to kiss her.

He took it in Ronnie's office, feet up on the desk, ankles crossed, looking at his shiny Cole-Haan loafers as he said, 'Harry, I was thinking of calling you, man. How you doing?'

Harry said just great. The way he always did, sitting on the other side of this desk times before, here to ask for investment money – oh, everything was just great – though he did happen to have a few points left over if they wanted in. A few points meaning half the budget for the movie. In financial shit up to his chin, no doubt as he was at this moment, Harry was just great.

'We got a deal going at Tower . . .'

'On *Mr Lovejoy*?'

'They're extremely high on it.'

'I hear you got Michael Weir.'

'Boy, this town. Word gets around, doesn't it?'

'So how can I help you?'

'I'm looking for a little working capital.'

'Like how much?'

'Couple hundred.'

'What's wrong with using the money we put in *Freaks*?'

'That's in escrow, I can't touch it.'

Meaning the man had spent it. So for the time being Catlett resigned himself to forget it. Move on to bigger things.

'You offering a participation in *Lovejoy*?'

'A small one, considering it's a twenty-million-dollar shoot, minimum. Maybe twenty-five.'

'So we're talking about like one percent.'

'Around there.'

'Or less.'

'Tell me what you want,' Harry said. 'Let's see if we can work it out.'

Listen to him. Cool for a man who was desperate or wouldn't have picked up the phone. 'I was about to call you, Harry.'

'Is that right?'

'Tell you how much I like *Lovejoy*.'

'You read it?'

'I think so much of it, man, I'm prepared to make you a deal you might not believe. But I also want to participate

194

actively. You understand what I'm saying? I want to work on the movie with you, be part of it, man.'

'I'd like to know where you got hold of a script.'

'Harry, let's me and you meet someplace and have a drink. I'll tell you how you can put your hands on a hundred and seventy thousand and you won't have to give me any points or pay interest on it. You pay me back at your convenience. How's that sound?'

'You serious?' Harry said.

No mention now of the script.

'Where you want to meet?' Catlett asked him.

'I don't care,' Harry said. 'Where do you?'

After going around on that Catlett called the Bear, named a restaurant and asked him to be there in half an hour. When Catlett left, going out through the working office where Marcella the pink woman sat behind her computer, he wondered what it was like to go to bed with a woman you would never think of going to bed with, if it was different.

A Mexican in a white busboy coat and crummy-looking pants brought drinks to them on Karen's patio. She sounded different, so polite saying, 'Thank you, Miguel. I'll see you tomorrow.' The Mexican didn't say anything. He was bow-legged and had big gnarled hands on him. After Miguel went in the house Karen said, 'Would you think he's only in his forties? He's been a migrant farm worker all his life. He came by one day asking to do yard work and I hired him as my houseman.'

Chili sipped his drink and said, 'Jesus, I don't think he put any tonic in this. It's good though.'

'Miguel's learning,' Karen said, and looked up at the trees. 'It's nice out here, isn't it? This is my favorite time of the day.'

She sounded different this evening. Neither of them said

anything for a minute or so, looking at the trees and the sky changing color. It reminded Chili a little of sitting with Fay as it got dark and they waited for Leo to come home; except Leo and Fay didn't have a swimming pool. He had thought they were waiting for Harry – the plan, to go out to dinner – till Karen said Harry had already stopped by. Changed his mind, made a phone call and left. Still upset about the meeting, among other things.

Chili took the 'among other things' to mean him. 'He doesn't think I'm doing anything for him.'

Karen turned to look at him. 'Are you?'

'What's he want? I'll do it.'

'He wants Michael . . . But listen,' Karen said, 'the way Harry's acting, that's his personality. To help him, you first have to break through this barrier he sets up – doing it *his* way, the independent producer, nobody knows anything but him. His last three pictures might've broken even, but didn't do nearly as well as his early stuff. I tried to tell him. You know why? You haven't kept up. If you're going to do low-budget exploitation you either have to go much heavier on the special effects, or you have to get outrageously campy, make pictures like *Assault of the Killer Bimbos*, *Surf Nazis Must Die*, *Space Sluts in the Slammer* – they're so bad they're fun. Or, you have to approach horror in a new and different way, like *Near Dark*, that I think is brilliant. A love story about a guy who falls for a vampire. But there's not one scene in a dark empty castle, the vampire dressed like Fred Astaire in white tie and tails. These are raunchy vampires; they roam around this flat, empty farmland out west in a station wagon looking for blood, hurrying to get what they need and stay out of the sun or they'll catch fire and burn up. It shows what it's really like to be a vampire,' Karen said. 'And I couldn't get Harry to go see it.'

Chili sipped his vodka and not much tonic, glad Harry

wasn't here, comfortable in the cushioned patio chair, more impressed by Karen every time he talked to her. She wasn't anything like Fay, but she'd understand Fay and could play her in a minute.

'You know all that stuff,' Chili said. 'I don't mean just what movies are about, but other things, the business.'

'I've been out here fifteen years and I pay attention,' Karen said. 'Harry's upset, and one of the reasons is my being offered a studio job. He said, "I don't believe it," because he still thinks of me as the girl he hired with nice tits and a great scream. My dad teaches quantum physics at a university and my mother's a real estate broker, has her own company and is incredibly successful; she has a super business mind. I'm not saying I follow after either one of them exactly, but I didn't come into the world on a bus to LA. I have a background. I know more about the film industry now than Harry does because I keep up, I know what's going on and I have good story sense. Elaine knows that, it's why she wants to hire me.'

'You gonna take the job?'

'I'm thinking about it,' Karen said. 'Meanwhile, poor Harry's off trying to raise money, so he can hire a writer . . .'

Chili paused, about to sip his drink.

'. . . and get deeper in debt. That's where he went, to talk to his investors.'

Chili said, 'You mean the limo guys?'

'I know it's the same ones he's been trying to avoid. I said, "Harry, you told me you've been dying to get out from under them," and he said he didn't have a choice.'

'He went to their office?'

'No, they're meeting somewhere . . . Tribeca, it's on Beverly Drive.'

Chili put his drink down. 'Can we have dinner there?'

Karen said, 'If you'd like,' and stared at him for maybe ten seconds before she said, 'Harry's a big boy,' and continued to stare as if wanting him to say something. 'Isn't he?'

Chili got up. He said, 'You ready?'

They were in the big corner booth upstairs at Tribeca, Catlett, Harry, now the Bear sliding in and Catlett had to stop what he was saying to introduce his associate, this former movie stuntman, bodybuilder and health nut in the Hawaiian shirt. So what did the health nut do? Immediately dove into the bread basket and started eating rolls thick with butter, getting crumbs in his beard and all over the table in front of him. Now Harry, watching him, grabbed a roll for himself before they were gone. Harry was on his second Scotch, Catlett still sipping his ice-cold Pouilly-Fuissé. Harry had ordered the meatloaf, which Catlett liked the sound of, basic food, indicating the man was in a basic frame of mind and would not get tricky on him. Catlett had ordered the shrimp salad, not wanting to make this one his dinner; he'd have that later on at Mateo's with people he liked, some cute woman who'd laugh at his wit and bullshit. The Bear ordered a beer – another simple soul – and would eat later, at home.

So far Catlett had explained once again he'd give Harry one hundred and seventy thousand dollars, interest and point free, pay it back when you can, for the privilege of working on *Lovejoy* and learning from the expert how moving pictures were made. Fringe benefits would come up later. All he wanted, Catlett had mentioned this time, was some kind of small credit up on the screen, head gofer, anything, his friends would get a kick out of seeing. Now then . . .

'I told you it was your boy, didn't I, let me have the script?'

Harry didn't know who he meant. 'My boy? . . .'

'Chili Palmer, from Miami, Florida.'

'He gave it to you?'

'Loaned it. Was the other night in your office.'

Harry said, 'Well, you *say* you read it,' not yet convinced.

'Ask me something.'

'All right, what's Lovejoy's brother-in-law's name?'

'You mean Stanley? I was thinking it wouldn't be bad if something happened to Stanley, the way he gets on your nerves. Even though as Lovejoy says to his sis, her and Stan have their own problems, being stuck with each other.'

Now the man couldn't have a doubt in his head, just questions.

'Why'd he show it to you?'

'I thought maybe you told him to.'

'I sent him to pick up a script, that's all.'

'Well, he called me, I went over. Man, I've been wondering why ever since. This town, you don't want to go showing your ideas around. I know of a guy left a script in one of the limos and the producer fired him. I thought that was heavy. The producer – I won't mention his name, one of the big power players – he said if the guy wasn't any more reliable than that he didn't want him around.'

Catlett sipped his wine, giving Harry a minute to think about it and then took a shot saying, 'I asked this Chili Palmer what his position was and he said you and him were partners, gonna produce the movie together. It surprised me, him coming in off the street and not knowing shit, you know, about the business. I noticed he didn't even know how to read a script, what some of the directions meant. In *fact* he's talking about producing the movie with you, he hadn't even *read* it. Man, that didn't sound right to me.'

Harry picked up his roll and took a bite out of it like he was eating an apple, crumbs dribbling down the front of him. The Bear, spreading butter on his, paused to watch this.

'I don't mean to sound like I'm sticking my nose in your

199

business,' Catlett said, going at him again, 'and if you don't care to tell me, don't. It's just I'm curious to know what this Chili Palmer does for you.'

'Not much,' Harry said.

Good, starting to speak.

'He run errands for you?'

'He has different functions, you might say.'

'Kind of a tough guy, huh? That was how he came on,' Catlett said. 'See, I suspected you had him around to do heavy work, deal with me and Ronnie, and that was something I couldn't get straight in my head. What would you need him for? Has Ronnie ever given you any trouble? I know I haven't. Ronnie might've shot off his mouth, but that's Ronnie. Man, he's from Santa Barbara and he's gonna let you know it. Anyway, Ronnie isn't in this deal – the one hundred and seventy thousand dollars I'm giving you as working capital in good faith. You're gonna find out, Harry, I know more about movies than most people in the business. You watch me.'

Harry said, 'When can I have the money?'

Getting right down to business. Never mind all the bullshit, huh? This was the meatloaf man.

'Whenever you want it, Harry. The money's in hundred-dollar bills inside one of those jock bags, you know? In a locker at the airport, waiting to be picked up.'

Harry looked at him. 'The airport?'

'It was waiting out there on another deal, one that didn't go through you don't want to know about,' Catlett said. 'Or maybe you should know something about it. I don't want you to get in any trouble. It was money put there to make a buy, if you know what I mean.'

Harry picked up his glass and took a drink on that one.

'Yeah?'

But was still interested, look at that. Anxious.

200

'What I'm saying to you, Harry, you could go out there, take the bag out of the locker and be on your way, nobody bother you. But you never know who's hanging around that airport.'

'You mean cops,' Harry said.

'Well, that's possible, yeah. Maybe Drug Enforcement individuals – I don't know. I was thinking more of other people in the product trade know buys are made out there, money changing hands. You understand what I'm saying? They the ones you have to watch out might rip you off. Like if you look, I don't mean like one of them, but kinda suspicious, you act nervous taking the bag out of the locker . . .'

'I don't know,' Harry said, shaking his head.

Wanting it, you could tell, but afraid.

'It's what I'm saying, it's not the kind of thing you do,' Catlett said. 'That's why I was thinking you could send your boy, Chili Palmer. He gets hit on the head you aren't out nothing.'

They took Chili's rented Toyota, down Rodeo to Wilshire to come back around on Beverly Drive. On the way he told Karen about going into a restaurant on Little Santa Monica when he first got here. Went in all dressed up and was put way in the back after waiting at the bar about an hour, while these people who looked like they'd been out camping would come in and get the empty front tables right away. He told her about the worn-out leather jacket Michael had been wearing.

'You buy them new like that,' Karen said. 'What did you think of him?'

Chili said he thought he was basically a nice guy, but it was hard to tell. 'He was *on* most of the time. I think he has trouble being just himself.'

'He do any imitations?'

'Michael Jackson.'

'He used to do Howard Cosell constantly.' She said, 'You know it isn't easy being Michael Weir.'

Chili didn't comment on that, thinking seven million ought to make it a *little* easier.

They were quiet and then she said, 'What's Nicki like?'

'She's a rock-and-roll singer.' He thought a moment and said, 'She doesn't shave under her arms.'

'Michael probably goes for that. He thinks he's earthy.'

'You still like him?'

'I don't hold anything against him. He's Michael Weir . . . and he's great.'

'You mean his acting.'

'What'd you think I meant, in bed? In bed he was funny.'

'Funny in what way?'

'He was *funny*. He said funny things.'

For a few moments they were quiet again.

'He's a lot shorter than I thought.'

'That's not his fault,' Karen said.

Chili dropped her off in front of Tribeca, a storefront kind of café with the name on the plate glass, and drove up the street looking for a place to park.

They weren't at that old-time-looking bar or anywhere on the main floor. Chili headed for the open stairway and started up. The place could be called the Manhattan or the Third Avenue, that's what it looked like, one of those typical overpriced New York bar-restaurants. The TriBeCa area, he thought of warehouses, buildings with lofts, but it was as good a name as any. He saw a railing along the upstairs, this end of it open, overlooking the bar. And he saw a guy standing near the top of the stairs, the guy a few steps down but not coming down, standing there waiting for him.

A guy in a Hawaiian shirt with beef on him and a full reddish-brown beard.

Moving up the stairs Chili got a good look at the guy and his size. Now he saw Bo Catlett appear above the guy to stand on the top step, almost directly behind him, and Chili knew the guy wasn't going to move. He got within three steps of the guy and stopped, but not looking up now, not wanting to put himself in that awkward position, his head bent back. He was looking at the guy's waist now at eye level, where the Hawaiian shirt bloused out of the elastic band of the guy's blue pants, double-knit and tight on him.

Catlett's voice said, 'I like you to meet my associate, the Bear. Movie stuntman and champion weight lifter, as you might've noticed. Picks up and throws out things I don't want.'

Chili looked at the thickness of the guy's body, at red and gold hibiscus blossoms and green leaves on a field of Hawaiian blue, but wouldn't look at his face now. He knew they were hibiscus, because Debbie used to grow them on Meridian Avenue before she flipped out and went back to Brooklyn.

Now the guy was saying, 'I know Chili Palmer. I know all about him.'

The Bear sucking in his stomach and acting tough, his crotch right there in Chili's face. This guy was as nuts as Debbie. You could tell he had his stomach sucked in, because the waistband was creased where the guy's gut ordinarily hung over and rolled it, the pants as out of shape as this guy trying to give him a hard time. But Chili didn't look up.

Catlett said, 'We think you ought to turn around and go back to Miami.'

Chili still didn't look up. Not yet.

The Bear said, 'Take your ten grand with you, while you still have it.'

And Chili almost looked up – this guy as much as telling him he had been in his hotel room, nothing to it, saw all that dough and left it – but he didn't. Chili kept his eyes on the guy's waist and saw the stomach move to press against the elastic band, the guy still putting on his show but giving his gut a breather. Chili looked at the guy's crotch one more time before moving his gaze up through the hibiscus till he was looking at the guy's bearded face.

Chili said, 'So you're a stuntman,' with the look he'd use on a slow pay. 'Are you any good?'

What the Bear did in that next moment was grin and turn his head to the side, as if too modest to answer and would let Catlett speak for him. It made the next move easier, the guy not even looking as Chili grabbed a handful of his crotch, stepped aside and yanked him off the stairs. The Bear yelled out of pain and fear and caught Chili's head with an elbow going by, but it was worth it to see that beefy guy roll all the way down the stairs to land on the main floor. Chili kept watching till he saw the guy move, then looked up at Catlett.

'Not bad, for a guy his size.'

Karen saw it.

There was a scene like it in an Eastwood picture only Clint grabs the guy a little higher. The thug asks him where he thinks he's going. She couldn't remember if Clint had a line. He's going upstairs in a hotel to have it out with Bobby Duvall. Grabs the guy with one hand and in a Reverse you see him tumble down the stairs to crash at the bottom. It was a western.

Karen had left the table within moments of seeing Catlett stop at the top of the stairs with the bearded guy, the Bear, in front of him, a few steps below, and knew they were waiting for Chili and something was going to happen. As a film sequence it would work from her point of view if she represented a third party in the scene. Then another setup to get the effect of it on her face. But there would have to be close shots too of what was going on. His hand grabbing the guy's crotch. A tight close-up reaction shot of the guy's face. As he begins to scream cut to a Reverse to see him go down the stairs. Catlett was down there now. They were leaving, the guy looking back this way, but not Catlett. Karen watched from the upstairs railing, people from tables around her now asking what happened. Chili was coming past the ones at the top of the stairs. She heard him say, 'I guess the guy fell.' Now he was looking at her. He came over and she said, 'What did he do to you?' Chili shook his head. He touched her arm and they moved through the tables to the corner booth where Harry was standing with his drink in his hand. Harry said, 'What was that all about?'

Karen sat at one end of the round booth so she'd have an angle on both of them at once and wouldn't have to turn her head looking from one to the other. She moved the shrimp salad that hadn't been touched away from her, and the half-glass of white wine. Chili brushed bread crumbs away from his place. He would look over, wanting to include her at first, telling them Catlett and the bearded guy, the Bear, had broken into his hotel room and gone through his things. Telling it matter-of-factly, making the point: 'These are the kind of people you're dealing with, Harry. They want me out of the way so they can have a piece of you.' Nice irony. The ex-mob guy telling Harry to look out for the limo guys, they're crooks.

Harry had been acting strange ever since she arrived and he introduced her to Catlett and Catlett introduced her to his friend the Bear and they let her stand there a few minutes, Harry's broad, nothing more, while Catlett spoke to him and placed a key on the table next to Harry's meatloaf. Most of it and the baked potato eaten; he hadn't touched his green beans. When Catlett got up he smiled and touched her arm and said it was a pleasure. A good-looking guy, he reminded her of Duke Ellington, dressed by Armani or out of that place on Melrose, Maxfield's, wearing about two thousand dollars' worth of clothes.

The key wasn't on the table now.

Harry said to Chili, 'You know what he is, you told me. So what? I need a hundred and a half, at least, and he's loaning it to me, no strings, I write any kind of agreement I want. All I have to do is pick up the dough. Okay? If you have a problem with him that's your problem. I don't.'

It seemed that simple till Chili asked, 'Is he giving you a check or cash?' and it got interesting. Harry said cash. He said it happened to be waiting right this moment in a locker at the airport. He said something about a business deal that didn't go through and Chili said, 'Jesus Christ, the guy's setting you up. Don't you see that? You pulled out of their *freaks* deal so he's teaching you a lesson. He's not giving you anything, Harry, he's paying you back.' Harry said he didn't know what he was talking about and Chili said, 'Harry, I could write a fuckin book on paybacks. You reach in that locker, you're gonna come out wearing handcuffs, I'm telling you.'

Karen wished she could write some of it down.

Harry said, 'Oh, is that right? I'm being set up? Then how come Catlett said I should send you out to get it, since you haven't done a fucking thing for me since you got into this?'

Karen watched Chili start to smile and for a moment it surprised her. Smiled and shook his head and said, 'Harry, I was wrong, I'm sorry. You're not the one he wants to set up.'

Harry was not the Harry she had known for fifteen years; he was too quiet. But pouty, acting offended, Harry realizing

206

he was into something he couldn't handle – that was it – and afraid of looking dumb.

Chili said, 'Give me the key. If it's there and I don't see a problem, I'll get it for you.'

Karen watched Harry turn his head to look at Chili as though he had a choice and was appraising him, thinking it over.

She watched Chili shrug. He said, 'It's up to you, Harry. But don't do it yourself, I'm telling you.'

She watched Harry put his hand in his coat pocket and bring out the key. He didn't hand it to Chili, he laid it on the table between them. He said, 'A hundred and seventy grand. I wonder if I'm ever gonna see you again.'

Harry left after that, which was fine with Chili. He and Karen went downstairs to sit at the bar for one, not sure if they'd eat here or go someplace else. She was full of questions, asking about the limo guys and how they made their money. Then asking if he was going out to the airport later this evening. He told her he was thinking of waiting till tomorrow around noon, when there'd be a lot of people there.

Right after that was when Karen said, 'Oh, I forgot to tell you. A friend of yours from Miami called the house.'

'Tommy Carlo?'

'No that wasn't it. I wrote it down,' Karen said. 'Ray something. Ray Bar-bone? . . .'

22

The way the lockers in the Delta terminal worked, you put in three quarters for twenty-four hours. If you expected to use the locker any longer than that, you left two bucks inside for each additional twenty-four hours and a locker attendant would come by and check the time and collect the money. Chili had to read the instructions, printed on each locker, twice before he figured it out. He did this before walking past the bank of lockers where C-018 was located, noticing the lockers on both sides of it had keys sticking out. He liked that as much as he liked all the travelers here today. This LAX, ten-thirty in the morning, was a busy airport.

Next thing he did was check the Arrivals monitor to see what flight he was waiting for if anybody should ask. The one that caught his eye was 83 from Newark, due in at twelve-forty. He imagined Debbie coming out of the gate carrying a makeup kit full of pills and with that pissed-off look she had. Hi, honey, how was the flight? It was awful. The food was awful, the stewardess was a snip and I have a headache. He seemed to be thinking of Debbie and his situation more, still married to her, since meeting Karen, even though he wasn't thinking of Karen in any serious way beyond – he wasn't sure what. The thing he liked about Karen, his past life and associations didn't seem to turn her on or off. She was natural with him, didn't put on airs. Also she was a knockout, she was smart, she was a movie star, or had been, and was starting to give him a certain look and call him Chil. All last night after the business with the stuntman, she had looked at him in a different way, he felt, than she did before. Like she wanted to know things about him. And she was quieter, even while asking a lot of questions, though she didn't ask if he was married or anything too personal. Dropping her off he thought she was going to ask him in. He believed she came close before changing her mind for some reason. Still looking at the Arrivals monitor he noticed Flight 89 from Atlanta up there, the one Bones had connected with from Miami and arrived on yesterday. Karen called him Ray Bar-bone, but didn't ask about him, so he didn't tell her what kind of pain in the ass this fuckin Bones was turning out to be: the way he kept showing up, Christ, for twelve years now, here he comes again, Bones the mob guy and playing it for all it was worth, but basically second-rate muscle, Bones could be handled. As long as he didn't have that big colored guy with him. Chili thinking he didn't need that one too, he already had a colored guy on his back, the dude. What was this? The first time in his life having trouble with colored guys.

In the gift shop Chili bought an LA Lakers T-shirt, purple and gold, and a black canvas athletic bag, a small one. The T-shirt went in the athletic bag inside the paper gift-shop bag. He looked around at the souvenirs, all the different kinds of mementos of Los Angeles, at the wall of books and magazines. There was a scruffy kid about eighteen who looked promising, checking out the skin magazines. Chili went up to him and said, 'You want to make five bucks, take you two minutes?' The kid looked at him but didn't answer. 'You go over to those lockers across the aisle there and put this in C-017.' The kid still didn't say anything. 'It's a surprise for my wife,' Chili said. 'But you have to do it quick, okay? While she's in the can.' That sounded as if it made sense, so the kid said yeah, okay. Chili gave him the paper bag his purchases were in, a five-dollar bill and three quarters. The kid left and came back with a key that had C-017 on the round flat part of it.

What Chili didn't do was look around the terminal to see if he could spot any suits – the way in movies you saw them standing around reading newspapers. That was bullshit. Maybe you could spot them if you were out here all the time doing business. Maybe the limo guys could spot them and that's why the hundred and seventy grand was sitting untouched in the locker. Chili had no doubt it was there or this wouldn't be a setup. The suits grab you with something incriminating, with what they called 'suspected drug money,' or there could be more than cash in the locker, some dope, to make the bust stick. There was no sense in looking around, because if it was a setup Catlett would have called it in and the suits would be here dressed all kinds of ways watching locker No. C-018, here and there but not standing anywhere near the locker, so why bother looking?

What Chili did, he left the airport for a couple of hours: drove over Manchester Avenue where he found an Italian place and had a plate of seafood linguine marinara and a split of red. While he was here he wrote the Newark flight number and arrival time on a piece of Sunset Marquis notepaper. It seemed like a lot of trouble, the whole thing, but it was better to have a story just in case, not have to make one up on the spot.

By half past twelve he was back in the Delta terminal waiting at the gate where 83 was due to arrive at twelve-forty. It was on the ground at five past one. He watched all the passengers come off the plane and out through the gate till he was standing there by himself. Okay, he turned and walked down the aisle now to the bank of thirty-three lockers, three high, where C-018 was about in the middle. He looked both ways, taking his time, waiting till a group of people was passing behind him, giving him a screen, giving him just time enough to open C-017, grab the black athletic bag, leaving the gift-shop bag inside, and close the locker. He got about ten yards down the aisle, heading for daylight, when the black guy in the suit coming toward him stopped right in his path.

'Excuse me, sir. Would you come with me, please?'

Now there was a big guy in a plaid wool shirt next to him and another guy, down the aisle, talking on his hand radio. All of them put in the open now. The black guy had his I.D. folder open. They were Drug Enforcement. As Chili said, 'What's wrong?' acting surprised. 'What's this about?' The black guy turned and started off.

The one in the plaid shirt said, 'Let's follow him and behave ourselves. What do you say?'

They took him to a door marked AUTHORIZED PERSONNEL ONLY the black guy opened with a key. It was bare and bright inside the office, fluorescent lights on. Nothing on the metal desk, not even an ashtray. There were three chairs, but they didn't ask him to sit down. The one in the plaid shirt told him to empty his pockets and place the contents on the desk, actually using the word *contents*. But that was as official-sounding as it got. Chili did as he was told acting bewildered, saying he thought they had the wrong person. The black guy opened his wallet and looked at the driver's license while the other one pulled the Lakers T-shirt out of the athletic bag and felt around inside. They glanced at each other without giving any kind of sign and the black guy said, 'You live in Miami?'

'That's right,' Chili said.

'What're you doing in Los Angeles?'

'I'm in the movie business,' Chili said.

They glanced at each other again. The black guy said, 'You're an investor, is that it?'

'I'm a producer,' Chili said, 'with ZigZag Productions.'

'You have a card in here?'

'Not yet, I just started.'

The one in the plaid shirt looked at the 'contents' on the desk and said, 'Is that everything?'

'That's it,' Chili said. He watched the black guy pick up the note with the Newark flight number and arrival time written on it. Chili said, 'I'd appreciate your telling me what this is about.' He could act nervous with these guys without trying too hard.

'I got a John Doe warrant here,' the one in the plaid shirt said. 'I can strip-search you if I want.'

'Pat him down,' the black guy said.

'Why don't I strip-search him?'

'Pat him down,' the black guy said.

Chili was starting to like the black guy, his quiet way, but couldn't say as much for the other one. The big guy in the plaid shirt put him against the wall, told him to spread his legs and did a thorough job going over him as the black guy asked what he was doing at the airport. Chili said he was supposed to meet his wife, but she wasn't on the flight. The black guy asked why, if he lived in Miami, his wife was coming from Newark? Chili said because they'd had a fight and she left him, went back to Brooklyn. He said he asked her to come out here, maybe with a change of scenery they could get back together and she said okay, but evidently changed her mind. He didn't mention it was twelve years ago she'd left him.

The black guy said, 'Your wife a Lakers fan?'

'I am,' Chili said. 'I'm a fan of everything that's LA. I love it out here.' And looked over his shoulder to give the guy a smile.

The black guy said he could go. Then, when Chili was at the desk, asked him, 'What was the number of the locker you used?'

Chili paused. 'It was C . . . either sixteen or seventeen. He said, 'Can I ask you – are you looking for a bomb? Something like that?'

'Something shouldn't be there,' the black guy said.

'Why don't you get the attendant to open all the lockers and take a look? Maybe you'll find it.'

'That's an idea,' the black guy said. 'I'll think about it.'

'That's what I'd do,' Chili said. 'I'd make sure I got the right guy next time.'

That was it. Time to collect his 'contents' and his new bag and leave. He didn't like the way the black guy was looking at him.

23

Chili didn't see the stuntman until he was up on the third level of the parking structure. There he was, the Hawaiian Bear, standing by the Toyota. So he must have been here all day. Walking up to him Chili said, 'I don't know how I could've missed you with that shirt on. It's the same as the other one you had on only the hibiscus are a different color, right?'

The Bear didn't answer the question. He looked okay, no cuts or bruises showing from his fall down the stairs. He said, 'So you didn't have the key with you.'

Chili said, 'You think I'd be standing here? You set somebody up and you want it to work, it has to be a surprise. Can you remember that?'

'You spotted them, huh?'

This guy was either dumb or he was making conversation.

'Who, the suits? If I know they're there, what's the difference which ones they are? Tell that colored guy you work for he blew it. Whose idea was it, yours or his?' The Bear didn't answer and Chili said, 'Did you see it work in some movie you got beat up in? There's quite a difference between movies and real life, isn't there?'

Now Chili was making conversation. For some reason he felt sorry for this guy in his Hawaiian shirt.

'What movies were you in I might've seen?'

The Bear hesitated as if he might be thinking of titles. He wasn't though. He said, 'I have to ask you for that key.'

'What're you talking about?'

'The locker key.'

'I know what one you mean,' Chili said. 'I can't believe what you're telling me. The setup didn't work so you want the key back?'

'Catlett says if you don't open the locker the deal's off.'

'You serious?' Chili said. 'This is how you guys do business? I can't believe you aren't dead.'

The Bear kept staring but didn't say anything.

'Look,' Chili said, 'you know as well as I do there's no fuckin way I'm gonna give you the key, outside of you point a gun at my head. Then we might have something to talk about. Otherwise . . . I'd like you to step away from the car.'

'I don't need a gun,' the Bear said. 'Where is it? If it isn't on you, it's around here someplace.'

Chili shook his head, tired of this, but still feeling a little sorry for the guy. The Bear didn't seem to have his heart in it; he was going through the motions, doing what he was told. Chili looked off in kind of a thoughtful way, turned to the Bear again and kicked him in the left knee, hard. The Bear stumbled, hunching over. Chili grabbed him by the hair with both hands, pulled his head down and brought his knee up into the guy's face. That straightened him and now Chili hit him high in the belly as hard as he could, right under the rib cage. The Bear gasped and sucked air with his mouth open trying to breathe, helpless now and in pain. Chili took him by the arm saying, 'Lie down on your back. Come on, if you want to breathe.' He got the Bear down on the concrete, straddled his midsection and reached down to lift him up by the waist of his pants, the same blue ones he had on yesterday, telling him, 'Take deep breaths through your mouth and let it out slow . . . That's it, like that.'

Once the Bear was breathing okay, checking his teeth now, feeling his nose. Chili said, 'Hey. Look at me,' and got him to raise his eyes. 'Tell your boss I don't ever want to see him again. He made a deal with Harry and a deal's a deal. I'm talking about if we get the dough out of the locker. We don't, then okay, there's no deal. But either way I don't want to see him coming around anymore. You understand? Will you tell him that?'

The Bear seemed to nod, closing and opening his eyes.

'What're you hanging around with a guy like that for? You were in the movies, right? A stuntman? What's he ever done he can talk about? The guy pimps you and you let him do it. You feel okay?'

'Not too bad,' the Bear said.

'How 'bout when you went down the stairs?'

He touched his left thigh. 'I think I pulled my quadriceps.'

'If I was you,' Chili said, 'I'd quit that guy so fast. No, first I'd kick him down some stairs, let him see what it's like. Then I'd quit.'

The Bear didn't say anything, but had a look in his eyes that maybe he was thinking about it.

'How many movies you been in?'

'About sixty.'

'No shit,' Chili said. 'What're some of 'em?'

The locker key was down on the first level of the parking structure, stuck in a crack where the pavement joined one of the concrete support posts. Chili made sure nobody was in sight before he picked it up.

Now he drove to the Avis lot to return the Toyota, walked over to National and took out a Cadillac Sedan de Ville, a black one. There was more to this than switching cars just in case. He felt he deserved a Cadillac. If he had one at home, he should have one out here. At least a Cadillac. Driving up

405 he began thinking that if somehow he got the cash out of that locker he'd tell Harry he wanted a ten percent commission on it, then turn in the Cadillac and lease a Mercedes or that expensive BMW. Karen said top agents and studio execs were driving BMWs now. She said a Rolls was too pretentious; low-key was in. Other things to remember: you don't 'take a meeting' anymore, you say you have 'a two-thirty at Tower.' If a studio passes on a script, you don't say 'they took a Pasadena.' That was out before it was in. Like 'so-and-so gives good phone.' If they say it's 'for a specialized audience' or it's 'a cast-driven script,' that's a pass. But what Elaine Levin gave *Lovejoy* was a 'soft pass,' which meant it was salvageable. There were a lot of terms you had to learn, as opposed to the shylock business where all you had to know how to say was 'Give me the fuckin money.' He'd call Karen later on, after he had a talk with Harry.

Pulling into the parking area beneath the Sunset Marquis he wondered if he should switch hotels. He liked this one, though, a lot. The people here were friendly, relaxed. They gave you free shampoo, suntan lotion, moisturizing cream. The food was good. You could cook in your room if you wanted. There were ashtrays everywhere you looked. A Sunset Marquis ashtray right there by the elevator, if you forgot to take one from your room when you checked out.

Chili unlocked the door to 325 and stepped inside, not too surprised to see the message light on the phone blinking. That would be Harry dying to know how he made out, Harry becoming a nervous wreck lately. He'd tell Harry it was still possible to get the money, but it wasn't going to be easy. Show Harry, first, he still needed him, then straighten him out about the limo guys – stay away from them. Chili took off his suitcoat, turned to drape it over one of the chairs at the counter and saw that someone had been in here.

Not the maid, someone else. The maid hadn't come in yet to clean up the room. You could tell, the newspapers on the sofa, the ashtray by the phone . . .

What had caught his eye, the cupboard doors in the kitchenette were open. Not all the way, but not closed tight either, the way he'd left them. But the desk drawer, Chili noticed, was closed, and he had left that one open about an inch. He had set the drawers in the bedroom the same way, some open an inch or so, some closed – a little nervous about security after the Bear had come in and tossed the place and didn't leave one clue that he'd been here. This one who'd come in either didn't know how to cover his moves or didn't care. The Bear had left the ten grand in the suitcase in the bedroom closet, but this one was different, this guy . . .

Chili was about to go in there and thought, Wait a minute. What if the guy's still here? As he fooled with that idea, looking toward the hall where you went into the bathroom or turned right and two steps took you into the bedroom, he knew who it was. Bones. There was no doubt in his mind now, that fuckin Bones had been here. Or was still here. In the bedroom.

There was one way to find out, but he didn't want to walk in there, maybe surprise him, even though Bones, if he was there, would have heard him come in. Except that you couldn't tell what Bones might do, the guy being either too dumb or crazy to act in a normal way.

What Chili did, he called out, 'Hey, Bones? I'm home.' Waited maybe ten seconds watching the hall and there he was.

Bones appeared extending a pistol in front of him, some kind of bluesteel automatic. In the other hand he was holding a paper laundry sack you found in hotel closets. Chili didn't have to guess what was in it. His ten grand. Bones waved the pistol at him.

218

'Get over there, by the sofa.'

'You don't need that,' Chili said. 'You want to sit down and talk, it's fine with me. Get this straightened out.'

Chili turned his back on him, walked over to the sofa and sat down. He watched Bones come in the room to stand by the counter, by the suitcoat hanging on the chair, and began to see what was going to happen.

Bones had on a shitty-looking light-gray suit with a yellow sport shirt, the top button fastened. It might be the style out here, but Bones looked like a Miami bookmaker and always would. Jesus, and gray shoes.

'I gave up looking for the drycleaner,' Chili said. 'This place's all freeways, you can drive around forever and never leave town. How'd you get in here?'

'I told them at the desk I was you,' Bones said. 'I acted stupid and they believed me.'

He came to the middle of the room, still pointing the gun, and held up the laundry sack.

'Where'd you get this?'

'Vegas. I won for a change.'

Bones stared at him, not saying anything. Then swung the sack to drop it on a chair.

'Get up and turn around.'

'What're you gonna do, search me?'

Chili got to his feet. Bones motioned with the gun and he turned to face the painting over the sofa that looked like a scene in Japan, misty pale green and tan ricefields, the sky overcast, not a lot going on there. He felt Bones lift his wallet out of his back pocket.

'You won the ten grand in Vegas?'

'That's where Leo went before he came here and I lost him.'

'Las Vegas.'

'Yeah, it's in Nevada.'

'Then how come the straps on the ten grand say Harrah's, Tahoe? Can you explain that to me?'

There were figures in the painting he hadn't noticed, people way out in the field picking rice.

Chili said, 'You sure it says that, Harrah's?'

He hadn't noticed any printing on the money straps either, or didn't remember.

'You're the stupidest fuckin guy I ever met in my life,' Bones said. 'Let's see what's in your pockets.'

Chili shoved his hands in and pulled the side pockets out.

'What you should've done was told me the guy was alive and skipped, soon as you found out.'

Chili heard the voice moving away. He looked over his shoulder to see Bones pulling his suitcoat from the back of the chair at the counter.

'Why would I do that?'

' 'Cause the guy's my customer now, stupid. His ass belongs to me.'

Bones laid the pistol on the counter, held the suitcoat up with one hand and felt through it with the other. Chili waited for his expression to change. There – his eyes opening wider.

'What have we here?' Bones said. His hand came out of the coat with the locker key.

Chili sat down in the sofa again.

'Give me my cigarettes. They're in the inside pocket.'

Bones threw the coat at him. 'Help yourself.' And held the key up to look at it. 'C-oh-one-eight.' Frowning now, putting on a show. 'I wonder what this's for, a locker? Yeah, but where is it?'

Chili sat back to smoke his cigarette and let it happen.

'I checked a bag at the airport, when I came.'

'Yeah? Which terminal?'

Chili hesitated. He said, 'Delta,' and it was done.

Bones said, 'You found Leo, didn't you? . . . Took the poor asshole's money and put it in a locker, ready to go.' Bones looked over. 'Why haven't you left?'

'I changed my mind. I like it here.'

'Well, there's nothing for you in Miami.'

Bones was nervous or anxious, touching his thin strands of hair, his collar, making sure it was buttoned.

'How much's in the locker? Just out of curiosity.'

Chili drew on his cigarette, taking his time. 'A hunnerd seventy thousand.'

'Jesus Christ, that drycleaner left with three hunnerd,' Bones said. 'I hadn't got here you would've pissed the rest of it away. You knew I was coming, right? That fuckin Tommy Carlo, I know he phoned you.'

'Yeah, but he didn't know why. 'Less you told him about the drycleaner.'

'I didn't tell him nothing.'

'What about Jimmy Cap, you tell him?'

Bones paused. He said, 'Look, there's no reason why you and I shouldn't get along. Forget all the bullshit going back to that time – I don't even remember how it started. You took a swing at me over some fuckin thing, whatever it was – forget it. You owe me eight grand, right? Forget that too. But, you don't say a fuckin word about this to anybody. It's strictly between you and I, right?'

'I get to keep the ten in the laundry bag,' Chili said.

Bones had to think about that one.

'Look,' Chili said, 'I was gonna pay you the eight I owe you out of the ten. See, but now you tell me I don't have to. So . . .'

'So I take two out of it and we're square,' Bones said. 'How's that?'

'Sounds good to me,' Chili said.

*

He looked up the number for the Drug Enforcement Administration in the phone book, dialed it and told the woman who answered he wanted to speak to the agent in charge. She asked what it was in regard to and he said a locker out at the airport, full of money.

A male voice came on saying, 'Who's speaking, please?'

'I can't tell you,' Chili said, 'it's an anonymous call.'

The male voice said, 'Are you the same anonymous asshole called last night?'

'No, this's a different one,' Chili said. 'Have you looked in that locker, C – oh-one-eight?'

There was a pause on the line.

'You're helping us out,' the male voice said. 'I'd like to know who this is.'

'I bet you would,' Chili said. 'You want to chat or you want me to tell you who to look for? The guy's on his way out right now.'

This DEA agent wouldn't give up. He said, 'You know there's a reward for information that leads to a conviction. That's why I have to know who this is.'

'I'll get my reward in heaven,' Chili said. 'The guy you want has a bullet scar in his head and is wearing gray shoes. You can't miss him.'

24

'This was Warren's office,' Karen said, 'before he was shipped off to Publicity. Warren Hurst, I think I mentioned him to you.'

'*Beth's Room*,' Chili said, sitting across from Karen at her big oak desk. 'The one that said if you did it your way they wouldn't have a movie.'

'You remember that.'

She said it with that nice look in her eyes she had been using on him lately. Interested, letting him know she liked him. The only difference today, she had on glasses, round ones with thin black frames. She was telling him now the office decor was pre-Warren, he hadn't been here long enough to redecorate; that it wouldn't be bad in a men's club, but she wasn't going to touch it. 'Not till I see if I get a vote here.'

Chili said, 'You don't fool around.'

'What, taking the job? Why not?'

Karen's shoulders moved in the beige silk blouse, the little ninety-pounder behind the big executive desk.

'I think I'll be good at it if they let me. Look at the scripts.'

She picked up one from a stack of about ten and moved it to another part of the desk.

'Elaine says all of them have spin in varying degrees. That means they're supposed to be good.'

She picked up another one. '*Beth's Room*, still under consideration.'

She picked up another and laid it down again.

'Elaine wants to know what I think.'

'Tell her the truth.'

'Don't worry.'

'I got an idea spinning around.'

'You told me about it.'

As he said, 'It's getting better,' Karen's phone buzzed.

She picked it up. 'Yeah?' Said, 'Tell him I'll call him back,' and looked at Chili as she hung up. 'Harry. That's the third time today.'

Chili said, 'I have to call him too, tell him what happened.'

And Karen said, 'That's right, you were going out to the airport,' her expression changing, her eyes losing that nice glow as they became serious. She took off her glasses as he told her about the DEA guys and hunched her shoulders leaning on the desk, looking right at him but maybe picturing it too, the scene. That was the feeling he had. He finished the part at the airport and she said, 'You really did that?' sounding amazed. 'So the money's still there?' He had to tell her about Bones then, and she listened to that part, every word of it, without blinking her eyes. When he finished she sat back in her chair for a moment thinking, still looking at him, then came forward again asking about Bones, who he was. So Chili had to take her all the way back to Vesuvio's and the leather coat.

This time when he finished Karen said, 'He'll tell the DEA guys you set it up. Won't he?'

'If they get him,' Chili said. 'Yeah, Bones'll try to put it on me. If they come around looking and I get hauled in, I say I don't know what he's talking about.'

'But they saw you there today,' Karen said, 'at the airport.'

'Yeah, well, they'd still have to prove I put the money in

224

the locker and there's no way they can do that, 'cause I didn't. I never touched that locker. If I see I'm in too deep I can always give 'em Catlett. But I don't want to go through all that right now. Even if I didn't have to post a bond it would be annoying, the way they keep after you asking questions. So I checked out of the Marquis. Now I have to find another place.'

She was giving him that amazed look again. 'You're serious.'

'Yeah, I tried the Chateau Marmont, see if I could get Jean Barlow's room, but they're full up. One thing I did, not knowing any better at the time, I told the DEA guys I was with ZigZag. They didn't write it down, so they might not remember it, and I didn't have a card to give them. But if they do, they'll look up Harry, try to find me that way.'

'What Harry will have trouble accepting,' Karen said, 'you didn't get the money, not that you could go to jail.'

'Yeah, I'll have to explain it to him. Once Bones found the key, the way his one-track mind works it was out of my hands. I had to let it happen.'

'I'd like to have seen that,' Karen said. She pushed out of her leather chair, came around the desk in a black skirt a few inches above her knees and leaned against the edge of the desk, close, looking down at him. He thought for a moment she was going to touch his face. She said, 'I'll bet you have scars . . .'

'A few.'

'I like your hair.'

'That's another story I could tell you sometime.'

She said, 'Why don't you hide out at my house?'

'Sleep in the maid's room?'

She said, 'We'll work something out.'

*

225

There was a certain look about the Mexican gardener that made Harry think of one of his maniacs: the little gnomelike one in *Grotesque Three* who took over after the original hideously disfigured maniac was burned to death in *Grotesque Two* and the picture went on to gross twenty million worldwide. The Mexican gardener coming this way across the lawn was bowlegged. Maybe that was it. *Grotesque Three* did almost eight million, which still wasn't bad. Or it was – of *course*, it was the shears the guy was carrying, the way he held them in front of him with both hands. The gnomelike maniac had used shears a lot.

Harry was on Karen's patio. Out here now as he kept moving, waiting for the phone to ring. Harry nodded to the Mexican approaching with the shears, wishing he'd point them down. 'How are you?'

'Miss Flores isn' home.'

'I know that,' Harry said.

'She's at work.'

'I know where she is,' Harry said, 'and she knows I'm here. It's okay, I'm a good friend of hers. We're amigos.'

This Mexican, with his dark skin and big nose, reminded Harry of an Aztec figure carved in relief on a stone wall. It got Harry thinking about human sacrifices, a blood cult four centuries old, virgins into the volcano . . . like movie ideas presented to a studio. The Mexican was saying something.

'What?'

'I ask you want a drink.'

'Do I want a drink – I thought you were the gardener.'

'The houseman, Miguel. I do outside, inside, everything.'

Harry said, *'You're* Miguel?' feeling a change in his mood, a sudden lift knowing Karen wasn't sleeping with her houseman, not this old guy and not that it made any difference, really, but he felt better in general and said, 'Yeah, Miguel, let me have a Scotch, lot of ice.'

Four times now Catlett had tried to get hold of the Bear: phoning his house from home, from the limo office, from his Porsche coming here and now here, in the turnaround part of the driveway at Karen Flores's French-looking house. Still no answer, only the Bear's recorded voice: Leave a message if you want. The only thing good happening Catlett could see was Harry's old Mercedes parked there, and Harry was the reason he'd come. Catlett went up to the door and rang the bell, set his sunglasses on straight, smoothed down his double-breasted navy blazer he wore with a white cotton shirt open wide at the throat and cream-colored pants.

The door swung in and the man standing there startled him, flashed him back in his mind to migrant camps and hundreds of guys with round, tired shoulders just like this one. Catlett said, 'Man, I haven't seen you since picking lettuce down the Imperial Valley. How you doing?' Found out this was Miguel the houseman and got taken out to the kitchen where his good friend Harry Zimm was sitting at the table with a drink, a bottle of Chivas Regal and a big pair of garden shears, the kind with ten-inch blades and wooden handles. Harry had that expectant look in his eyes, hoping for news.

'You hear anything?'

'I was about to ask you,' Catlett said. 'There's been plenty of time to do it.'

He turned his head and there was Miguel the houseman asking what would he like to drink, this stoop-labor field hand, Catlett thinking Karen Flores must be a strange kind of lady.

'Let me have a glass of chilled white wine. Some Pouilly-Fuissé, you happen to have it in the house.'

Harry said, 'Well, I guess he ran with it.'

Harry sounding tired out, depressed.

'Or, as I mentioned could happen if he wasn't careful,' Catlett said, 'somebody hit him on the head. Or, there's the chance he got busted.'

'What he got was the money,' Harry said. 'I called his hotel. They said he checked out.'

'He could've done that before.'

'I spoke to him at ten this morning. He was just leaving.'

'That's right, that's what I heard.'

From the Bear, phoning as he tailed him, the Bear in communication up to that time.

'He didn't check out,' Harry said, ''till two-thirty this afternoon.'

Catlett said, 'Hmmmmm,' to Harry, nothing to Miguel, noticing the man's broken fingernails, big knuckles, handing him the glass of wine; or when Miguel said he was leaving, going home, and walked out the back door to the garage.

Harry looked so depressed he seemed in a daze.

'I didn't think he'd do it. I said to him, "I wonder if I'll ever see you again." But I honestly thought I would.'

Catlett sat down with Harry at the table wondering why, if Chili Palmer was going to run with it, he didn't take a flight out while he was at the airport. Why come back to the hotel? The Bear would have the answer if he could ever locate the Bear.

'Harry, you can't trust nobody like that, has those bad connections. This man come in off the street, nobody speaking for him, you don't know who he is.'

'He was working for Mesas. I know the people there and they know him. They use him for collections.'

'They know the guy that takes out the garbage too. Harry. How'd he find you right away if I couldn't?'

'Through Frank DePhillips.'

'Man, what does that tell you? What you're saying to me right there?'

'I was staying here that night . . .'

'Yeah, with Karen?'

'We're in bed, we hear a noise. Voices. We listen awhile. It's the TV, downstairs. Karen says, "But it can't just come on by itself." I tell her, "That's right, somebody had to push the button." So I go down . . .'

'You have a gun?'

'Where do I get a gun? Karen doesn't own one. No, I went downstairs figuring it has to be somebody she knows. Some friend of hers probably stoned, thinks he's a riot. I walk in the study, the TV goes off – it was the Letterman show – the light comes on and there's Chili sitting at the desk.'

'Chili Palmer,' Catlett said, 'yeah. Sneaky, huh? You should've known right then, just from the way he does things. Man breaks in the house . . .'

'The patio door was open.'

'Yeah? Was there a sign on it, "Come on in"? Harry, you walk in where you don't belong it's breaking and entering, whether you have to break in or not. Chili Palmer commits a felony against the law and you take him in, make him your partner.'

'He isn't my partner,' Harry said, and took a drink from his glass. 'I don't know what he is.'

That was okay as far as it went. But what Catlett wanted would be for Harry to kick and scream, call the man names. A no-good lying motherfucker would cover it. Harry though, for some reason, didn't seem all the way unsold yet on Chili Palmer. So Catlett reset his gold-frame sunglasses and went at him again saying, 'The man robs you and you tell me you don't know what he *is*? If he managed to get his hands on the hundred and seventy thousand and took off with it . . . Harry, you paying attention?'

'Yeah, if he got it, what?'

'Or, if he messed up out there and *they* got it, but

229

somehow or other they didn't get *him* . . . What I'm saying is either way, Harry, it was your money. You understand? Soon as I presented you with the key to the locker it was the same as giving you the money. So you the one he ripped off, huh?'

Harry was looking at him with a frown turning all of a sudden from worried to mean.

'You're saying I still owe it to you? A hundred and seventy grand I haven't even *seen*?'

It wasn't the point Catlett had intended to make. Yeah, but it was true. He opened his hands, helpless, and said to Harry, 'Man, you owe me *some*thing.'

Karen had given him a key to the front door, in case her houseman had already left.

Chili dropped his suitcase in the foyer, checked the study, the living room, then moved down the back hall to the kitchen. He knew Harry's car, could guess who the Porsche belonged to and got it right – Mr Bo Catlett in the kitchen with Harry, Catlett looking this way through his hotdog sunglasses. It was in Chili's mind to grab a frying pan from the rack, go over the table with it and whop him across the head. Right now, not say a word. But he was no sooner in the kitchen Catlett was on his feet, Christ, holding a pair of shears in front of him. Chili said, 'You knew I was coming, huh?' looking at the shears, the blades gunmetal, clamped together. 'The Bear tell you?'

He wanted Catlett to answer, keep it between them and settle with this guy. But now Harry got into it, Harry again, ruining the moment.

'I don't know how many times I tried to call you,' Harry said. 'Where've you been?'

'Talking to federal agents,' Chili said, still looking at Catlett. 'DEA, the ones were waiting for me.'

'They let you go?' Harry said.

'It didn't take too long.'

Catlett said, 'Uh-huh. Harry, you understand what he saying? If he was talking to federal agents, how come he's here talking to us?'

Chili said, 'I didn't have the key on me.'

Catlett said, 'You didn't have the key . . .' and let his voice trail off. 'All right, why would they pick you up then, if you didn't have the key?'

'They thought I opened the locker.'

'But you didn't?'

'Ask the Bear, he saw it.'

'Is that right? You talk to him?'

'After. He wanted me to give him back the key,' Chili said, and watched Catlett take that and run with it.

'Sure, 'cause I told him, anything goes wrong, see if you can help out. Like take the key off your hands, case you get followed and picked up again they won't find it on you.' Looking at Harry: 'I told you it could happen, didn't I? That's why I said don't you go out there, send your man here.' Looking at Chili again. 'You know what I'm talking about. You experienced in shit where you have to keep your eyes open. Was I wrong? If you still have the key, what's the problem? Wait for it to cool and try again. Only be more careful next time.'

Chili said, 'That's all you have to say?'

Catlett frowned in his sunglasses, 'I don't see what the problem is.'

'I told you, they were waiting for me.'

'You're the type they go for, man. I can't help it how you look.'

This guy was not only sure of himself, he was starting to get cocky, insulting even. Chili fingered the button holding his double-breasted jacket closed. He said, 'I'll make you a deal. If you can get out of here before I take my coat off, I

231

won't clean the floor with you, get your yacht-club outfit all messed up.'

Catlett shook his head, acting tired. He said, 'Harry, you hear this?'

'Harry, stay out of it. This's between me and him,' Chili said, undoing the button to let the jacket come open. He said to Catlett, 'You have your choice.'

'You don't know me,' Catlett said, his voice quiet now. 'You only think you do.'

'I know if I wanted to,' Chili said, 'I could take those shears away from you and cut your nuts off. You want to stay around, take a chance?'

'I think the party's getting rough,' Catlett said. 'Harry, this make any sense to you?'

'It will, when I tell him how they knew I was coming,' Chili said, holding the coat open now to slip it off his shoulders. 'You want to add something to that? Ask me how I found out?'

Catlett shrugged, keeping whatever he felt about it to himself, behind his sunglasses. He said, 'What's the difference? I'm not gonna get into it with you,' and laid the shears on the table. 'This kind of shit is not my style.' He moved to the door saying, 'Whatever is, huh, Harry? But you still need all kinds of money, don't you?' and walked out of the kitchen, into the hall.

Chili reached across the table to pick up the glass of wine, ice-cold on the tips of his fingers, and took a sip, Harry watching him.

'What it comes down to after all that, you didn't get the money.'

Chili stood listening till he heard the front door close.

'There's more to it, Harry.'

'But you still have the key?'

232

'There's a lot more to it,' Chili said, pulling a chair out from the table.

Turning out of Karen's drive, Catlett was busy handling all the stuff flashing in his head at once. He had to talk to the Bear, find out before he did anything else what happened at the airport, where the key was, how Chili Palmer knew he was informed on unless he was lying, telling Harry stories now, except the only good thing about it was Harry needed money more than he needed Chili Palmer, but Chili Palmer still had to be removed from the situation. There was something else flashing in his head, that suitcase . . . And Catlett had to crank the wheel, quick, waking up to the BMW turning in directly in front of him. The cars came side by side, the windows going down, the woman's face in the BMW a bit higher than his. Catlett put his sunglasses up on his head. He smiled, seeing late sun reflected in her sunglasses, not smiling. He said, 'Miss Flores, this is my pleasure. Harry Zimm might've mentioned my name to you. Bo Catlett?'

She kept looking, though her face didn't change.

So he said, 'Can I tell you I've always been one of your biggest fans?'

Her face still didn't change as she said, 'What're you doing here?'

He said, 'I was with Harry,' acting a little surprised on account of her tone. 'We had a meeting.'

Her face *still* didn't change, this time saying to him, 'If I ever see you here again I'll call the police.'

The BMW was there and then it wasn't and he was looking at shrubs. Man. Whatever the woman had heard about him couldn't have been too good. Like Chili Palmer had been talking to her. Already today, with everything going on he had taken the time. Came back from the airport, checked out of his hotel . . . And there was that other thing that had flashed in his head to think about, the black nylon suitcase sitting in her front hall by the door.

The suitcase hadn't been there before Chili Palmer came.

Checked out of the hotel and was moving in with Karen Flores. Sure, the one he wanted in the movie as the girl. Checked out in case the DEA people wanted to look him up again and came here to hide. Which presented new possibilities, didn't it? Catlett drove down the hill thinking of some, deciding which one he might use. The one he liked best was the simplest. Shoot the motherfucker and have it done.

For a few moments he wasn't aware of her standing in the doorway.

Karen watched him sitting alone at the table. Saw the bottle of Scotch, the garden shears, saw him raise his glass of wine and take a sip. He had a cigarette going too. She watched him draw on the cigarette and raise his head to exhale a thin stream of smoke. Karen the camera again watching him, this guy who had told her in a matter-of-fact way federal agents might pick him up and he might have to post bond. . . She wanted to know what happened while Catlett was here. Where was Harry and why the garden shears? She had questions to ask and something amazing to tell him – Chili Palmer in his pinstripe suit, tough guy from Miami. Not a movie tough guy, a real one. She kept watching him with her camera eye wondering if, real or not, he could be acting. If he was, he was awfully good.

'Not a worry in the world,' Karen said.

He looked over. 'Hey, how you doing?'

'You really aren't worried, are you?'

He said, 'About what?'

And she had to smile because that was an act, the bland

expression. But he wasn't serious about it, he was smiling now and that seemed natural.

'Where's Harry?'

'I think he's in the bathroom. He didn't say where he was going, but that'd be my guess.'

She said, 'Catlett was here? . . .'

'Yeah, did you see him?'

'I almost ran into him, on his way out.'

'I think basically he's all the way out now,' Chili said. 'I explained the whole thing to Harry, told him if he ever saw the guy again he oughta have his brain looked at. Harry kept nodding, yeah, he understood, till I got to the part, Bones walking out with the locker key? He hasn't said a word to me since.'

'He does that,' Karen said, 'he pouts.'

She wondered again about the shears, but was more anxious to tell him the latest amazing development.

'Meanwhile, back at the studio, Elaine spoke to Michael . . .'

Right away Chili said, 'Hey, where's Harry?' looking toward the door. 'He's got to hear this.'

'He wants to meet with *you*,' Karen said. 'He didn't mention Harry.'

She kept her eyes on Chili, who didn't say anything now, staring at her as she sat down across the table from him.

'You told Michael about the drycleaner and the shylock.'

'That's what he wants to talk about?'

'And he told Elaine it was the best pitch he's ever heard. Now Elaine wants to hear it.'

'Yeah, but it wasn't a pitch. He was pretending he was a shylock, wondering what it'd be like. So I gave him a situation, that's all.'

'He wants to have dinner with you this evening, at Jimmy's. That is,' Karen said, watching him, 'if you can make it.'

He said, 'Is it a nice place?' with his bland look, eyebrows raised.

And she said, 'You think it's funny. You *do*. But you're going to meet with him, aren't you?'

'It depends,' Chili said. 'Who pays?'

'You don't have a script. You have the beginning of an idea that doesn't go anywhere . . .'

'I've added to it. There's a girl in it now.'

'Yeah – and what happens? What's the *story*?'

'You mean what's the theme? I'm still thinking about the visual fabric, as they say.'

'I can't believe you're serious.'

'The guy wants to talk – I know how to do that. But Harry has to be there too.'

'Or you won't meet with him?'

'Why's it have to be like that? Get his permission. Harry comes along, he's there, right? What's Michael gonna do, tell him to leave? We'll talk about *Lovejoy*, bring it up, see what happens. If Michael says no, Harry'll have a chance to argue with him. He won't blame me if the guy doesn't want to do it.'

'You're serious,' Karen said.

'I don't see what's the big deal.'

'Right, it's only a movie.' She had to smile at him. 'Fifteen years in Hollywood . . . I'd give anything to be there.'

'You can come. Why not?'

She was shaking her head as Harry walked in and Chili said, 'Michael called. He wants to meet.'

'Well, it's about time,' Harry said.

Karen shook her head again, this time slowly, in amazement. Harry, pouring himself a Scotch, didn't notice. But Chili did. He gave her his innocent look, with the eyebrows.

25

When he asked Karen if it was a nice place he was kidding and she never said, or told him who was supposed to pay. As soon as they walked in through the dark cocktail lounge area, Chili knew dinner for three would run at least a hundred bucks with wine.

He and Harry were taken to a table in the middle of the front section, eight-thirty, the restaurant crowded. Michael had made the reservation, but didn't show up till after nine. Then it took him about ten minutes to get to the table, stopping off to say hello to people sticking their hands out at him, Michael pleasant about it, smiling at everybody. Like Momo coming into a joint on 86th Street, getting the treatment. Only Momo would have a suit on, as most of the guys did here; Michael was wearing his World War Two flight jacket with a dark T-shirt under it.

As soon as he sat down at the table he looked at their drinks, ordered a Perrier and then started fanning the air in front of him.

'Would you guys mind terribly not smoking?'

Harry stubbed his cigarette out in a hurry saying of course not, he was trying to quit anyway. Chili took another drag on his and blew it out past the empty chair at the table, toward the entrance to the room where a little guy with dark shiny hair was standing there looking around as the maître d' hurried up to him, the maître d' giving him the same treatment he had given Michael, though the guy was not a movie star or Chili would have known Him. Chili believed ninety percent of the guys in Hollywood had dark hair and looking around the room confirmed it. What he saw was a lot of hair, dark hair on the guys, different shades of blond hair on the women; older guys with younger women, girls, which was what he had expected. He observed this as Michael was saying that, according to a study he read, smokers exercised less than nonsmokers, were not as likely to use seat belts, were more prone to argue, missed work more often than nonsmokers, and were two-point-two times more likely to be dissatisfied with their lives, not to mention they were two-point-six times more likely to have bronchitis and emphysema.

Harry was saying, 'They made a study, huh? Gee, that's interesting, I'd like to read it,' as the maître d' was looking this way now and the little guy with the dark shiny hair was coming to the table. Chili noticed he had on a dark-gray shirt and tie with a dark-gray sport coat and light-gray pants that looked like pajamas. Drab colors, but the guy still had a shiny appearance. He pulled out the empty chair and sat down. A waiter tried to push his chair in and the guy waved him away, turning the chair and hunching toward Michael, his back to Chili. As this was happening Michael said, 'Buddy—' sounding a little surprised.

So this was Michael's agent.

Buddy was supposed to know Harry, but didn't even glance at him. He started right in with, 'They want you to take a meeting with this producer they keep talking about. You believe it? The guy's a fucking *writer*, I mean he writes *books*, not even screenplays, but he wants this broad as the producer. I never heard of this in my life.'

'I want the property,' Michael said.

'Don't worry about it, you'll get the property. I said to the

238

guy's agent, "The fuck *is* this, you trying to hold a gun to my head? We have to take the broad?" Which is out of the question. I said, "What if there's no communication between she and Michael? What's she made, three pictures?" One did okay, the other two barely earned back negative costs.'

'I want that book,' Michael said.

'Michael, you'll get the book, soon as we get done with this pissing contest. If it was a director – yeah, I can understand he's got a producer he likes to work with. But this is a fucking *writer*. I said to his agent, "Hey, Michael doesn't *have* to option this book, you know." And the agent goes, "And we don't have to sell it." I go, "Well, what the fuck is the guy writing for, he doesn't want to sell his work?" You ever hear anything like that?'

'You have to understand his motivation,' Michael said. 'A writer can spend years working on a book he isn't sure will ever sell. What makes him do it?'

'Money. The idea of hitting big,' Buddy said. 'Selling one to Michael Weir. What else? Look, what we do, we say okay to the meeting. The broad arrives, we ask her to wait a minute, be right with you. I call the guy's agent and I say, "Do we have a deal? Come on, we have a deal or not? We don't have a deal, I'm sending the broad home." Put it to them like that, I guarantee you within five minutes we'll have a deal.'

Chili watched Michael playing with a book of matches that would never be used for lighting cigarettes, Michael saying, 'How you handle it is up to you.'

Buddy said, 'I'll give you a call.'

Getting up he seemed to notice Harry for the first time, Harry waiting to be recognized, Harry saying, 'Buddy, how you doing?' The agent nodded, said yeah, great. Chili watched him glance this way now – like, what, another one? Where'd these guys come from? Michael didn't tell him. He said one more time he wanted that book. Buddy told him it was his, and left.

Harry said, 'Well now . . .'

But there was something Chili wanted to know and he said to Michael, 'What he mentioned to you there . . . You mind my asking – what if the other agent says okay, you got a deal? Then will you have the meeting with the woman, the producer?'

'I don't know, I suppose,' Michael said, 'we'd talk to her. I'm not really involved in this.'

Harry said, 'Chil, it has nothing to do with Michael.'

And now Michael was nodding. 'All it amounts to is a power play, the dance of the agents, circling each other for position.'

'With the woman in the middle,' Chili said, 'not knowing what's going on. I was thinking she's sitting there like a hostage. Use her to get what you want.'

'Hey, come on, man. All I want is a book.'

'They say no deal, what do you do, shoot her?'

Chili smiled.

Michael didn't.

He said, 'Why is everybody giving me a hard time?'

It was dark and Catlett still hadn't spoken to the Bear. Had been calling him since coming home and getting no answer, the Bear's machine turned off. Right now Catlett was standing out on his deck looking at the night, trying to get his head to settle.

Looking at the view he started thinking about his great-great-grandfather with the cavalry sword, because that original Bo Catlett had lived on a mountain and must've had a view of his own, but without any lit-up swimming pools and girls laughing or, tonight, the cool sound of Jobim coming from down there. The original Bo Catlett had his view, had his sword, had his squaw wife – but what did he *do*? This Catlett's grandmother said, that time before she died, 'Oh, he had plenty to do,' but never said what. So this Catlett started thinking of western movies, wondering what people outside of cowboys did back then. They lived in little towns that had one street, wore six-guns and were always crossing the street going someplace, the extras in the movies. The stuntmen were always getting shot off of horses or off of roofs or falling through the railings on upstairs porches and balconies. Fall against the railing shot and it would give way every time, like the carpenters of the Old West didn't know shit about putting up railings. Bump against a railing shot, man, you're going through it . . .

And here he was leaning against a railing himself, his head having come all the way around a hundred years back to now.

You could bump against this railing all you wanted. It was California redwood, bolted together, built solid. The drop was about the same as looking down from a hotel room on the twelfth floor he had stayed in one time. If you fell through like in a movie, you wouldn't come close to that swimming pool. You'd hit on the slope partway down and from there it would be like falling down stairs, only you'd land in the scrub and shit where the coyotes hid. . . Seeing this and thinking, Invite Chili Palmer out here.

Thinking, I don't know why, Officer, but it just give way on him.

Catlett picked up the phone from a deck chair, punched a number for about the twentieth time today and got him. *Damn*. The Bear's voice came on and Catlett said, 'How you doing this evening?' having decided hours ago to be cool with the Bear, save his emotions.

'The guy faked them out,' the Bear said.

'This Chili Palmer you speaking of? I *know* that much.'

'You see on the news the drug bust at LAX? They picked up a guy from Miami. Alleged member of organized crime.'

'You watching the news?' Catlett said. 'What else? Watch some sitcoms 'stead of calling me?'

'I had to take Farrah to Costa Mesa, to her mother's. She had the news on and that's when I saw it. Then I had to stay a while and visit, talk about how I'm always late with the check. I got back, I had to eat I figured you'd have talked to Harry, found out what happened. But I didn't actually give a shit if you did or not. I don't work for you no more, or Ronnie. I quit.'

Catlett said, 'This the man use to jump offa high buildings talking?'

'Into air bags,' the Bear said. 'There's no cushion under what you're doing. I got responsibilities, I got Farrah to think about.'

'You always had Farrah. Took her on buys with you.'

'I'm out of it. Cat. Ronnie picked up two keys for Palm Desert. I'll drop off the rest tomorrow morning and I'm done.'

'Been giving it serious thought, huh?'

'All the way down to Costa Mesa and back.'

'How 'bout we talk about it tomorrow? Tonight, later on, I got one for you doesn't involve any heavy work. Chili Palmer's staying with that woman, Karen? I need you to get me in the house.'

'I'm already an accessory on one count,' the Bear said. 'You want to get in, bust a window.'

'I'm thinking she might have an alarm system.'

'Good, so don't do it.'

'Something happened to you, huh? Like that tumble down the stairs shook you up.'

'Or straightened me out,' the Bear said. 'It's different. It isn't like a stunt gag, you're ready, you know what's gonna

242

happen. This guy doesn't fool around, he comes right at you. You talked to him, yeah, but you don't know him.'

Catlett said, 'Uh-huh,' and said, 'Bear, I had an idea. Listen to this.'

Making it sound as though he was starting over and they were still friends.

'You get your saw – no, get your wrench, and fix my deck railing to give way like they do in movies. You know what I'm saying? Like when the guy gets hit he falls against it and it gives way on him? All you do is loosen the bolts that hold the upright part of the rail to the deck. So then I invite Chili Palmer out here to look at my view. Get him to lean over the railing, see what's down there . . . Huh? What you think?'

'This isn't a movie. Cat. This guy's real.'

'It could be done though. Sure, loosen some bolts. I can see it . . . Except how would I get him out here? So I better go in the woman's house and do him. You helping me.'

There was a silence on the line before the Bear said, 'I'm not gonna do it.'

'You sure?'

'I told you, I quit.'

'I hate being alone, Bear.'

'That's too fucking bad.'

'I hate it so much, man, if I go down I'll plea-deal you in. Give 'em this ace burglar now one of the West Coast dope kings, if they go easy on the Cat. You dig? Tell 'em where you live, where you keep the product, all that shit they love to hear.'

There was that silence again. This time all the Bear said was 'Why?' in a quiet tone of voice.

' 'Cause I'm a mean motherfucker,' Catlett said. 'Why you think?' and hung up the phone.

It was fun playing with the Bear, putting fear in a man his size. Now forget him. He hadn't needed the Bear to do Yayo

243

or the gas station man in Bakersfield or the fools he did over business, the one in his car waiting at a light, the other one on his front steps. He didn't sit down and *plan* doing those people. He saw the need and did them. Do this one the same way and don't think so much, worrying if there was an alarm system in the house. Harry said Chili Palmer had come in the house at night. He didn't say nothing about any alarm system going off. Chili Palmer had come in the house and turned the TV on and Harry had to go downstairs being the man, but without a gun, 'cause there wasn't a gun in the house, was there?

It took Harry about two minutes to decide on the Norwegian salmon – anxious to talk, get things going – and another Scotch. Chili kept reading the menu while Michael told them about the curious negative influence his father became in motivating his career. Harry was willing to bet Chili, after all the time he spent on the menu, would order a steak; and he did, the filet rare, baked potato, house salad, the soup, a half-dozen bluepoints and, yeah, another Scotch. But Michael wasn't finished telling about his dad, this tyrant who manu-factured hairpieces and wanted his sonny to follow him in the rug trade, the head-waiter standing by. Then Michael had to look at the menu for a while, Harry willing to bet anything he wouldn't order from it. It was an unwritten rule in Hollywood, actors never ordered straight from the menu; they'd think of something they had to have that wasn't on it, or they'd tell exactly how they wanted the entree prepared, the way their mother back in Queens used to fix it. The seven-million dollar actor in the jacket a bum wouldn't wear told the headwaiter he felt like an omelet, hesitant about it, almost apologetic. Could he have a cheese omelet with shallots, but with the shallots only slightly browned? The headwaiter said yes, of course. Then could he have some

244

kind of light tomato sauce over it with just a hint of garlic but, please, no oregano? Of course. And fresh peas in the tomato sauce? Harry wanted to tell him, Michael, you can have any fucking thing you want. You want boiled goat? They'll send out for it if they don't have one. Jesus, what you had to go through with actors. The ideal situation would be if you could make movies without them.

'What fascinates me about this one,' Michael said, 'is the chance to play an essentially cliché-type character in a way that's never been done before, against his accepted image.'

Harry liked the sound of that. He wished he could light up, so he could enjoy it more. Chili, busy eating ice cream, might or might not be paying attention.

'It's not unlike the way I saw Bonaparte in *Elba*,' Michael said. 'The script had him morose, dour, bound by his destiny to play the tragic figure. I thought, yeah, that's the portrait we've all seen, with the hand shoved inside his coat. But why were his troops so loyal? Why were they willing to follow this neurotic guy, with the original Napoleon complex, to hell and back time after time, until finally Waterloo?'

Harry thinking, *To Hell and Back*, Audie Murphy, about 1955.

As Michael said, 'What I did was separate the man from the historic figure, visualize a dichotomy, imagine him off-stage making love, getting drunk, generally kicking back . . .' Michael grinned. 'No pun intended.'

Harry didn't get it.

'And you know what? I saw him rather impish in his off moments. Maybe because he was a little guy and I had to play him that way. I saw him childlike with a love of life, a mischievous glow. I have him telling jokes, mimicking his generals, I do one like a French Howard Cosell. I drink wine, smoke hash and giggle, I moon Josephine a couple of times

in the film . . . Anyway it's this human side that my grena-
diers sense, the reason they love *me*, not the historic figure,
and are willing to die for me.'

'Sure,' Harry said, 'you bring out that human side you've
got the audience empathizing with you.'

Chili said, 'Why'd he put his hand in his coat like that?'

'It was a fashionable way to pose,' Michael said. 'And
that's what I'm talking about. There's the pose of the character, as most people see him, and there's the real person
who laughs and cries and makes love. I think the romance
angle in our story is critically important, that it isn't simply a
jump in the sack for either of them. These two become
deeply in love. There's even a certain reverence about it, the
way they fuck. Do you know what I mean? And it's totally in
contrast to the guy's accepted character.'

'From the way he appears in the beginning,' Harry said.

Michael didn't even glance over. He went on saying to
Chili – no doubt because Chili had spoken to him about it
that other time – 'Once their lives are in danger and you have
the mob guy coming after them, it not only heightens tension, it adds a wistful element to their love. Now, because
they have more to live for, they also have more to lose.'

Harry said. 'The mob guy?'

Michael, the typical actor, onstage, ignored that one too. A
simple, honest question, for Christ sake.

'I also have to consider, I mean as the character, this is
another man's wife I'm sleeping with. I know the guy's a
schmuck, he's a sneak . . . By the way, what does he do?'

'He's an agent,' Chili said, 'and his wife, he handles, is a
rock-and-roll singer.'

Michael nodded. 'Like Nicki. I like that. I don't mean for
the part, but a character like her.'

Harry stared at Chili now, Chili eating his ice cream and

246

refusing to look over this way, Chili telling Michael, 'We're still working on the ending.'

Michael said, 'You are?' sounding surprised. 'I thought you were bringing the script.'

'You have the first draft,' Harry said, wanting to start over, make some sense out of this. 'The one you read I sent to your house?'

He saw Michael shaking his head with that surprised look and Chili saying right away, 'Basically it's the ending has to be fixed, but there some other parts too.' The hell was he talking about? Now Michael was looking at his watch.

'Elaine wants us to come by tomorrow, sometime in the afternoon. How does that sound?'

Harry saw Chili nodding, so he nodded.

'I have to run,' Michael said. 'But what I hope to see, they begin to have misgivings about wanting the money. It becomes their moral dilemma and they try to rationalize keeping it, but in the end they can't.' Looking at Chili the whole time. 'Can they?'

'Which money,' Harry said, 'are we talking about?'

That got Michael's attention, finally, but with a kind of bewildered look on his face. 'The three hundred large. What other money is there? I'm not being facetious, I'm asking, since I haven't read the script. I think their idea, ultimately, would be to let the husband keep it, knowing he'll get caught sooner or later. No, wait.' Michael paused. 'The mob guy gets to the husband first, the agent, and whacks him, knocks him off. But he doesn't have the money. Somehow the lovers have gotten hold of it. We see it piled on a bed. Make it a million – why not? The mob guy, who scares hell out of the audience, is closing in but the lovers don't know it. So now you've got the big scene coming up. But just before it happens . . . Well, it could be after, either way, but it's the shylock who makes the decision, they can't keep it.'

247

Harry said. 'The *Shylock*?'

Michael turned to him saying, 'Look at me, Harry.'

Harry was already looking at him.

Now Chili was saying. 'That's not bad. I think you got it down.'

Harry turned to Chili and back to Michael again.

'Jesus Christ, you mean all this time . . .'

But Michael wasn't listening. He was getting up from the table saying, 'I should keep quiet, I know, till I've read the script, but I've got a feeling about this one. I'm that shylock. Really, it scares me how well I know him. I could do this one tomorrow, no further preparation.'

'What am I thinking?' Chili said.

Michael grinned at him. 'Well, I might need a week to get ready. But I'll see you tomorrow, right? At Tower.' He started to go, paused and said, 'Chil, work on that moral dilemma. Harry? Remember that time you turned me down for *Slime Creatures*? I'm glad you did. I might've gotten typecast.'

Michael table-hopped and touched hands all the way out. Harry watched him before turning to Chili.

'All that time he's talking about your movie.'

Chili nodded.

'That's what we came for?'

Chili nodded.

'You told Michael about your movie when you saw him that time? You never talked about *Lovejoy*?'

Chili finished his ice cream. He said, 'Harry,' getting his cigarettes out, 'let's light up and have an after-dinner drink. What do you say?'

26

Karen was waiting for him. He saw her coming away from the front steps in a heavy-knit white sweater as he got out of the car. They walked around to the patio side of the house and over to the swimming pool that was like a pond with a clear bottom, leaves, dark shapes on the surface, Chili telling about the dinner with Michael, most of what happened, and finally asking her, 'Guess who paid?'

Karen said that, first of all, high-priced actors never picked up the check. They had no idea what things cost. They seldom knew their zip code and quite often didn't know their own phone number. Especially guys who changed the number every time they dumped a girlfriend. Telling him this quietly in the dark. He felt they could be in a woods far away from any people or sounds or lights, unless you looked at the house and saw dim ones in some of the windows. They could have walked in the house when he got out of the car, but she was waiting for him with the idea of coming out here. It told him they were going to end up in bed before too long. He wasn't sure how he knew this, other than being alone in the dark seemed to set the mood, the idea of moonlight and a nice smell in the air, except the moon was pretty much clouded over. Her waiting for him outside was the tip-off. He didn't ask himself why she wanted to go to bed with him. It never entered his mind.

'So who paid, you or Harry?'

'I did.'

'You felt sorry for him.'

'Well, yeah, maybe. Twice in one day I have to explain something where he's already made up his mind I'm trying to stick him. Michael left, we sat there another hour and talked. You know what his omelet cost?'

'Twenty bucks?'

'Twenty-two-fifty.'

'And he ate maybe half of it,' Karen said.

'Not even that. The whole shot came to two and a quarter, with the tip, and we didn't have any wine.'

'Harry went home?'

'Yeah, feeling sorry for himself. I said to him, "This wasn't my idea, I didn't call it. If you wanted to ask him about *Lovejoy*, why didn't you?" Harry says, "What, follow him out to the parking lot?" Harry had a point. Michael does all the talking and then he's gone, never mentioned the check. You know, at least offered. No – see you tomorrow at the meeting. Now I either have to make up something quick or forget the whole thing. Or let him do it. Michael knows more about it than I do anyway. All the time at dinner he's telling me how it should work: that the love part should be important and how he wants to play the shylock as a nice guy – like people don't mind paying him a hunnerd and fifty percent interest. You know what I'm saying?'

'That's what Michael does,' Karen said. 'He turns the story around to suit himself and then walks away. The shylock becomes a brain surgeon. The drycleaner – who knows?'

'I'm thinking of making him an agent,' Chili said, 'and his wife, Fay, a rock-and-roll singer. It's a little different'n what I told you and Harry. She comes here with the shylock and they fall in love looking for Leo. Also there's a mob guy that's after them.'

Karen stopped and turned to him. 'His name Ray Bones?'

'Yeah, but I think I'll change it. I don't want to get sued. I've had enough of Ray Bones to last me the rest of my life.'

They started walking again, strolling toward the house. Karen's shoulders hunched in the bulky sweater, hands shoved into the sleeves. She said, 'What about Catlett?'

'He's not in it.'

She said, 'Are you sure? You have an idea for a movie based on something that actually happened, but now you're beginning to fictionalize. Which is okay, like bringing Fay into it more . . .'

Chili said, 'After I saw that's what *Lovejoy* needed.'

'That's fine – but what exactly are you keeping and what are you throwing away?'

'Well, if I have Bones as the bad guy, what do I need Catlett for? It's not about making a movie, it's about getting your hands on money without getting killed. Or it's about a moral dilemma, as Michael says. If they do get their hands on the money, can they keep it? Michael says no.'

'So you resolve that,' Karen said. 'You have action, suspense, romance, good characters . . . You have that wonderful scene with Bones in the hotel room. He takes the locker key and you set him up.' She paused and said, 'It's cool the way it works, but you can't end the picture with it. What happens next, at the airport, is offstage. But if it did play as a scene you wouldn't be in it.'

'You mean the shylock.'

Karen said, 'Yeah, right,' thinking of something else. 'What you might do is play the hotel room scene with Leo instead of Bones – it's too good to throw away. Leo finds the key, leaves to pick up the money and you call the DEA.'

'I wouldn't do that.'

'But you did.'

'Yeah, to Bones. I wouldn't do it to Leo.'

She said, 'Well . . . I don't know. I like Catlett as a

251

character, if you could use him somehow. Doesn't he fit into this at all?'

'He's Harry's problem.'

'Isn't Harry in it?'

'I left that part out, the shylock looking for him.'

He thought of Catlett again. He thought of the Bear, the Bear falling down the restaurant stairs, but didn't see how he could use that either.

Karen said, 'I wouldn't throw anything away just yet,' as they reached the patio and she turned to him. She looked cold, hugging herself with her hands in the sweater sleeves. 'What're you going to call it, *Chili's Hollywood Adventure*?'

'That's a different story. I like it, though, so far.'

She said, 'What happens next?'

He said, 'I'm ready if you are.'

He'd open his eyes and she'd be watching him, the first time smiling, and he remembered her telling him Michael said funny things. Then she'd close her eyes and he'd close his, moving with her, all the time moving, and he'd open his eyes and she'd be looking at him again, face-to-face in the lamp-light She was feeling it, not just going through the motions, he could tell by her face, a certain look around her nose and mouth that was almost a snarl, but her eyes would still be looking: like she was riding a bike with no hands to look at something she was holding, doing two different things at once: her body turned on and having a good time, but her mind still working on its own, watching, until her eyes glazed over and it became more the way it usually was in those final moments of hanging on, no time to think or do anything but ride it out. She opened her eyes with kind of a dreamy look, thoughtful, and said it was like falling back-wards . . . a time you could let go knowing you were safe. He wondered if she analyzed everything she did and had been

252

watching, before, to see her effect on him. When Karen left the bed, went into the bathroom and came back a few minutes later, he got to see all of her at once – a picture he now had for life – before she turned the lamp off and got back in bed.

Chili had his arm ready in case Karen wanted to snuggle in, as they usually did after, but she stayed on her side and was quiet. They were alone in a different kind of dark now that they'd made love, a dark for sleeping. He thought, Okay, fine. Though had expected there would be a little more to it. It surprised him when she said, lying there in the dark, 'I've been watching you.'

'I noticed that.'

'I think you could be an actor. I know you're acting sometimes, but you don't show it.'

'You thought I was faking?'

'No, I don't mean *then*.'

'What was I doing? I was auditioning?'

'We made love,' Karen said, 'Because we wanted to. That was the only reason.'

'Yeah, but you were watching.'

'For a minute.'

'A *minute* – it was a lot longer'n that.'

'Why're you getting mad? I say I think you could be an actor, you take it the wrong way.'

'I don't like being watched.'

'That could be a problem.'

'Why would it?'

'If you want to act.'

'I never said I did.'

'You don't want to, then don't.'

It was quiet for a minute or so.

'You don't mean become a movie star. More like a character actor.'

253

'Let's talk about it in the morning. I'm beat.'

'I ever made a movie, you know who'd go see it? My mother and my two aunts. Tommy, he'd go, for a laugh.'

Karen didn't say anything, meaning that was the end of it.

He could see himself in different movies Robert De Niro had been in. He could maybe do an Al Pacino movie, play a hard-on . . . He couldn't see himself in ones, like say the one where the three guys get stuck with a baby. They don't know how to take care of it and you see these big grown-up assholes acting cute. Put on a surprised look and that was as far as they could take it. People liked that cute shit, they went to see it. But, man, that would be hard, try and act cute.

What else could he play? Himself? The shylock?

No, he'd start trying to act like himself and it wouldn't work, because acting wasn't as easy as it looked. He knew that much. No, what he needed . . .

He heard Karen's voice in the dark say, 'I forgot to tell you. The Bear called.'

Chili said, 'Yeah?' even though for some reason he wasn't surprised. 'He say what he wanted?'

'He left a number.'

'I'll call him in the morning.'

The Bear could wait. What he needed to think about was an ending. And maybe a title. *Get Michael*. Except that wasn't the movie, that was real life. He kept getting the two mixed up, *Chili's Hollywood Adventure* and whatever the other one was . . .

He must have heard the sounds coming from downstairs, because something woke him up before he heard Karen say, 'Not again.' He turned over on his back and was looking at a faint square of light from the window reflected on the ceiling. Karen said, 'It's Harry, downstairs.' He could hear the sounds as faint voices now, a movie playing on the TV in the study. 'Harry pulling the same stunt on you,' Karen said. 'He was drinking, I'm sure of it, and got this wonderful idea.' He saw Karen sitting up, her face and breasts in profile. Another picture to keep. The clock on her side of the bed – seeing it behind her – said 4:36.

'If he was drinking all night . . .' Chili let the words trail off before saying, 'he'd be out of it, wouldn't he? How could he drive?'

'Ask him,' Karen said, 'he's waiting for you.'

She turned to fix her pillows, puff them up, and sunk back in the bed.

'If I know Harry he'll act surprised to see you. "Oh, did I wake you up? Gee, I'm sorry." What happened at dinner, well, not forgotten, but put aside. This is Harry the survivor. Sometime during the past five hours or so he realized that if his project is dead, he'd better quick get a piece of yours. He'll offer to take over as producer . . .'

'I don't know,' Chili said, wanting to listen for sounds, different ones than the TV.

But Karen kept talking.

'He'll get a writer, probably Murray, and handle all negotiations. He'll already have a plot idea and that's why he's here at four-thirty in the morning. He'll say he couldn't wait to tell you. But the real reason is he wants to be annoying. He still resents what he thinks you pulled on him, stealing Michael, and I know he doesn't like the idea of us being together . . .'

Telling him all that until he said, 'I don't think it's Harry.'

And that stopped Karen long enough for him to hear the TV again and what sounded like gunshots and that sharp whining sound of ricochets, bullets singing off rocks.

Karen said, 'If it isn't Harry . . .'

'I don't know for sure,' Chili said, 'and I hope I'm wrong

255

and you're right.' It was a western. He heard John Wayne's voice now. John Wayne talking to the West's most unlikely cowboy, Dean Martin. Getting out of bed he said to Karen, 'I think it's *Rio Bravo*.'

Catlett sat in the dark with the big-screen TV on loud the way Harry said Chili Palmer had done it; the difference was a movie instead of David Letterman and Ronnie's Hardballer .45 in his hand resting on the desk and pointed at the door part open. He believed the John Wayne movie was *El Dorado*, the big gunfight going on now with the sound turned up so high it was making him deaf, but he wanted Chili Palmer to hear it and come down thinking it was Harry paying him back. He'd checked to make sure Harry was home and not here and after so many rings he almost hung up, got Harry on the line slurring his words bad, the man almost all the way gone. He told Harry to go to bed before he fell down and hurt himself. All there was to do now was do it. Chili Palmer walks in the door – let him say something if he wanted, but don't say nothing back. Do him once, twice, whatever it took and leave the way he had come in, through the door on the patio he found unlocked.

He had waited this long so as not to be seen or run into by other cars on the street. Most went to bed early in this town, but some stayed out to party and drove home drunk when the bars closed or in a nod. Four A.M. was the quietest time. He had been here now since four-twenty. Shit. If Chili Palmer didn't come down in the next two minutes he'd have to go upstairs and find him.

Chili put on his pants and shoes, Karen watching him, and got out the Lakers T-shirt he'd bought at the airport to go with Karen's Lakers T-shirt if he got lucky. But when he did, when they came upstairs earlier and jumped in bed, he wasn't thinking of T-shirts. This one fit pretty well. Karen probably couldn't see what it was. He walked over to the bedroom door and stood listening. He was pretty sure the movie was *Rio Bravo*.

After about a minute Karen said, 'Are you going down?'

He turned to look at her.

'I don't know.'

She said, 'Then I will,' getting out of bed. 'You're as bad as Harry.'

He watched her pull on the bulky sweater and a pair of jeans. She looked about twenty. When she came over to the door he raised his hand and then laid it on her shoulder.

'What if it isn't Harry?'

'Someone else comes in and pulls exactly the same stunt?' She was calm about it. He liked that.

'I think Harry might've told Catlett, and that's who it is.'

She said, 'Oh.'

Maybe accepting it, he wasn't sure. 'Or it could be somebody Catlett sent. You don't have a gun, do you? Any kind would be fine.'

Karen shook her head. 'I could call the police.'

'Maybe you better. Or call Harry first, see if he's home.'

She moved past him to the bed, sat on the edge as she picked up the phone from the night table, punched Harry's number and waited. And waited. Karen shook her head. 'He's not home.'

'He could be asleep, passed out.'

'It's Harry,' Karen said, coming away from the bed. 'I'm sure. Paying you back.'

Maybe, though it wasn't Chili's idea of a payback, the kind that kept you looking over your shoulder waiting to happen. He wanted to believe Karen was right. It was Harry trying to be funny. She knew Harry a lot better than he did. He wanted so much to believe her that he said, 'Okay, I'll go. I'll sneak down the stairs.' He looked through the doorway to the big open area that reached from the foyer below at a high domed ceiling above the curved staircase and the upstairs landing. 'You stand over there by the railing, okay? You can see the door to the study. I don't want any surprises. You see anything at all, let me know.'

'How?' Karen said.

'I don't know, but I'll be watching you.'

Time to do it. Catlett got up from the desk with the big Hardballer ready to fire. He moved past the lit-up noisy screen where John Wayne and Dean Martin were snooting bad guys and ducking bullets singing off walls, the bad guys falling through those rickety porch railings. *El Dorado* was the name of it. Fine sound effects to go with what he was about to do. Loud, but not as loud as the Hardballer would be once he had it pointed at Chili Palmer. Catlett moved through the doorway into the front hall, heard his heels click on the tile and turned enough to face the stairway. He bent his head back to look at the upstairs railing that curved around the open part of the second floor and looked back at the stairway: did it quick to catch something dark there partway down, a shape against the light-colored wall. There was that moment he had to decide was it Chili Palmer or the woman and said Chili Palmer, though right then didn't care if he had to do them both, he was this far. Catlett raised the Hardballer to put it on the shape, got it almost aimed and a scream came at him out of the dark – a scream that filled the house and was all over him and he started firing before he was ready, firing as that scream kept screaming, firing at that shape dropping flat on the stairs, firing till that fucking scream turned him around without thinking and he ran down a hall to the back of the house and got out of there.

*

The first thing Karen said was, 'I haven't screamed in ten years,' amazed that she could still belt one out. Chili told her it was a terrific scream, she ought to be in the movies. The second thing she said was, 'We'd better call the police.' And he said, not yet, okay? But didn't say why.

Now they were downstairs: Karen waiting in the kitchen, lights on, the television off, Chili looking around outside. She watched him come in shaking his head and noticed his purple and gold T-shirt for the first time.

'You said last night the Bear called?'

She nodded toward the counter saying, 'The number's by the phone,' and watched him walk over and look at the notepad next to it. 'I have a T-shirt like that only it's white.'

He said, 'I know you do.'

'Is that why you got one?'

She watched him with the phone in his hand now punching numbers. He waited and said, 'Bear? Chili Palmer.' She watched him listen for several moments before he said, 'Yeah, well he tried. Tell me where he lives.' He listened and said, 'I'll find it.' Then listened again, longer, for at least a minute, and said, 'It's up to you,' and hung up.

'You didn't answer my question,' Karen said. 'Is that why you bought it?'

He said, 'I guess so,' and turned to walk out.

'You're going to Catlett's house – why?'

'I'm not gonna spend another twelve years waiting for something to fall on me.'

'What did the Bear want?'

'He's gonna meet me there.'

27

Catlett had put on Marvin Gaye to pick him up, Marvin Gaye's voice filling the house now with 'I'll Be Doggone.' No sun yet: barely starting to get light out on the deck.

This tape he was playing had all of Catlett's favorites on it gathered from other tapes and records. It had 'The Star-Spangled Banner' on it, Marvin Gaye doing our national anthem, and had 'Ain't No Mountain High Enough' he did with Tammi Terrell, deceased. Both of them now. Marvin Gaye, the Prince of Motown, shot dead by his own father in the hot moment of an argument, a pitiful waste . . . Catlett thinking, And you can't shoot a man *needs* to be done?

If it was the man, Chili Palmer, on the stairs and not the woman. Trying to decide which was what had thrown him off at the time and then the scream coming to finish the job, a scream like he hadn't heard since *Slime Creatures*, Karen Flores doing her famous scream, which meant it must have been Chili Palmer on the stairs and maybe he did hit him and the job was done, 'cause Chili Palmer had gone down, shot . . . Or had dropped down to get out of the way. All that had been in his head coming home, thinking Karen Flores would call the cops when she quit screaming. That was the reason he wiped the gun clean and almost chucked it in some weeds going up Laurel Canyon; but didn't.

Came home, put his car in the garage part of the house, ran inside and changed from his black race-car-driver coveralls to his white silk dressing gown, barefoot. Mussed up the bed, mussed up his hair and then combed it again, Marvin Gaye doing his 'Sexual Healing' now when he heard the car outside the front and thought of cops. He knew they couldn't have a court-signed search warrant this soon, so didn't worry about the gun; he went to the front window with a sleepy innocent expression ready. But it wasn't even a car. The headlights aimed at the house close went off and it was a van parked in the drive; the Bear getting out now, coming to the door with a suitcase.

Catlett let him in saying, 'You know what time it is?' What anybody would say.

'I want to get rid of this,' the Bear said, holding the Black Watch plaid suitcase Yayo had brought. 'I came by last night after you called me, but you weren't home, so I came in to leave this stuff,' the Bear said, talking all at once, 'but then I thought no, I better deliver it in person and you check what's in here. Less what Ronnie took out for Palm Desert.'

Catlett said, 'Wait now. You came in my house last night?'

'I just told you I did,' the Bear said.

This stove-up muscle-bound stuntman sounding arrogant. Catlett took it as strange. He said, 'Bear, why you talking to me like that? I thought you and I got along pretty good, never argued too much. I always considered you my friend, Bear.'

'I'm the one falls down the goddamn stairs,' the Bear said. 'But you take a fall, that other kind, and I go with you, huh? Well, I don't need a friend that bad.'

'What?' Catlett frowned at him. 'What I said on the phone to you? Man, I was putting you on is all. How'm I gonna scare you? I said, 'cause I was a mean motherfucker, right? When do I ever talk like that?'

'It's what you are, whether you say it or not,' the Bear said. 'I'll tell you right now, I don't fucking trust you. I want you

261

to look in this suitcase and see what's in it, so you don't say later on I took any.'

Catlett watched the Bear lay the bag on the floor and get down on his knees to zip it open.

'Eight keys,' the Bear said, 'right?'

'Right. You want a receipt?'

He watched the Bear zip the bag closed and said to him on the floor, 'Listen to Marvin Gaye doing "Ain't That Peculiar," Bear. Ain't it, though. You coming by this time of day, can't wait? How come you haven't asked me anything?'

Catlett watched the Bear get to his feet, the size of him rising up in that shirt full of flowers.

'You haven't asked did I get in the woman's house without you helping me. Did I do what I went in there for.'

'You didn't,' the Bear said, 'or you'd have told me soon as I walked in. Then you'd give me some shit about keeping my mouth shut, saying I'm in it too.'

Look at that, Catlett thought, surprised, but not taking it as strange anymore, seeing how the Bear's mind was working.

'I told you I quit and I meant it.'

Telling him more than that.

'What's wrong with me?' Catlett said. 'You talked to Chili Palmer, didn't you? Since you quit. When was it, last night? . . . This morning?'

The Bear didn't answer, or have to, Catlett seeing the dumbass half-a-grin on the Bear's face, trying to look wise, the Bear here because Chili Palmer was coming.

Catlett said, 'Bear, I'm glad you stopped by,' and left him, went in the bedroom and got the big .45 out of the bureau where he'd put it, slipped it in the pocket of his dressing gown and had to keep hold of it on account of the gun's weight and size. He heard two sounds then, as if timed to come one right after the other:

262

Heard a car drive up to the front.

And heard Marvin Gaye begin his 'Star-Spangled Banner,' recorded at the Forum before an NBA All-Star game: Marvin's soul version accompanied by a lone set of drums. Listen to it. A way to start this show by dawn's early light. Marvin's soul inspiring Catlett, setting his mood, telling him to be cool.

Chili found the house looking for a van parked in front, a little stucco Spanish ranch house, half two-car garage, it looked like, till he was inside and saw how the house was built out into space. Across the living room the doors to the deck were wide open. All he could see out there was sky starting to show light. He wanted to have a look and must have surprised Catlett and the Bear when he walked past them saying, 'So this's one of those houses you see way up hanging over the cliff.' Meaning from Laurel Canyon Drive. It didn't get any kind of comment.

He half turned in the doorway, light behind him now, to see the Hawaiian Bear standing by a suitcase on the floor, Mr Catlett in his bathrobe, hands shoved in the pockets, soul music coming from somewhere in the white living room. Hardly any color showing at five-thirty in the morning. White carpeting, white sectional pieces forming a square, white artwork on the walls that might have spots of color. Green plants showed dark, the suitcase on the floor, dark, Catlett's face dark, his bare feet in the white carpeting dark. He would say he hadn't been out of the house. It didn't matter. Chili knew where to begin and was about to when he realized, Jesus Christ, it was the national anthem playing, some guy doing it as blues.

Chili got his mind back on Catlett and started over saying, 'I've been shot at before – once by accident, twice on purpose. I'm still here and I'm gonna be here as long as I want.

That means you're gonna have to be somewhere else, not anywhere near me or Harry. If you understand what I'm saying I won't have to pick you up and throw you off that fuckin balcony.'

'My turn,' Catlett said, feeling Marvin Gaye behind him and the big .45 in his right hand, inside the silky pocket.

He moved toward Chili Palmer saying, 'You mean out there, *that* balcony? That's my sun deck, man. You gonna try your rough stuff I want to move us off my seventy-bucks-a-yard carpeting, so it don't get messed up.'

The way Chili Palmer stood looking at him Catlett thought he'd have to show the gun; but the man moved, walked out on the deck looking across to where the canyon road cut through to climb over into the Valley. Catlett glanced aside, motioning to the Bear to go out there too.

'Say you been shot at before,' Catlett said, following them out. 'I can believe it. What I can't understand is you're not dead.'

'I been lucky,' Chili said, 'but I'm not gonna press it. Okay, what can I do, go to the cops and complain? I read in the paper a guy was knocked off and dumped out'n the desert 'cause he was trying to ace this woman out of a movie deal and she had him killed. I was surprised – you know, it's only a movie. But it's high stakes, so I guess it can happen. I look at me and you in maybe the same kind of situation. I get shot at over it and I think, you bet your ass it can happen. But I'm in and you're out. You understand? That's the way it's gonna be.'

'It cost forty million and some to make that movie,' Catlett said, 'the one the guy was killed over. But you know what? The movie bombed, man, and everybody lost money. It's high stakes and it's high risk, too. What I'm saying, I'm not gonna let you be in my way.'

He heard Marvin Gaye coming to 'home of the brave,' the end of the anthem, and felt a need to hurry, get this done. Time to bring out the Hardballer and he did, putting it on Chili Palmer standing in the middle of the deck.

'You broke in my house and I have a witness to it,' Catlett said, glancing at the Bear. 'Witness or accessory, I'll go either way.' He said to Chili Palmer, standing there looking stupid in a purple Lakers T-shirt and suit pants, 'Only no sound effects this time, huh? John Wayne and Dean Martin shooting bad guys in *El Dorado*.'

'It was *Rio Bravo*,' Chili said.

'Robert Mitchum was the drunk in *El Dorado*, Dean Martin in *Rio Bravo*, practically the same part. John Wayne, he also did the same thing in both. He played John Wayne.'

Chili couldn't tell if Catlett believed him or not, but it was true. He had won five bucks off Tommy Carlo one time betting which movie Dean Martin was in. He could mention it though he doubted it would interest Catlett much. So he got down to what this was all about and said to him, 'Okay, you win. I go back to Miami and you become the mogul, how's that? I'm not gonna argue with anybody holding a gun on me.' The biggest fuckin automatic he'd ever seen in his life. 'I'll leave today. You want, you can see me get on the plane.' Catlett kept pointing the gun, but with a fairly calm look on his face. Chili had a feeling the guy was going to say okay, go. And then maybe threaten that if he ever saw him again . . .

But it was the Bear, for Christ sake, who got into it then, the Bear saying, 'I'm a witness, Cat. Go ahead, do it.' And Chili saw the gun barrel come up an inch or so to point right at his chest.

'You don't have to,' Chili said, 'I'm telling you. It's not worth it, man.'

That fuckin Bear, now what was he doing? Taking Catlett by the arm, telling him, 'You got to set it up, have a story for when they ask you how it happened. If I'm in it, I won't do it any other way. It's like I used to choreograph fight scenes,' the Bear said. 'You're over there and he's coming at you. You don't want to shoot him and he knows it. So you keep backing away till the last second and you don't have any choice.'

'Like I say, "I warned him, Officer," ' Catlett said, getting into it, ' "but he kept coming at me . . ." Hey, but he should have a weapon, a knife or something.'

'We'll get it later,' the Bear said. 'He's here . . .' The Bear took Chili's shoulders in both hands and moved him two steps back, toward the door, then motioned to Catlett. 'You're around on that side. Yeah, right there. Okay, now you start backing away. Go ahead.'

Catlett said, 'You worked this in a movie, huh?'

'Now you go toward him,' the Bear said to Chili.

Chili didn't move. He said, 'You're out of your fuckin mind,' and tried to turn, get out of there, but the Bear got behind him to grab hold of his shoulders again.

'This's okay where he is,' the Bear said to Catlett. 'You understand why we're doing this. You see it happen, you're able to remember each step when you tell it.'

Chili watched Catlett, about five feet from the railing, the view of Laurel Canyon behind him, give the Bear a nod. 'Don't worry, man.'

'Okay, when I say go,' the Bear said, 'I duck out of the way. Give it two beats and move to the railing, quick, you're desperate now. Grab it with your hand, turn and press your back against it for support as you aim the piece with both hands. You ready?'

Catlett nodded, half turned, ready.

'Go!'

Chili wanted to turn, make a dive for the living room, but the Bear was still behind him, his big arms going around him tight and he couldn't twist free, couldn't move because the Bear hadn't moved, the Bear not even trying to get out of the way.

That's why Chili was looking right at Catlett as Catlett looking back took two quick barefoot steps to the railing, got his left hand on it, the gun pointing out of his other hand, and kept going, screaming as the railing fell away behind him and Catlett, it seemed for a moment, hung there grabbing at space.

The guy who had sung the national anthem was doing 'Ain't No Mountain High Enough.' Which wasn't exactly true, Chili thought, standing at the edge of the deck looking down. He could see Catlett, the white silk robe, lying in weeds and scraggly bushes, more than a hundred feet from here, not moving. The Bear came up to stand next to him and Chili said, 'Jesus, how'd that happen?'

The Bear started taking bolts and nuts, old used ones, out of his pants pockets. Wiping each one on his shirt before dropping it over the side, he said, 'Beats the shit out of me.'

Looking at sky, Catlett knew everything he should have known while he was still up there looking at Chili Palmer instead of the Bear, the Bear too dumb to have the idea himself, shit, he had *given* the Bear the idea and the Bear had come in his house last night, even *told* him he did, but he kept seeing Chili Palmer instead of the Bear. Even knowing he was going to do them both he had listened to the Bear 'cause it sounded like movies and he said yeah, not taking even half a minute to look at it good . . . But, shit, even if he *had* taken the half a minute and said forget it and then did them both, he wouldn't know what the Bear had done to his deck, no, he'd walk out there some night hearing bossa nova

267

or the nice sound of that girl laughing, look over the rail at the lit-up swimming pool down there in the dark, movie people having some fun, knowing how to live. He believed he was almost in their yard, but couldn't turn his head to look, couldn't move, couldn't feel nothing . . .

28

The way Chili told it when he got back to Karen's and they were in the kitchen: 'He fell off his sun deck and was killed.'

She said, 'He fell off his sun deck.'

'The railing gave way on him for some reason. When he leaned on it.'

She said, 'The railing gave way . . .'

'Yeah, and he fell. I'd say about a hunnerd feet.'

'You went down, looked at him?'

'The Bear did. I never would've made it, it's steep.'

'It was an accident?' Karen said. 'I mean you didn't hit him or push him and he happened to fall?'

'I'll take a polygraph neither one of us touched him.'

'But you didn't call the police.'

'Not with a suitcase full of cocaine in the house. Also he had that gun in his hand. He still wanted to shoot me.'

Karen poured their coffee. She sat across from him at the kitchen table and watched him put two spoons of sugar in his and stir it slowly, carefully, smoking a cigarette. He looked up at her. She thought he was going to ask if she was still watching him, but he didn't. He smiled, stirring his coffee. He said after a moment, not smiling now, 'You think I might've done it. I say I didn't, but you still think I might've. What can I tell you?'

Karen didn't say anything. He was a cool guy. Or seemed cool because she didn't know him and maybe never would.

She thought. All right, the guy fell off his sun deck. She said to Chili, 'Were you scared?'

'You bet I was scared.'

'You don't act like it.'

'I was scared then, not now. How long you want me to be scared?'

There was a silence. She heard him blow on his coffee and take a sip.

'The meeting's at two-thirty,' Karen said. 'Harry wants to pick us up.'

They sat around the coffee table in the living room part of Elaine's office at Tower waiting for Michael to get off the phone. Chili listened to Harry saying that as soon as this guy told him the story he knew they had a picture. Elaine saying that from what she'd heard so far it did sound off-trail, a shylock not your usual good guy. Harry saying that was the beauty of it, a hard-on type metamorphosized by his love of a woman. Elaine saying she hoped he didn't soften up too much, become limp. Chili thinking, Jesus Christ. Michael came over from Elaine's desk and took a seat next to Karen on the hard sofa. Chili, in his dark-blue suit, looked at Michael in his beat-up flight jacket thinking, What if it's that same fuckin jacket was at Vesuvio's?

They waited while Michael put his hand on Karen's leg, told her she looked great, then started explaining to everybody why he was leaving his agent who – they wouldn't believe this – could *not* acquire a property Michael wanted, could *not* make a deal with the writer, and if an agent couldn't make a deal with a writer, for Christ sake . . . Until Chili said, 'You want to talk about that one or this one?' It got a surprised look from Michael and Harry, deadpan reactions from Karen and Elaine, and the meeting started.

*

270

Elaine: 'Mr Palmer?'

Chili: 'Okay. Open at the drycleaning shop. You see the shylock talking to Fay, the wife.'

Michael: 'I thought the guy was an agent.'

Chili: 'I changed him back to a drycleaner.'

Michael: 'You still don't have a script?'

Karen: 'They're working on the moral dilemma.'

Michael: 'That writes itself. I want to know what happens.'

Chili: 'Yeah, that's what I'm telling you.'

Michael: 'Let's go to the third act and then come back if we want. You build to a climactic scene. What is it?'

Chili: 'You're referring to the action, with Ray Carlo.'

Michael: 'Who's Ray Carlo?'

Chili: 'He was Bones, I changed his name. Okay, Randy finally catches up with Leo . . .'

Michael: 'Wait. Who the fuck is Randy?'

Chili: 'Randy's the shylock. You need a nice-guy name. You don't want to call him Lefty, Cockeye, Joe Loop, one of those.'

Elaine: 'Sonny's nice.'

Chili: 'It's not bad. I know a Lucky, a Jojo, Momo, Jimmy Cap, Cowboy, Sucky, Chooch . . .'

Elaine: 'Sucky?'

Michael: 'Okay, I'm Randy, for the moment anyway. What happens?'

Chili: 'They catch up with Leo the drycleaner, Randy leans on him a little, not much, and Leo tells them, okay, the dough's out at the airport in a locker. So Randy and Fay have the key and are at the moral dilemma part when Ray Carlo shows up. Actually he's already there, searching the place when they get home from Leo's. Carlo, he's got a gun, takes the key offa Randy and Randy says okay, you win, the

271

dough's out at the airport. Ray Carlo leaves to go get it and Randy calls the FBI.'

Michael: 'All he's doing is picking up money. What would they arrest him for?'

Chili: 'They'd at least give him a hard time. Randy knows this and wants to see it, so he and Fay go out to the airport. They see the bust and look at each other with surprise, 'cause what's in that locker is not money but cocaine. You understand? Leo was setting *them* up, or anybody that got on to him.'

Michael, frowning: 'That's how it ends?'

Chili: 'No, you still have Leo.'

Michael: 'I thought Carlo was the heavy.'

Chili, noticing the way Karen was staring at him: 'That's what you're suppose to think. No, that's the surprise. Leo's the bad guy, from the beginning.'

Elaine: 'Good. I like Leo.'

Harry: 'Leo has delusions of grandeur, wants to be famous, hobnob with movie stars, entertainers.'

Elaine: 'He could be fun to watch, while the other guy's just a heavy.'

Michael: 'Leo's a schmuck.'

Elaine: 'He's sort of schmucky, that's all right.'

Karen: 'He could have some funny lines, out of desperation.'

Michael: 'Wait a minute—'

Chili: 'Yeah, he could be funny. I still think, though, he oughta fall off the balcony.'

There was a silence.

Michael, quietly: 'Okay . . . what balcony?'

Chili: 'Leo's apartment, twenty floors up overlooking Sunset. He's with this starlet, they're drinking, doing coke, when Fay and Randy walk in. Basically what happens, here's Leo and here's the guy he's been paying for years and was always scared to death of. But right now Leo's flying on coke and booze and doesn't know enough to be scared of *any*thing, this little drycleaner. What he wants to do is put the shylock down – you know what I mean? Dishonor him, this guy he thinks of as a hard-on, a regular mob kind of guy.' Chili paused. 'Suddenly Leo jumps up on the cement railing of the balcony and says, "Let's see if you got the nerve to do this, tough guy." The starlet screams. Fay yells at him to get down. The shylock doesn't do nothing, he watches, 'cause he knows this guy basically is a loser. He watches Leo take three steps and that's it, off he goes, screaming all the way down twenty floors to the pavement.'

There was a silence again.

Michael: 'That's how it ends?'

Chili: 'After that, they find the money in the closet. They have another moral dilemma talk, a short one, and take off for Mexico in a brand-new Mercedes.'

Michael, to Elaine: 'You know what I do in this picture? I stand around and watch.'

Chili: 'You want to shoot somebody? Or, hey, you want to play Leo? Take the dive?'

Elaine: 'I don't know why, but Leo fascinates me. The little drycleaner with all that money. I'd like to see what he does with it.'

Harry: 'Sure, the guy must think he's died and gone to heaven.'

Michael: 'Elaine—'

Elaine: 'He wouldn't have to take the dive, would he?'

Karen: 'Not if he lives on the ground floor.'

Michael: 'Is it a comedy? At this point, who knows?' Grins. 'I can see why you don't have a script. All you have is an idea, and you know what ideas are worth.'

Chili: 'Michael?'

Michael: 'I'm going to London tomorrow. New York a few

days and then grab the Concorde. But I'll put my writer on it first. By the time I get back next month we should have a treatment we can play with and then go right into a first draft.'

Chili: 'Michael, look at me.'

Michael, grinning, 'Right. That's what it's all about, right there, the look.'

Chili: 'You don't mind my saying, Michael, I don't see you as the shylock.'

Michael: 'Really . . . Why not?'

Chili: 'You're too short.'

Harry waited till they were in the car, driving along the street of sound stages toward the main gate.

'You have to be out of your mind, talk to a guaranteed box-office star like that. You blew any chance of getting him.'

Chili, in the backseat, kept quiet. It was too hard to explain why during the meeting he started seeing Michael as Leo, thinking that if he wanted to play Leo, great; and after that couldn't see him as the shylock. It had nothing to do with the fact he didn't like the guy or trust him or would never loan him money, the guy was still a great actor.

Karen said, 'Harry, we knew going in he'd back out sooner or later, it's what he does.'

'Then what was the meeting for?'

'Elaine, she loves the whole idea, except the ending. You heard her, she thinks Pacino would be perfect.'

Chili said, 'He's kinda short too, isn't he?'

'They all are,' Karen said. 'You shoot up.'

They drove through the gate and followed a side street to Hollywood Boulevard.

'What if,' Chili said, 'Leo hops on the railing and makes a speech. Says how he sweated, worked his ass off all his life as a drycleaner, but he's had these few weeks of living like a movie star and now he can die happy. In other words he commits suicide. Steps off the balcony and the audience walks out in tears. What do you think?'

Karen said, 'Uh-huh . . .' Harry said he wanted a drink and Karen said that wasn't a bad idea. Chili didn't say anything, giving it some more thought. Fuckin endings, man, they weren't as easy as they looked.

blog and newsletter

For literary discussion, author insight,
book news, exclusive content,
recipes and giveaways, visit the
Weidenfeld & Nicolson blog and
sign up for the newsletter at:

www.wnblog.co.uk

For breaking news, reviews and exclusive competitions
Follow us 🐦 @wnbooks
Find us 📘 facebook.com/WeidenfeldandNicolson